Revelation 2:10

Do not be afraid of what you are about to suffer. I tell you, the devil will put some of you in prison to test you, and you will suffer persecution for ten days. Be faithful, even to the point of death, and I will give you the crown of life.

Psalm 23

A Psalm of David.

[1] The LORD is my shepherd, I shall not be in want.

[2] He makes me lie down in green pastures,

  he leads me beside quiet waters,

[3] he restores my soul.

  He guides me in paths of righteousness

  for his name's sake.

[4] Even though I walk

  through the valley of the shadow of death,

  I will fear no evil,

  for you are with me;

  your rod and your staff,

  they comfort me.

[5] You prepare a table before me

  in the presence of my enemies.

  You anoint my head with oil;

  My Cup Overflows.

[6] Surely goodness and love will follow me

  all the days of my life,

  and I will dwell in the house of the LORD forever.

My Cup Overflows

Psalm 103:17-18

[17]But from everlasting to everlasting the LORD's love is with those who fear him, and his righteousness with their children's children—[18]with those who keep his covenant and remember to obey his precepts.

My Cup Overflows

An Inspiring Testimony of the Martyrdom
of Reverend Yang-wŏn Son and His Two Sons

By
Tong-hŭi Son

Translated by
Ava Lawrence

My Cup Overflows

Fourth edition published in the Republic of Korea on 10 May 2007
by Daesung.com, a subsidiary of the Daesung Group.

Daesung.com Co., Ltd.
11th Floor, Dongduk Bldg.
151-8 Gwanhun-dong, Jongno-gu
Seoul, Korea 110-300
www.daesungbook.com
Tel: +82 2 3700 1729
Fax: +82 2 3700 1701
Email: jcrbooks@korea.com
© 2006 by Tong-hŭi Son

Cover image: *Peace* by Young Joo Kim, Acrylic on Canvas. Used with
permission.

ISBN 978-89-958974-1-6
Printed in Korea

Recommendations

My Cup Overflows is an admirably simple and straightforward account by Tong-hŭi Son of the ministry and martyrdom of her father, the Reverend Yang-wŏn Son, and the martyrdoms of her two brothers. I was deeply moved and impressed by it, and I hope that it will be widely read by Christians in the West who may not realize how similar the sufferings of Korean Christians in the twentieth century were to those of Christians in the Roman Empire in the first three centuries of the Church.

Rev. Professor C.E.B. Cranfield, D.D., F.B.A.
Professor Emeritus of Theolgy, University of Durham

This stirring account of the remarkable life and cruel death of Reverend Yang-wŏn Son of Korea will capture your heart and draw you closer to our Lord. Ministry to lepers, imprisonment by the Japanese, two sons murdered by the Communists, then himself martyred—he is truly one of the great heroes of the faith and highest examples of faithfulness to our Lord. My own heart is deeply moved.

Dr. Bill Bright
Late Founder, Campus Crusade for Christ International

Reverend Yang-wŏn Son's story is the most moving that I have ever read. He shows us the true meaning of love by forgiving the murderer of his two oldest sons—even adopting the murderer as a son into his own home. I recommend this touching account of love, forgiveness, and dying for one's beliefs to anyone and everyone.

John A. Linton, M.D., Ph.D.
Medical Director, International Health Care Center
Severance Hospital, Seoul, Korea

What is the secret to the rapid development of Korean churches despite their short 100-year history? This is a question we are often asked. There could be several answers, but I believe that this was possible because we had great Christians like Reverend Yang-wŏn Son in this country.

Reverend Yang-wŏn Son was a pastor and a leader of our nation. He was an apostle of love who cared for lepers and a leading light who died for his beliefs. He went to prison because he refused to worship the Japanese emperor.

Most of all, he was a true follower of Jesus Christ. He showed us what real love and forgiveness are by adopting a leftist student who killed his own two sons. His story is well known among Christians and non-Christians and still affects many people. I think it is appropriate that people call him the "Atomic Bomb of Love."

I am glad to hear that the English version of Reverend Yang-wŏn Son's biography is going to be published. I strongly recommend this English version and trust that his story will greatly impact not only readers in Korea but also people all over the world.

Dr. Billy Kim
President, FEBC-Korea,
President, Baptist World Alliance

This book introduces a very stirring story that shows us the great power of God's love. Reverend Yang-wŏn Son dedicated his whole life to ministry among lepers and remained faithful to Jesus during the five years of tortuous imprisonment for refusing to worship at Shinto shrines. He went so far as to adopt the young Communist who had killed his own two sons. He not only forgave him but was such a wonderful father that his adopted son chose to enter a theological seminary. Reverend Son was surely the "Atomic Bomb of Love."

Reverend Yang-wŏn Son defended the church during the Korean War and was finally martyred by the Communists. However, his ardent faith still lives on in our hearts because of the love of Jesus Christ.

Reverend David Yonggi Cho
Yoido Full Gospel Church

This is, without a doubt, a life-changing book that I would recommend to everyone. Reverend Yang-wŏn Son is one of the most challenging and convicting martyrs in Christian history.

He was tortured and suffered in Japanese prisons for five years because of his refusal to worship the Shinto gods. He forgave and adopted a young Communist boy who was also the murderer of his two eldest sons. Furthermore, he spent his entire life ministering to lepers. He was truly a disciple who followed the Lord, even at the cost of his own life.

Dr. Joon Gon Kim
President, Korea Campus Crusade for Christ

This marvelous book by Tong-hŭi Son deals with the saintly career and martyrdoms of her father, Reverend Yang-wŏn Son, and her two brothers. Devoting their lives to Christian principles of self-sacrifice and love, the Son Family fulfilled God's commandments to love even their persecutors and not to worship other gods or idols. The saga of their tragic but triumphal death unfolds against the background of oppressive Japanese colonial rule over Korea (1910-1945), the socio-political upheaval that followed the division of the country along the 38th parallel (1945-1948), and the Korean War (1950-1953). The authoress offers a rare insight into how a devout Korean Protestant minister and his family continued to guard their faith in the midst of a series of satanic challenges, including Japanese orders to worship at Shinto shrines, the massacre of Christians by the Communists during the Yŏsu-Sunch'ŏn Mutiny (1948), and the Korean War.

I urge complacent, self-professing Christians living in this age of demoralized values to read this book as a mirror of reflection. I recommend it also to non-Christians who question

God's existence and to those who are about to accept Jesus Christ as their Savior. Finally, I recommend it to those who want to know and understand how South Korea, once the home of resplendent Confucian civilization, transformed over the past century into becoming Asia's premier Christian nation.

Young Ick Lew, Ph.D.
Chair Professor of Korean Studies,
Yonsei University, Seoul, Korea

Contents

PART THREE
Endure with the Spirit of a Martyr!

Preface

Recalling Painful Memories

All people have painful memories that they don't want to relive. Some have been separated from their loved ones against their will or have suffered the loss of parents or siblings because of an accident. I suppose we experience more pain than joy through the passage of life.

The longer we live, it seems our wounds multiply and get deeper. The generation of Koreans who went through the Japanese occupation and the Korean War live on with numerous sorrowful memories that words cannot express. I too am one of them.

Though fifty-five years have passed since our liberation from Japan, the joy of freedom still moves me to tears in the same way it did then. My heart aches with a longing for my loved ones that is far stronger than any fear of death itself. The division of our nation grieves me to no end. Whenever I think about these sorrows, I feel pain rush throughout my whole body, causing even greater excruciating pain.

Yet I am about to trace back through these painful memories that still trigger tears and great longing, only because I trust that God's sovereign power and infinite love will shine through and guide me through the process.

Many years ago, Reverend Yong-jun An wrote a book called *The Atomic Bomb of Love* (in Korean) or *The Seed Must Die* (in English) about my two brothers and my father who were martyred. It moved many Christians worldwide and was later translated into five languages and was made into a motion picture. But I still felt that parts of Reverend An's book were not exactly accurate and that it lacked important information about my family. For many years, I felt the need to reveal the detailed truths about our times of trial. I wanted to record the unexaggerated facts about my family, whom I knew best.

Fortunately, I kept a diary from my high school years in which I wrote the details of the experiences that my family endured together. For decades, it was hidden at the bottom of a drawer, but it has stood the test of time.

If God lives, how could He allow such things to happen? Why did He single out my family to suffer such unbearable anguish? My heart often screamed such questions in indignation as I wrote about my experiences in my diary. I felt that I must not keep this memoir, my most painful possession, to myself. So I resolved to reveal to later generations of Korean Christians, perhaps to the whole world, the way it really was. Now toward the end of my life, I am making that promise a reality. As I read my tattered old diary, still full of charged emotions that had not been filtered out of my life, I experienced anew God's great love and sovereignty, which replaced the indignation and crushing sorrow of my early years.

Although I don't possess great writing skills, I found the courage to write this account, not out of pride but out of trust that God would be with me until the book's completion. It is my wish that each reader and the church at large will be encouraged in their walk with Christ.

For the sake of accuracy, I sought information about my father's martyrdom from Mr. Ch'ang-su Kim, who was imprisoned in the same prison cell as my father and was a classmate of my brother Tong-sin. He was the one who remained with my father until the moment of his death. He was later able to miraculously escape from a firing squad. He currently lives in Seoul and remains in close contact with my family to this day.

Concerning the actual accounts of my brothers' martyrdoms, I recorded the events based on the recollections of Dr. Che-min Na, who was also a friend of Tong-sin and who was later involved in the prosecution of the murderer. Dr. Na is the son of my father's best friend, Reverend Tŏk-hwan Na. When my two brothers were alive, they served in Reverend Na's church. Because my two older brothers, Tong-in and Tong-sin, are mentioned so frequently in this book and their names so similar, I've changed their names to Matthew (Tong-in, the oldest) and John (Tong-sin, the second) for the sake of clarity.

I would like to take this opportunity to express my profound gratitude to my aunt, Mrs. Tŏk-sun Hwang; my uncle, Reverend Mun-jun Son; Reverend Kwang-il Yi of the Aeyangwŏn Leprosy Clinic, as well as the many patients there; Reverend Yong-jun An; the editorial staff at Daesung.com; and Dr. Jung Joo Kim—all of whom have helped make this book possible.

Tong-hŭi Son
Pusan, Korea

Background Notes

Koreans Living under Japanese Occupation

Readers unfamiliar with Korea's modern history may wonder what exactly life was like under Japanese occupation from 1910 to 1945. As the author notes, indoctrination began at an early age: "When my father turned eleven, he entered Ch'irwŏn Public Elementary School. At that time, the Japanese forced every Korean to bow down in worship toward the east where the Japanese emperor, Hirohito, lived." This type of indoctrination was not simply a matter of political subjugation but a matter of serious spiritual dilemma for Korean Christians. According to Dr. Jung Joo Kim, professor of theology at Yonsei University in Seoul, bowing down at Shinto shrines "implies worship of the Japanese emperor as the one and only god," which is obviously a violation of the First Commandment. "Most of all," the author goes on, "the Japanese overlords outlawed all religions other than the worship of their own emperor as a sign of submission to their conquerors."

The Japanese also instituted a comprehensive "assimilation policy." Put simply, the author writes, "It was an extremely difficult time for every Korean to be Korean." In fact, rather than "assimilation," the Japanese strived for the "obliteration" of Korean culture. Basically, as Professor Kim points out, the "Japanese government forced all Koreans to change their names to Japanese names and even forbid them to speak Korean." The author recalls that "history books were rewritten in favor of Japan and to denigrate Korea; school textbooks were altered to uplift Japanese culture," and by making the children ignorant of their Korean heritage, they "thus cease[d] to be Korean."

Why were ancestral rites problematic for Korean Christians?

Early on in the book, the author discusses her grandfather Chong-il Son's conversion to Christianity. She goes on to mention that his espousal of Christian faith involved not only the refusal to bow down before ancestral altars during the rites ceremonies but also his dramatic upheaval of the ritual table and burning of the ritual vessels. Professor Kim notes that Confucian traditional rites "demanded that the descendants worship their ancestors...as gods or spirits that needed to be appeased by some formal animal rites. Otherwise, family members felt that they would be harmed by these spirits."

Again, Korean Christians, while comfortable in honoring the memory of their ancestors, did not consider them gods. Furthermore, a person's soul after death is in the hands of God and therefore does not need to be appeased or worshipped.

How were lepers (Hansen's disease patients) treated before 1909?

Since Reverend Son's commitment to the patients at Aeyangwŏn is one of the focal points of this book, it is important to realize that before 1909 and before the building of the first leprosaria by missionaries, lepers were treated as if they were under a divine curse. Therefore, families cast them out or hid them from the public. No proper treatment was given to them nor was any asylum provided before the missionaries arrived.

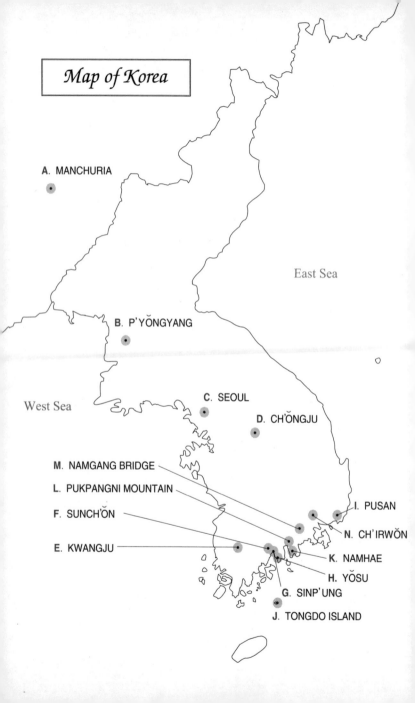

Map of Korea

A. MANCHURIA

East Sea

B. P'YŎNGYANG

West Sea

C. SEOUL

D. CH'ŎNGJU

M. NAMGANG BRIDGE

L. PUKPANGNI MOUNTAIN

F. SUNCH'ŎN

I. PUSAN

N. CH'IRWŎN

E. KWANGJU

K. NAMHAE

H. YŎSU

G. SINP'UNG

J. TONGDO ISLAND

A. MANCHURIA

- Rev. Son's father, Chong-il Son, fled to Harbin, Manchuria to live with his second son Mun-jun.
- He later died here in 1945, four months before Liberation.

B. P'YŎNGYANG

- At age 34 Rev. Son began his studies at P'yŏngyang Bible College.
- Rev. Son served the Nŭngnado Church as pastor in 1935.
- In 1938 the 27th Presbyterian General Assembly decided to worship the Shinto gods.

C. SEOUL

- Rev. Son was held at Kyŏngsŏng Detention Center during the course of his first imprisonment in 1943.
- Rev. Son preached in Namdaemun Church after Liberation in 1945.
- Tong-hŭi attended Ewha Girls' High School after her brothers were killed in Sunch'ŏn.

D. CH'ŎNGJU

- Rev. Son was taken to Ch'ŏngju Probation Center in November 1943.

E. KWANGJU

- Rev. Son, after his arrest in 1940, was initially taken to the Kwangju Detention Center.
- Rev. Son was in Kwangju Prison from July 21, 1941. He received a life sentence on May 17, 1943.

F. SUNCH'ŎN

- Matthew attended high school, John attended middle school, and Tong-hŭi and Tong-jang attended elementary school here.
- Matthew and John were shot on October 21, 1948 behind Sunch'ŏn Police Station as part of the Yŏsu-Sunch'ŏn Mutiny.

G. SINP'UNG

- The Son children took the train from Sinp'ung Train Station to attend school in Sunch'ŏn.

H. YŎSU

- Rev. Son first arrested by police from Yŏsu Police Station on September 25, 1940.
- Yŏsu-Sunch'ŏn Mutiny, fall 1948.
- Rev. Son was arrested again on September 13, 1950 by officials of the Yŏsu Department of Internal Affairs.
  He was later gunned down on the outskirts of Yŏsu in Mip'yŏng Orchard while on a forced march to Sunch'ŏn on September 28, 1950.

I. PUSAN

- Site of Kammandong Leprosarium where Rev. Son first began working with lepers.
- Pŏmnaetkol Mountain, where the Son Family lived in the early 1940s while their father was in prison.
- Aerinwŏn, the orphanage where Tong-hŭi and Tong-jang were sent in 1944.
- Ch'ŏl-min Kang, murderer of Rev. Son's two oldest sons, studied at Korea Bible Institute here.

J. TONGDO ISLAND

- Aeyangwŏn "Garden of Loving Care" Leprosarium was moved here in 1925. Rev. Son served 1,200 lepers as their pastor.

K. NAMHAE

- Matthew hid here to avoid being drafted into the Japanese army.

L. PUKPANGNI MOUNTAIN

- John lived here with seven lepers from Aeyangwŏn to avoid the draft.

M. NAMGANG BRIDGE

- Lepers who lived under the bridge helped the Son Family.

N. CH'IRWŎN

- Ancestral burial place of the Son Family and where Rev. Son grew up.
- His father, Chong-il Son founded Ch'irwŏn Church here.

Son Family Tree

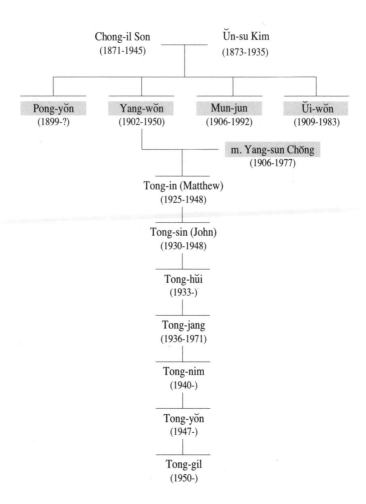

PART ONE

Lord, Give Me Holy Love
so that I May Truly Love Aeyangwŏn

1 John 4:7-12

[7]Dear friends, let us love one another, for love comes from God. Everyone who loves has been born of God and knows God. [8]Whoever does not love does not know God, because God is love. [9]This is how God showed his love among us: He sent his one and only Son into the world that we might live through him. [10]This is love: not that we loved God, but that he loved us and sent his Son as an atoning sacrifice for our sins. [11]Dear friends, since God so loved us, we also ought to love one another. [12]No one has ever seen God; but if we love one another, God lives in us and his love is made complete in us.

1. Three Graves

Far into the ocean off the coast of South Chŏlla Province, the picturesque Namhae (South Sea) Island floats about and the tiny islands of Odongdo, Tolsando, and Kŭmodo shine brightly like small pebbles under the sun. From where I stand on a neighboring island, here on the hill where the Aeyangwŏn Leprosarium rests, the briny sea breezes feel familiar and the ocean waves crash monotonously below. A forest of pines and broadleaf trees stand tall around the entrance to the leprosarium; they are silent witnesses to the passage of many years.

It's so peaceful at ebb tide. The women gather cockles and short-necked clams in the tide pools while holding up their long skirts. The older patients at Aeyangwŏn converse on garden benches with their worn faces bright and happy, unaware of the outside world.

Although the leprosarium appears to be quite beautiful and tranquil, it is home to many lepers who have led sorrowful lives under adverse circumstances. Still, they are a family in one faith and live and die by prayer. Sent from towns throughout the country, their infirmity prohibits them from living with their own relatives. Yet in this place, they have a common kinship in Christ that links them closer to each other than to their own flesh and blood.

Built as a leprosarium at Yangrim in Kwangju City, Aeyangwŏn—Garden of Loving Care—originally began as an outreach program organized by the Southern Presbyterian

Church Mission in 1909. In 1925, it was relocated to its present place on Tongdo Island. Beginning with only nine lepers, Aeyangwŏn grew to a population of 1,200 while my father, Reverend Yang-wŏn Son, served as their pastor. Later, in an active settlement program for the lepers, about 300 patients were moved to Namwŏn, South Chŏlla Province, as well as to nearby Sŏngam Church. At present, only 700 remain.

The Aeyangwŏn Church stands tall like a symbol of hope and faith for the leprosy patients. Since my father's death, it has been renovated and now stands in a much better condition. Behind the church, one can walk along the banks of Tongdo Island, next to the ocean, and find a well-kept cemetery. Looking out over the ocean expanse, three graves lie peacefully. This is where my father and two brothers rest. My brothers were killed on the same day—Matthew was twenty-five and John only nineteen. My father stood firm through all sorts of trials and persecution because he was able to see God's love and hidden truth behind all the suffering. His earthly life came to an end at the age of forty-eight.

Each of them, through no fault of his own, was killed by a firing squad. Yet even up to the very last moment before their deaths, they steadfastly praised the Lord and accepted death with joy. But for me, then only a young adolescent girl, their deaths were unforgettable tragedies that I struggled to overcome. If the murderers were somehow captured, I honestly desired to stone them to death. Although I could quote from memory God's commandment to love our enemies, I just couldn't bring myself to doing so. Grinding my teeth, I was seized with bitterness and anger and could not remain still. My heart pounded violently, filled only with indignation and sorrow.

Originally founded in 1909, Aeyangwŏn Church is where my father served as pastor.

Whenever I recall my dreamy adolescent days spent with my beloved parents and two loving brothers, I see their bright smiling faces shine like stars, causing me to plunge deeper and deeper into reminiscence.

Watching my father live among lepers, pouring Christ's love into their hearts and souls, I felt profound awe, boundless respect, and child-like trust within my young heart. But still, the terrifying sound of gunshots refused to disappear from my ears. Even my dreams wouldn't let me forget the sound of the soldiers' jackboots approaching ever closer.

Like most high school girls, I wanted to spread my wings

and live out my dreams. But both of my wings broke when I lost my two brothers. If that were not enough to bear, my fate was worsened two years later when my father also fell, struck by bullets fired by his own countrymen. I screamed out in anguish and even denied God in whom I had so firmly believed.

I don't know how I survived such trials. Though it was foolish to measure God's wondrous sovereignty with man's limited understanding, my mind was so parched at the time that there was no room for His understanding. Whenever I miss those who have gone to heaven ahead of me, I visit Aeyangwŏn, though not as often as I would like to. Aeyangwŏn's like the Garden of Eden to me. As I turn my feet toward the sea, I recall so many happy memories of my family. Oh, how Matthew used to fish in that beautiful water! How happy I felt, drifting off to sleep underneath the turtle-shaped rock while listening to him sing! Though that rock still remains where it stood years ago, nowhere is my beloved brother to be found. The sea was my best friend, a place of refuge. It was like my dependable brothers. I used to stand on the seashore and send my sorrows away with the waves.

My father, Yang-wŏn Son.

Many leprosy patients who were alive when my father was alive still remain at Aeyangwŏn, but their hair is white and their backs are hunched. It surprises me every time I ask them to tell me a story about my father how they remember the littlest details of his life as though it had happened yesterday. Whenever I visit, they take turns sharing bits of their memories of my father all through the deep night. Sometimes their stories are funny and make us burst into laughter, and sometimes they bring up sad memories that move us to tears. Today, even after several decades, their deep love for my father remains vivid in their hearts.

I enjoy meeting the patients who remember my father, but my visit to the three graves and my father's memorial, which was built behind the graves, is far more precious to me. When my father was alive, he had no desire to become the best, and likewise, his memorial site was made small. It has, nevertheless, become a famous sacred place with more than 40,000 pilgrims visiting each year. Many church groups visit to learn about the beautiful spirit of this man and his two sons and how they were martyred for their faith. The more this world spins out of order, the more it seems necessary to embrace the beautiful flowers that have blossomed through sacrifice and the seeds of the Gospel that have scattered around the world because of those flowers.

In 1991, land was purchased for the memorial building, and construction was completed on April 27, 1993. I remember the time when Reverend Kwang-il Yi and eleven elders visited our home in Pusan. For many hours, they stressed the need for a proper memorial site. Although several thousand pilgrims visit every month in order to strengthen and renew their own faith, the elders felt that there was a void surrounding the silent graves. They believed it was time to build a memorial building. Visitors often drove many hours to reach Aeyangwŏn. It would not be proper to allow them to leave after only a few minutes of prayer in front of the graves.

Since only a few leprosy patients who witnessed my

father's and my two brothers' deaths first-hand remain at Aeyangwŏn, everyone agreed to seize the opportunity to organize all the information about the three men in order to preserve the memory of their sacrifices. One by one, the lepers left for heaven by the call of God. Now, not many of the patients who personally knew my father remain at Aeyangwŏn. Even the ones who remain are so old that no one knows when they will also leave to be with the Lord. Their last wish before death was to construct a memorial building with their own hands in memory of their beloved Pastor Yang-wŏn Son so that his solid faith would be remembered for many generations to come. Reverend Kwang-il Yi explained that the purpose of the memorial was to continue the spirit of martyrdom.

Now on display are my father's old Bible, hymnal, letters he wrote during his imprisonment, a few articles of clothing, and my brothers' books and possessions. Below the memorial building are the three graves, surrounded by thick pine trees that stand like a massive folding screen. The solemnity of this serene setting overpowers every person who visits, moving them to adjust their clothing and bow their heads in reverent awe. We planted young pine trees when my brothers and my father were buried, and now the trees have grown to become magnificent watchmen that tower over the three graves and protect them from the whirling winds. Though they sway gently in the sea breeze, they remain silent, oblivious to the pain of the lingering memories of that place.

Though fifty-two years have passed, I can clearly recall the moment we said our last good-byes right here where these three graves now stand. I remember how my mother, hysterical with grief, wailed aloud and called out to her sons, "Matthew! John!" and to her husband, "Dear, how do you expect me to go

The Three Graves at Aeyangwŏn: the graves of my parents, buried together, and my brothers, Matthew and John.

on living without you?" I can still see my youthful form standing stiffly next to her. I too was stricken with grief and called out, "If you leave me behind, from whom will I receive such love?" Yet the pine trees stand still and silent, pretending not to remember those sorrowful days. No matter how greatly one's life is marked by adversity, could it ever be filled with as much pain and suffering as were the lives that were led by the occupants of these three graves? Now, I will tell the true story behind these three graves.

2. Grandfather's Fiery Faith

Founded between 3,000 and 2,000 B.C., Korea is known as the Land of the Morning Calm. Yet throughout its history, the peace-loving Korean people rarely found lasting peace, because of ongoing attacks from imperialistic neighbors: China, Japan, and Russia. Each of these powerful nations was vying for control of the tiny Korean Peninsula because of its strategic location as a valuable stepping-stone for further Asian expansion. But strong resistance by the Koreans drove them away, time and time again. The Korean people fought bravely for centuries to keep their nation free and independent, and this struggle continued even into the final years of the Chosŏn Dynasty, Korea's last royal dynasty.

In 1860, watching China struggle to preserve her own sovereignty in the face of colonialism by Great Britain, France, and Russia, the Taewŏn'gun (1820 - 1898)—Korea's *de facto* ruler and father of King Kojong (r. 1863 - 1907)—decided to make Korea a "Hermit Kingdom" in order to repulse the Western powers. He shut all the ports and erected a *ch'ŏkhwa* monument[1] with an inscription exhorting the people to resist foreigners and Western influence, including their religions. During the Taewŏn'gun's reign, serious religious persecutions broke out against all foreign religions, mainly Roman Catholicism and Protestantism. Many newly converted Christians were put to death as a result. In addition, the Confucian values of government and society, which had been so deeply rooted in Korean life and history, were made increasingly irrelevant to the actual situation in light of accelerated transformations during the nineteenth century.

But King Kojong was more in tune with the changing times. After he came to power in 1873, he began to open ports in order to encourage and develop commerce and to adopt Western technology and weapons. He considered this the best route to achieve prosperity and preserve national independence. A wise ruler, King Kojong was keenly aware of Japan's territorial ambitions for his land and China. Japan had been active in the arms trade with European nations and was rapidly becoming a strong military power.

In order to counteract Japan's growing power, King Kojong and Queen Min welcomed foreign advisers and diplomats to Seoul, namely Paul Georg von Möllendorff from Germany, Dr. Horace N. Allen from the United States, Collin de Plancy from France, and Sir John Newell Jordan from Great Britain. Thanks to the positive influence of Dr. Allen, who came as a Christian missionary, the religious persecutions initiated by the Taewŏn'gun had ended, and Christians were once again free to gather and worship. It was since 1885 that many Protestant missionaries continued to arrive in Korea to finally begin the task of sowing the seeds of the Gospel in earnest. This was the situation in Korea immediately prior to my family's becoming rooted in the Christian faith.

My grandfather, Chong-il Son, lived in a poor farming village located in South Kyŏngsang Province. In May 1905, my grandfather accepted Christ at the age of thirty-eight because of the witness of an elderly neighbor, who one day called my grandfather in a low voice, "Mr. Son, I've come to tell you something." Grandfather looked out to see that it was one of his neighbors. The man had strong political convictions, so he would frequently visit my grandfather to share his concerns and indignation about Japan's suspicious territorial ambitions, which had become increasingly more overt since the assassination of Queen Min by the Japanese.

During the Sino-Japanese War of 1894-95, Japan sent a large number of advisers to Korea with the promise to support the modernization of Korea. But along with the advisers came Japanese soldiers and *sōshi* (ruffians). In mid-1895, Queen Min, upon discovering Japan's territorial ambitions for her nation, turned to Western diplomats, especially the Russians, for help in counteracting growing Japanese domination. When the Japanese became aware of the Queen's pro-Russian tendencies, they plotted to permanently eliminate her and her followers. They hoped that the Taewŏn'gun's hatred for his daughter-in-law would garner his cooperation with their plan. As before, the Taewŏn'gun ruled the government, but this time under Japanese auspices. The assassination was to be executed while a clash between the palace guards and soldiers, who were apparently discontent with the scheduled disbandment of their training unit, was to occur.

At three o'clock in the morning of October 8, 1895, a large number of Japanese soldiers and *sōshi*, who were disguised as criminals of some sort, reached Kyŏngbok Palace, opened fire on the royal guards, and ransacked the palace. This time, there was no way Queen Min could escape. When the Japanese troops found her, they immediately hacked her into pieces and set her remains aflame in order to hide the evidence of her murder. Many palace guards were killed, as well as the minister of the royal household. The Japanese troops occupied the palace and seized King Kojong in order to restore their pro-Japanese government. This barbarous act provoked widespread indignation throughout the country and the world. The Japanese government, however, pretended to know nothing about it and sent a special envoy to inquire about the matter. Minister Miura Gorō and some forty others who were responsible for the murder were arrested and imprisoned in Hiroshima where they were put on trial. But all of them were freed shortly on the grounds of "insufficient evidence." After punishing the guilty with a mere slap on the wrist, Japan tried to continue with its "reform program" in Korea, but the Korean people suspected the dubious plans of the Japanese and became indignant.

My grandfather knew also that there was something suspicious about the current situation. He and his neighbor agreed about the matter, so when they met up each day, they shared their anger and grief, deploring the evils of the turbulent times they lived in. Though they were poor, uneducated farmers, they knew it wouldn't be right to allow the Japanese to rule Korea by military force.

On one particular day, they were discussing the unpredictable fate of the nation and the Japanese oppression that was becoming increasingly more severe. My grandfather's heart burned with patriotism. As he stood up to drink a glass of cold water in order to calm his anxious mind, the elderly neighbor urged him to sit back down and whispered, "Please listen to me carefully. I've wanted to do this for a long time. Today, I want to give you the greatest gift you'll ever receive— Jesus." The neighbor spoke quietly but fervently about what he knew about Jesus and the Gospel. This was the beginning of Chong-il Son's faith. Though unexplainable, from that day on in my grandfather's heart, a brand new faith began to sprout and the name of Jesus Christ was deeply etched.

My grandfather looked forward to the following Sunday.

His heart pounded as he entered the church that morning. Everyone there received him warmly. His elderly neighbor grabbed his hands with both of his, for he was too overjoyed to know what to do. During his first experience at the worship service, Grandfather felt a mysterious presence warmly surround him, relieving him of any discomfort and awkwardness. A church member prayed for him and the prayer deeply moved him, filling his heart with endless emotions:

> *Dear heavenly Father, Your beloved son has come. After wandering through this mazelike life, he's now found the right path and turned around. During the past years, he's been pricked by numerous thorns of sin and fallen into the pit, wounding himself, but now this son has come to trust You, Father. Give him an indomitable spirit that will never give in to the adversities of the world. Let him be a candle in this nation that still stands in darkness. Let him be the precious seed that spreads the Gospel in this uncultivated land.*

At that very moment, Grandfather accepted Jesus Christ as his personal Lord and Savior. Raging flames burned within his heart, creating an ardent passion for God. This consuming fire was not extinguished until it burned up all the dross that was in his heart. Grandfather's old self disappeared. In one moment, Jesus captured his soul and changed him. Grandfather was born again. Beginning with the shunning of alcohol and tobacco, he grew to be a devout Christian and a new creation in Christ.

He regularly stayed up throughout the night, often until dawn, immersing himself in the reading of Scripture. He witnessed to whomever he met. It was an unbelievable transformation. But the more my grandfather's faith grew, the more severe the persecutions and mocking from the elders of the Son Clan grew. Even the person closest to him, his wife, did not attempt to understand him.

"Believe in Jesus! Trust in Jesus!" Grandfather announced these words every day in the streets. The village women used to make great fun of him and considered him crazy. My grandmother could do nothing but sigh; her cheeks flushed with embarrassment.

"That...that husband of mine! Once he comes home, I'll beat it out of him!" she would fume. Her fists clenched as she waited for his return. Grandmother had long been upset by her husband's abnormal behavior. One day when he entered through the brushwood gate of their home, she yelled, "Are you crazy? Why are you going about mumbling like a crazy man? Won't you please stop talking about that Jesus? Don't make a scene! You embarrass me so much that I want to die." Heated words were exchanged between the two that night.

My grandfather's conversion to Christianity caused such a great uproar in the close-knit Son Clan that some considered him a lunatic. Based on the teachings of Confucius, every part of our body is given to us by our parents, thus not a single hair on our heads should be treated lightly, and filial piety was the most highly upheld virtue in Korean society. Grandfather cut his topknot off and kept his hair short to signify his decision to follow the teachings of Jesus. This was enough to be considered crazy in those days. And if that wasn't extreme enough, he not only refused to bow down in front of our ancestors' graves but also overturned the table with ceremonial food offerings that had been carefully prepared for the ritual of ancestor worship.

Grandfather suddenly quit smoking and drinking—habits

he had greatly enjoyed. Every chance he had, "in season and out of season," he spoke only of Jesus Christ. In the eyes of the obstinate village people whose minds were deeply embedded in Confucian ethics, my grandfather could not be seen as a man in his right mind. It wasn't only the villagers but also family members and relatives who concluded that Chong-il Son had gone insane.

Every year whenever there was a festive day set aside to pay homage to one's ancestors at their graves, Grandfather's heart became troubled. So he came to the conclusion that his changed life alone could not overcome walls of misunderstanding. *No matter what may happen*, he thought, *my faith cannot be changed. Even if a sword should cut my throat, I will still declare that my Lord is God alone. I must make this clear to all who are around me.*

Grandfather concluded that there was no way to keep his faith pure without directly confronting Confucian ideas about ancestor worship. He came up with a disturbing plan and decided to carry it out on the Lunar New Year holiday, the biggest holiday in Korea.

On this morning, the entire Son Clan gathered and began the ritual of bowing before the graves of their ancestors. While all of them were bowing down, Grandfather stood still like a statue and then suddenly overturned the offering table, which was covered with all kinds of fruits and vegetables and ritual vessels. Everything was scattered about. Some things broke and some washed away in the nearby stream. All of a sudden, chaos broke out at the graveside. Everyone was so dumbfounded by Grandfather's behavior that they stood aghast for some time. No one had ever expected this to happen. It was an unimaginable desecration against all the tenants of filial piety.

When they recovered from their momentary shock, all the elders jumped on my grandfather and began to beat him mercilessly. The assault continued for nearly an hour.

"You must be insane to do such a thing!" they said as they kicked him repeatedly. "You've been bewitched by that foreign demon and we must drive it out of you!" They continued to punch him with their fists.

Grandfather received the hailstorm of anger without resistance. When the beating did not quell their wrath, they even hung his limp body upside down, high on a tall persimmon tree. Nevertheless, Grandfather remained steadfast in his conviction despite the wounds he suffered all over his body. Even while hanging there, he spoke vigorously.

"If you please, sirs, listen to me! God is the only God and we must not worship any other but Him alone. Do not bow down before the dead! It displeases God!"

"You, you, lunatic!" they replied.

In belief that it was pointless to do anything more to him, they shook their heads, clucked their tongues in disgust, and turned back to go home. But the incident didn't end there.

Several days passed and Grandmother was out visiting a neighboring village. While she was out, Grandfather searched the storage shed and pulled out all of the ritual vessels that were kept for the purpose of ancestral worship. Then he started a fire in the yard and threw all of the items into the blaze. The flames grew hot and leaped high. As he watched them burn, he was convinced that any tool used for idol worship ought to be burned up. But the blowing wind carried the sparks to a sheaf of straw that was piled up in the corner. All the people in the neighborhood came running over, and after a clamor of activity, they barely managed to bring the fire under control.

Once the fire was extinguished, the people asked how the fire started. When they discovered that Grandfather had caused it while burning the sacred instruments of ancestor worship, they were shocked and stared at him in disbelief, believing him to be mad. They turned away and shook their heads. Because of this incident, my grandfather had to endure another storm.

During those days of feudalistic customs, Grandfather was considered a madman in the eyes of the villagers. A rumor spread that he had become mentally ill.

In the midst of much opposition and misunderstanding, Grandfather's faith did not fade nor did he stop witnessing to the Truth. He was finally able to see the fruit of his perseverance—first with Grandmother's conversion and later when other relatives came to Jesus one by one. Those who had openly despised him at first were now overwhelmed by his testimony and his love.

Grandfather's transformed life and unyielding faith softened and melted their hearts, but only because God's blessings and protection were with him the entire time. From that time on when all the family members believed in Christ, early morning prayers, family worship every morning and evening, tithing, and keeping the Lord's Day holy all became unbreakable family traditions.

My father, Yang-wŏn Son, was seven years old at that time. My grandfather sent him to Sunday school. When it rained, Grandfather carried him on his back to Sunday school and later brought him home on time. He always said, "Learning about God is not something we can skip because it rains or snows."

My grandfather had three sons—Yang-wŏn, whose childhood name was Yŏn-jun; Mun-jun; and Ŭi-wŏn—and a daughter named

Pong-yŏn. All three of his sons became pastors. Like father, like son. Under the faithful guidance of my grandfather, it was not acceptable that just one of them become a prodigal son. The fact that not one or two but all three of his sons went into full-time ministry was not only the result of God's blessings and sovereignty but also proof of Grandfather's deep faith.

My grandfather's faith grew and he later became an elder in his church. In fact, he founded the Ch'irwŏn Church at a place where there had been no churches. In the spring of 1923, a revival meeting was held at Ch'irwŏn Church to raise funds for constructing the church building. The famous Reverend Sŏn-ju Kil[2] was invited as the main speaker. At that time, my grandfather's entire wealth consisted of five rice fields, which amounted to about twenty-five acres. Grandfather offered all he had, except for the kitchenware, toward building the church. I was told at first that he decided to give only three of the fields, but Grandmother decided to give away the other two as well. Therefore, the other relatives pointed their fingers at him in scorn and said, "Now you've gone bankrupt for the sake of building a church." Far from understanding, they only criticized my grandfather.

In reply, he told them, "In this world, there are many different ways to go bankrupt and self-destruct. A fire can burn down your house, a business can crumble down, and a debauched lifestyle with alcohol, prostitutes and gambling can reduce a man to utter poverty. Even if I go bankrupt building the holy temple of God, the church will remain and absolutely nothing lost. Don't you agree?" With these words, he comforted himself, for it was much too difficult alone to even obtain one's daily bread at that time.

Moreover, a great earthquake occurred in Tokyo where his

second son Mun-jun was studying. Thousands of people lost their lives in Tokyo and he didn't know whether his son was dead or alive. He couldn't eat or sleep; he only prayed. In time, however, a letter from his son in Tokyo arrived, along with a cheque that was large enough to purchase eight rice fields. My uncle had earned that money for his hard work in restoration and relief efforts after the earthquake. There are much too many miraculous anecdotes about my grandfather's life to mention them all here.

Yet Grandfather wasn't unreasonable or extreme in his thinking. He only expressed his profound faith without regard for the views of other people or the Japanese overlords. Like any patriot, he possessed a prime concern for the fate of his country. Ten years after the murder of Queen Min, Japan took control of the country by force and soon forced Emperor Kojong to abdicate his throne. Rumor spread in 1919 that the emperor, who had refused to sign the annexation documents that would thus give Japan possession of our nation, was poisoned to death by the Japanese. On the day of Emperor Kojong's funeral, the Korean people seized the opportunity to hold a peaceful demonstration, known as the March First Movement, against the Japanese atrocities.

The Korean people reasoned that a nationwide demonstration for freedom from Japan would focus attention on this tiny peninsula and thus pressure Japan to abandon its colonial rule and allow Korea to govern itself once again. It was decided that the demonstration be nonviolent because an armed uprising against the Japanese would only lead to a quick defeat, especially since Japan possessed greater military strength and modern weapons. In a hostile demonstration, Japan would excuse its own retaliation as necessary to quell

The roots of our familly's faith, Grandmother Ŭn-su Kim and Grandfather Chong-il Son.

armed rebels.

On March 1, 1919, thirty-three leaders of the Korean independence movement assembled at Pagoda Park in Seoul and publicly read their own Declaration of Independence, proclaiming to the world that Korea has the right to exist as a free and independent nation and that Japan illegally annexed Korea against the will of the Korean people. After this proclamation, the demonstrators marched into the streets, not only in Seoul but in every community in Korea. As previously agreed, the demonstration remained peaceful with no armed revolt or violence. Thousands of people who had come to Seoul for Emperor Kojong's funeral immediately joined the demonstration, marching and waving the national flag. Over two million people took part and Koreans abroad immediately followed suit. It seemed that every Korean alive demanded the nation's freedom.

In response, the frightened Japanese reacted with violence. Japanese police and soldiers fired indiscriminately into the large, unarmed crowds, killing over 7,000 people and wounding about 15,000. They also began to burn down houses and churches, where many people were trapped inside. Later, about 46,000 more were arrested and tortured, including about 10,000 women and school children who were tried and executed. Grandfather took the lead in the March First Movement. He was arrested by the Japanese police and suffered imprisonment at Masan Prison for approximately one year.

My grandfather lived a poor and simple life, desiring only to leave an inheritance of faith in Jesus Christ to his descendants rather than earthly properties and expensive material treasures. When the elder prayed for my grandfather at church for the first time, he sowed the seed of the Gospel in the hearts of my grandfather's children. Grandfather spent his whole entire life spreading the Gospel and living for the glory of the kingdom of God.

3. Grandfather's Great Heritage

My father was born on June 3, 1902, as the oldest son of Chong-il Son and Ŭn-Su Kim. Growing up among kind-hearted people in a country setting where water was clean and landscapes were beautiful, Father enjoyed a happy childhood. Supported by strong Christian family values and Grandfather's passion, my father grew up receiving a Christian education. It was he who wholly inherited my grandfather's fiery faith and who was trained to become a servant of God since his early years. He was a boy who was wise but not self-righteous, gentle but not weak.

In 1913, when my father turned eleven, he entered Ch'irwŏn Public Elementary School. At that time, the Japanese forced every Korean to bow down in worship toward the east where the Japanese emperor, Hirohito, lived. It was an extremely difficult time for every Korean to be Korean because of Japan's attempts to completely erase Korean culture. History books were rewritten in favor of Japan and to denigrate Korea; school textbooks were altered to uplift Japanese culture; and the Japanese prohibited all use of the Korean language, even in careless play, in order to make the children ignorant of their Korean heritage and thus cease to be Korean. Most of all, the Japanese overlords outlawed all religions other than the worship of their own emperor as a sign of submission to their conquerors. Japanese teachers were assigned to every public school in Korea. Even the private school curriculum was strictly regulated and censored.

Moreover, the school my father attended had a Japanese principal and was more overtly strict in keeping the rule of emperor worship than were the other schools in the neighborhood. The principal was an extremely cruel man and an absolute materialist. He opposed to Christianity without even giving any sort of consideration. For my father, the act of simply entering the school was painful.

Every morning, the students and teachers were gathered together and forced to bow down towards the Japanese emperor. Most of the children bowed down without much reluctance. Some of the Christian students had a terrible dislike for the rule but succumbed to the ritual out of fear of possible torture for disobedience. Truly, the reaches of our weak nation's sorrows were not exclusive of children.

My father, however, could not dare violate the higher law of God about idol worship. Keeping to the Ten Commandments was one important lesson that my grandfather repeatedly drilled into his sons. No matter how fearful the thought of punishment might have seemed to Father, he knew that nothing was more fearful than the thought of having God's wrath upon him should he violate the Scriptures. Thus, while all the other students bowed down toward Japan, my father alone stood still with his head up high, praying to God.

Because of his insolence, the ruthless Japanese principal did not overlook my father's actions. Even though the principal repeatedly warned him and threatened him, my father resolutely refused to bow down. The principal, incensed by Father's stubbornness, said, "You say you refuse to bow down toward the emperor because you believe in Jesus. Believing in Jesus is your right and freedom, but violating the laws of the country is a serious crime!" The principal had long since intended to punish my father, so the tone of his voice and his frowning facial expression turned extremely hostile.

My father knew, however, that the principal was more displeased with the fact that he was Christian rather than because he had violated the law. Though still a child, my father remained calm and bold, and said: "I too want to keep the laws of the country. But I believe that in everything and every situation, there are exceptions. I cannot violate God's higher law in order to obey man's law. If the emperor were here in front of me, I would bow out of respect as I would to anyone who is my elder. But you randomly force us to bow toward the east. This to me is an obvious expression of idol worship."

The depth of Father's faith was great enough to match the stubborn resolve of any adult. His reply was sound and full of unbreakable determination.

"Damn you! Confound you! Do you mean to say that the god you believe in is more almighty and powerful than the emperor, our nation's rising sun?" the principal questioned my father.

"Yes! God is the only true God in the whole universe," my father replied.

The Japanese principal, flushed with anger, gave a few more threats, but in the end, he failed to break the young boy's firm loyalty to his God. The arguments of the principal were merely absurd sophisms, whereas my father's replies were based on the absolute truth of the Scriptures. The schoolmaster held the grip of power in his hands and, greatly offended by my father's rebuff, the schoolmaster spat in my father's face and slapped him repeatedly across the face until his cheeks were swollen and bleeding. And finally, huffing and puffing in his fury, the schoolmaster scowled, "How dare you! I ought to kick you out of school!"

When my father returned home severely bruised and bleeding, Grandfather prayed for him in earnest. "Lord, I thank You for giving this lowly servant's son such honor to endure this trial. It is said that the more the beating, the stronger the iron becomes. In the days to come, beat my son with a bigger hammer and with more crushing force in order to prepare him for a greater purpose. Please do not spare him from the pain of Your hammering until he becomes a worthy servant in Your sight."

As Father listened to Grandfather's prayer, he considered expulsion from school a trifling matter. From the very beginning, he had not been afraid of the principal's empty threats. He thought, *Why should I be afraid of anyone or anything when the almighty God is on my side?*

The Japanese principal was transferred to a different assignment before he could even expel my father from school. God, indeed, expelled the principal! As a result, Father was able to complete primary school without further complications.

When the time came for him to move on to middle school, my father could not pursue further schooling because of the family's financial situation. My grandfather, a poor farmer in a poor country, earnestly desired for his son to receive higher education, but his finances would not allow for it. Likewise, my father could not shake off his burning desire to study further. He believed that he must learn many things if he were to become God's servant. He could not let lack of money stand in the way of education.

After much thought, my father decided that he would study in Seoul while earning a living and paying his tuition. He entered Chungdong Middle School. He studied by day and worked by night, wandering through the streets and alleys, selling egg rolls in the cold. Those were difficult, miserable days for him, not only because of physical fatigue and heartbreaking loneliness but especially due to the ridicule he endured for his belief in God. Wherever he went, he encountered much persecution for his Christian faith. And whenever he sold fewer egg rolls than the others, his boss and co-workers would taunt him and mock him saying, "You said that nothing is impossible with your God. Why then can't He help you sell all your egg rolls, huh? Your so-called 'almighty God' can't even feed you!"

But what was far more difficult to endure than their ridicule was being forced to work on the Lord's Day. Sundays were the busiest of days for egg roll sales and my father's boss could not understand why my father insisted on keeping that day holy. Though his boss vainly attempted to force my father to change his mind, Father was not a man who would violate the Lord's Day for the sake of money or even academics. Regardless of whether he would be forced to starve or forfeit his schooling as a consequence, he believed that it was a higher priority to worship at church on Sunday. To compensate his boss for not working on Sundays, he got up earlier than the others and cleaned every inch and corner of the house.

In the end, the boss failed to break Father's faith. Yet it didn't mean he accepted my father's religious convictions. When he knew he could not change my father's beliefs, he said, "You are good at everything you do and there's nothing about you that I cannot tolerate except for your faith in Jesus," and fired him.

It was a bitter cold day and, though my father begged his boss to keep him for just one more day, his pleas were in vain.

Now, with no place to go, my father had no choice but to hop from one friend's place to the next, hoping that at least one of them would be kind enough to invite him in. None of them, however, were Christian nor could they understand his situation. They advised him to beg his boss for forgiveness and ask for his job back. "If you insist upon following your religious convictions and work your way through school, you won't find any work here in Seoul," they informed him.

For the next few days, Father lived off of what little he had saved, but he soon ran out of money and went hungry for three days. The only money that remained in his pocket was 70 chŏn—his tithe to the church. *Even if I starve to death, I still won't steal the tithe*, he reminded himself. He gave it all to Anguktong Church as an offering.

During that time, it was extremely difficult for a hired worker to keep the Lord's Day holy. Despite his circumstances, my father moved from one workplace to another during the weekdays and worked his way through school. If his boss demanded that he work on Sundays, he did not hesitate to quit and search for another job. Father continued with his studies despite these challenges.

Then one day in March, following the March First Movement, he was suddenly called down to the principal's office.

"Is your father's name Chong-il Son?" the principal asked my father.

"Yes, it is," Father replied with caution, not knowing the reason behind the sudden questioning.

"You are expelled from this school!" the principal exclaimed without further explanation.

That was it. That was the end of it. Reluctantly, my father

put his schooling aside and returned to his hometown. Only later did he discover that his expulsion was the result of Grandfather's imprisonment at Masan Prison for his participation in the March First Movement. The Japanese reasoned that they could not allow the son of a rebel to be educated.

After about a year, Father decided to continue his studies in Japan. Just as he had done in Seoul, he supported himself while studying. By day, he worked as a delivery boy for the newspapers and for a milk company; in the evenings, he attended classes at Tsugamo Middle School. Living and working in Japan was far more difficult than his life at Chungdong Middle School, but he silently endured it to obtain his education. Of course, living in Japan, the birthplace of Shinto worship, did not weaken my father's faith. On Sundays, he didn't do his deliveries but rather attended Tokyo Mission Church and participated in street evangelism, carrying a drum through the streets in order to gather people to hear the preaching of the Gospel.

Whenever his heart was heavy and anxious, he would search for a quiet spot in the forest or even in a cemetery and pray aloud. He often went to the marshes where big mosquitoes were in abundance in order to chase away his sleep while he prayed throughout the night. When he would begin to drift off to sleep, fatigued by his laborious work, the mosquitoes would bite him so much that he wouldn't be able to fall asleep. He carried his Bible everywhere and read the Scriptures every chance he got.

Whenever he was homesick, he wrote to his family with much love. The very thought of his homeland made his heart burn with love and strengthened his resolve to return as soon as possible in order to preach the Gospel. *There's no time to lose,* he would remind himself.

In 1923, after graduating from Tsugamo Middle School, he returned to Korea to be an evangelist. Just as his father had always prayed, my father decided to become a seed planted in the uncultivated land of Korea. When Grandfather was released from prison and returned home, Father told him of his decision. "Father, I want to become a pastor so that I may be a light that shines brightly in this dark land. I think the greatest, most worthwhile work a man can do is to serve as a pastor."

Grandfather's eyes sparkled with tears as he said: "Indeed, you have chosen well. Ever since you were young, I've been praying for this day and have trusted that God would make it happen. Now, hearing these words directly from your mouth, I am absolutely overwhelmed with joy. As your father, I will pray for you until the day I die."

During those days, many people wanted to pursue theological studies in order to become pastors, but they couldn't fulfill their desires because of strong opposition from their parents and relatives. They knew very well that the difficult road to serving in ministry would be like walking through a thicket of thorn bushes. But things were different for my father. He at least had his parents' support and encouragement from the start. This was definitely a great blessing from God.

Father immediately entered Kyŏngnam Bible College[3] in March 1926 and began soaking up the profound truths of the sixty-six books of the Bible in earnest. Grandfather was Father's greatest supporter. Now that his beloved oldest son would become God's servant, he spared no pain or efforts for this purpose. Truly, Grandfather's faith was a fiery faith.

Whenever I think of my grandfather, Luke 9:62 and

Matthew 10:37-39 come to mind. I suppose it is because Grandfather recited these Scripture verses when the Japanese police seized my father on September 25, 1940. As the authorities were dragging my father away, Grandfather calmly told him, as though he knew they would be his last words to his oldest son, "My son, engrave these words deep into your heart...Luke 9:62 and Matthew 10:37-39."

I was only a little girl when Grandfather passed away, but I wept uncontrollably as I read these verses at his funeral:

Jesus replied, "No one who puts his hand to the plow and looks back is fit for service in the kingdom of God."

(Luke 9:62)

"Anyone who loves his father or mother more than me is not worthy of me; anyone who loves his son or daughter more than me is not worthy of me; and anyone who does not take his cross and follow me is not worthy of me. Whoever finds his life will lose it, and whoever loses his life for my sake will find it." *(Matthew 10:37-39)*

4. The 27th Presbyterian General Assembly

In 1924, at the age of twenty-three, my father married Yang-sun Chŏng while attending Kyŏngnam Bible College. His bride had been born and raised in the same hometown; she was eighteen on her wedding day. In my father's eyes, Yang-sun looked dazzling in her wedding attire as she shyly waited to be wed. I'm sure my mother would never have imagined what the future had in store for her; never would she have suspected that her husband and their first two sons would later perish on the altar of martyrdom; and never would she have imagined that she would have to raise her younger children alone in such a cruel world.

Greeting his new bride, my father's heart was full of joy and fluttered with hope. In the midst of the noisy, festive occasion, he committed himself to loving his beautiful wife until death. Finally, the ceremony was over and the couple left for their honeymoon. Arriving at the bride's home, he bowed in a respectful manner to greet his mother- and father-in-law. During their visit, while they sat talking leisurely with one another, several Christians from the local church came to meet my father. They had heard that he was a devout Christian and an evangelist. After discussing the Scriptures and the grace of God, one of the visitors asked my father if he would preach at their church during their Wednesday evening worship service. Father, never one to refuse an opportunity to share his faith, gladly accepted their invitation.

At the appointed hour, Father stood at the pulpit and

preached fervently about God's extravagant love for humanity and the grace given through Jesus Christ. Reminding the congregation of Jesus' unlimited power that showed up through His miracles, my father encouraged them not to lose hope while living in a world full of hardship, confusion and faithlessness. On that day, many were profoundly moved by the young evangelist's message.

Among them was a deaconess, Mrs. Na, who lived at the Kammandong Leprosarium in Pusan. It was purely by God's guidance that she happened to attend the service. Listening to my father's sermon, she was so moved that she felt as if her heart was burning with fire. In hindsight, it was his sermon on that particular day that became a providential event, opening the door for my father's work as pastor to lepers. It was the beginning of his journey through the thorny thicket.

Mrs. Na spoke very highly of this young evangelist to the patients at the leprosarium. "Listen, I've never been as moved as I was that night. Though still very young, he preached well. God's Word is, indeed, powerful! Oh, how my heart was stirred by his sermon! I can't express it in words!"

Listening to her, the lepers in Kammandong decided to invite my father to hold a series of revival meetings. When Father was contacted, he accepted without hesitation.

When the much-anticipated meetings began, all of the lepers who burned with a yearning for God's Word gathered and were filled with joy each hour, praising God aloud because of His abundant grace. Though their bodies were weakened by disease, their hearts were so moved that they could not help but to clap their hands and raise their voices in praise. It was certainly an enraptured time with the Holy Spirit.

Many were unwilling to leave after the meetings had

ended, for the meetings had left a strong impression on their hearts. After some time, the lepers still could not forget my father and longed to experience the excitement of his revival meetings once more.

"We must invite Evangelist Son again. Listen, if all of us eat one less spoonful of rice, then we can save 600 spoonfuls, couldn't we? We can support him and his family, and they could come live with us. Where can we hear more gracious words from God than through him?"

All of them agreed to invite my father back to live among them. That's how he took his first step in working with lepers: first at Kammandong in Pusan and then finally at Aeyangwŏn, where he shared both the joys and sorrows of the lepers. Strangely, from this first step into ministry until the day he died, the word "leper" followed my father like a shadow. The lepers, who needed affection more than anyone, genuinely thirsted for God's Word. More important than medicinal treatment of their wounds, the Scripture brought much-needed comfort and healing to their wounded hearts. Though their bodies were inflicted with disease, their spirits were pure like the morning dew. Through his ministry, Father brought them cool, refreshing spring water. This was how he started his pastoral ministry. Concurrently, he served as an evangelist for ten years beginning at the age of twenty-four. His ministry responsibilities covered five cities: Pusan, Masan, T'ongyŏng, Chinju, and Kŏch'ang. In Pusan, there were about seventy churches. Father served in and preached to the smaller congregations that were without pastors. His monthly income was only about 45 wŏn.

Although Father thought it would be important to serve immediately, he knew it would be best to put more efforts into his studies for the time in order to bear more fruit later. At the age of thirty-four, he deeply felt the need for further education and resigned his position in Pusan to enter P'yŏngyang Bible College. On April 5, 1935, my father began serving at Nŭngnado Church in P'yŏngyang as their pastor.

It was during this time that the Japanese began to oppress the Korean people and force them to worship at Shinto shrines. Japanese oppression began in northern P'yŏngyang. In 1937, the year the directive was promulgated, Japan was engaged in war in the Pacific, as well as in China. As Japan's defeat drew nearer, her demands and oppression of the Korean people increased. Korea was used as a supply base at the outbreak of Japan's war with China. Not only did the Japanese confiscate food and metal in order to send them to Japan, but they also took some 2.6 million people into forced labor, and another 723,900 Korean youth for service in the Japanese army abroad. But more than anything, the demand to bow at Shinto shrines tortured Korean Christians the most. Many Christians were arrested for refusing to obey, and many Bible schools were forced to close down as part of the notorious "assimilation policy."

Henceforth, all Korean educational institutions were forced to use the Japanese language exclusively. All meetings and ceremonies, including church worship services, were ordered to begin with an oath of allegiance to the Japanese emperor. Every Korean was coerced to worship at Japanese Shinto shrines. Later, the Korean people were ordered to change their names to Japanese names, and refusal to bow down before Shinto shrines became a crime of blasphemy against the deity of the emperor.

Just as we Christians believe in God as our absolute deity,

the Japanese worshipped Emperor Hirohito as their absolute god. Of course, Christians considered this an idolatrous act against God. Japan, on the contrary, put their trust in the force of superior guns and swords. Many Koreans were made to fear the Japanese more than they feared God. Foolishly, many in the Korean churches surrendered to Japan's physical pressures. More and more churches sought to flatter Japan's unrighteous policy by justifying their compromise with poor excuses. These Christians reasoned that worship at Shinto shrines was merely participation in a national ceremony rather than a religious one.

On September 9, 1938, at eight o'clock in the evening in P'yŏngyang, the 27th General Assembly of the Presbyterian Church began with an awe-inspiring atmosphere. On that day, there was an election for officers. More than 800 people were in attendance, including many leaders. Also scattered throughout the meeting were some 97 Japanese police officers who glared at the attendees with suspicion while they monitored the progress of the meetings. The atmosphere was extremely grave. For the position of president, Reverend T'aek-ki Hong of the Northern P'yŏngyang Provincial Mission was elected; Reverend Kil-ch'ang Kim of the Kyŏngnam Mission was elected vice-president.

On the following day, September 10, the General Assembly decided to worship the Shinto gods, proclaiming that it was merely a patriotic national ceremony rather than blasphemy against God. Over 90 percent of the church leaders bowed down at the shrine, which set the example for others to do the same. As a result, the compromising Christian leaders were allowed to live comfortably in luxury under the protection of imperialistic Japan. The General Assembly of Korea voted and agreed to participate in Shinto worship. People in positions of leadership demanded that the Bible be changed and hymns be eliminated. In doing so, the Church in Korea closed the final curtain on God with great lamentations.

Naturally, resistance to Shinto worship had to persist through the sacrifice of the few who shared a strong conviction, not by any grand denominational assembly. As a result, persecution and sacrifice followed. By 1945, more than 2,000 precious children of God had been imprisoned and tortured, 200 churches were forced to close their doors, and many Christians were martyred.

Later when Korea was liberated from Japanese colonial rule, the General Assembly held another meeting and concluded that worship of Shinto gods was a sin that violated God's first and second commandments. But even after liberation, some of the pastors who had previously agreed to Shinto worship remained unrepentant and even began to criticize the martyrs as being inflexible and ultra-conservatives. They also said that the martyrs had dug their own graves because they lacked flexibility and that they were unable to adapt to the laws of Japan: "If, at that time, all the churches of Korea had opposed to Shinto worship, who would be left to carry on the responsibilities of leading the Church in Korea now? We are the ones who led the Korean Church in spite of having been forced to worship at Shinto shrines."

Their justification was that they mutely followed Japanese policies in order to make this country into a kingdom of God some time later in the future. The people who committed this idolatry were highly judgmental toward the recently released Christian prisoners, as well as the martyrs who endured all kinds of suffering in prison.

The twisted logic of those who compromised was an

attempt to ostracize those who suffered for following Christ, and to argue that they were too foolish and proud. They claimed that "Shinto worship is a matter of individual conscience and not a religious issue, and therefore, repentance shouldn't be an issue for them. It's a decision that each individual should make apart from the coercion of others." Far from being repentant, they rationalized their sins with shameless logic.

But not all of the pastors who participated in Shinto worship were hard-hearted and lacking conscience. Though they knew Shinto worship went against God's will, some of the pastors had decided to worship the Shinto gods because of pressure from their families, especially from their wives. Reverend Pae was one of them. He was imprisoned for his refusal to bow down, but his wife came to see him and begged him, with a pathetic appeal, to give in to the Japanese: "Because of your stubbornness, your children and I are going to die!" His will was broken. Reverend Pae was released after participating in Shinto worship at the prison. His capitulation was a sad result of weak faith and lack of support from his wife.

P'yŏngyang Bible College had trained many Christian workers for the past thirty-three years, but now it was forced to close its doors in the whirlwind of enforced Shinto worship. Because of this, Father didn't receive his certificate of graduation until he was thirty-seven, and he received it by mail. In those days, my father frequently climbed up the mountain to pray. On the mountain, there was a designated prayer place, and once he climbed up, he didn't come down for several days, submerging himself only in prayer. He would take some uncooked rice along with him, soak it in water, and eat a handful each day while he was in prayer. Once he began praying at night, he wouldn't move from that one spot until dawn. It didn't matter to him whether it rained or snowed. When my father prayed out loud on the mountain, his voice was so loud that the people who lived in the village below the mountain used to say, "Oh my, that fox must have come out again."

Once, in the middle of the night while Father was praying on the mountain, a sudden storm and flood struck. Wrapped in darkness, he lost his sense of direction. Father grabbed onto whatever he could get a hold of—tree branches, roots and weeds—but he was swept away by muddy water. Then he saw a light from far away and managed to get there. It was a Buddhist temple.

"Hello, is anyone there?" my father called out.

A monk came out and stared intently at him. "If you are human, come in," screamed the monk loudly, "but if you are a ghost, get out of here now!"

"I am human," my father declared before he walked in.

After receiving his diploma, Father became a Pusan District Deputy Missionary and preached all around town to oppose the worship of the Shinto gods. My father put his head together with Reverend Sang-dong Han and Reverend Ki-ch'ŏl Chu to discuss how they would go about teaching naïve Christians that worshipping the Shinto gods was a great sin against God. Each of them was assigned to the south and north of Korea, and they diligently traveled about preaching and teaching. Therefore, the hands of the Japanese police were always in close pursuit to arrest my father. All three of these men were eventually arrested after only one year of ministry. All three of them were eventually martyred—Reverend Ki-ch'ŏl

Chu in February 1938; Reverend Sang-dong Han in June 1940; and my father, Reverend Yang-wŏn Son, on September 25, 1940.

The circumstances before his arrest would not have permitted Father to serve at Aeyangwŏn, but he was enabled to do so because of God's sovereign call.

5. *Lord, Let Me Love Aeyangwŏn!*

On July 14, 1939, Father began his new post at Aeyangwŏn as a Bible teacher. Despite the decision of the South Kyŏngsang Provincial Mission leaders to actively participate in Shinto worship, my father openly opposed and could no longer work for them. As a result, the organization refused to ordain him and later took away his position as a Bible teacher. They justified their actions by spreading a rumor that my father had been reading books by Uchimura Kanzō,[4] Japanese founder of *Mukyokai* (Nonchurch Christianity), and that his reasoning thus could not be trusted. But the real reason why they stripped my father of his position was his opposition to Shinto worship. Moreover, just before Father was arrested, the General Assembly of Pusan had been engaged in heavy discussions over the issue of Shinto worship and accused him of being a cult leader.

"Do you think you alone possess a special faith? Because of you, we might all suffer dire consequences. Why do you go around conducting revival meetings without permission? Get out of our mission group right now!" The entire organization had turned against him. Only after Korea was liberated from the Japanese did the South Kyŏngsang Provincial Mission leaders admit their faults and formally ordain him as pastor at Masan Munch'ang Church.

In the autumn of 1937 while he was still a second-year student at P'yŏngyang Bible College, Father was invited to lead a revival meeting at Aeyangwŏn. Because the leprosy patients received such grace through his preaching, they decided to call him to be their permanent pastor. At the same time, a friend from Bible College, Reverend Hyŏng-mo Kim, wrote a letter of introduction for my father to send to Reverend James Kelly Unger (whose name was pronounced "Wŏngari" by the Korean people), who was at the time in charge of the Aeyangwŏn ministry. In those days, the monthly pay was 65 wŏn. Reverend Unger and Dr. Robert M. Wilson, both of whom had dedicated their lives to mission work among the lepers, were both men of integrity and deep faith. They gladly welcomed my father. Reverend Unger put Father in charge of leading the congregation of lepers. For the first time, my father was able to meet those who would later become a part of our family.

Living with crooked fingers, disfigured faces and no eyebrows,[5] these men and women had been rejected by their own parents and abused by society. They had no other home now but Aeyangwŏn. What pain they must have felt being unwanted and despised! They had nobody unto whom they could entrust their diseased bodies until they found Aeyangwŏn. On more than one occasion, nearly all of them had attempted or contemplated suicide.

From time to time, some of the patients recovered completely from leprosy, only bearing the scars of the disease on their faces, legs and arms, and thus were able to return to living "normal" lives in society. But for most of them, Aeyangwŏn was their only home until the day they died.

Before they came to Aeyangwŏn, they had never been treated as human beings. Even their own family members would turn their heads away from them most of the time. The faith of the lepers was far more fervent than that of many healthy people. Scripture reading and prayer were the most important part of their daily lives. Far more effective than medicine, one word of prayer and one verse of Scripture brought heavenly peace to their hearts. At Aeyangwŏn, one could hear sounds of prayers and hymns from every direction, inch, and corner. They attended early-morning prayer services, family worship services, and all-night prayer meetings. They tried to cope with their difficult lives through faith and tears, and lived on only because they held onto heavenly hopes.

Father loved each of them dearly. Though he was our biological father, he seemed more as though he were the father of the lepers. He often said of them, "Though their bodies are diseased, they possess much purer souls than the hypocrites outside." He did his best to bring healing to their souls and minds. This song that he composed expresses well the deep sentiment of his heart:

Lord, Let Me Love Aeyangwŏn!

Lord, let me love Aeyangwŏn with all my heart.
Let me love these people as You love them.
They have been rejected by the world,
And they have been driven away from the love of their
*   parents and brothers and sisters.*
Even if all the people of the world despise them and
*   keep them at a distance,*
Oh Lord, let me truly love them still.

Oh Lord, let me love them more than my parents,
*   my brothers and sisters, and my wife and children.*
Even if I were to become as one of them and live with a
disfigured body,

Let me truly love them still.
If You will for me to live as one of them, I will shout for joy
   with them for as long as I live.
Oh Lord, let me truly love them as You do with Your gentle
   touch.

Lord, even if they shun me and may betray me,
   Still, let me truly love them
   and never abandon them for as long as I live.
Even if I were to be driven out of this place,
Let me love them and pray for them
   with the love You have shown for as long as I live.

Oh, Lord, though I love them,
Let me not love with an artificial, conditional love.
Let me not love for the sake of people
   but for the sake of You.
Lord, let me love these people.
But let me not love them more than I love You, my Lord,
You are my source of love, oh Lord;
   I love because You loved first.
How could I ever love anyone more than I love You,
   my Lord?
But let me love them more than myself,
   my parents, my wife, and my children.
And let my love for Aeyangwŏn
   come next to my love for You, my Lord.

And Lord, let not my love
   be out of selfish desires for glory in this world,
   or for some reward after life.

But let my love for these poor souls be pure,
  for I love only because You loved first.

O Lord, though I don't know how long
  my days are in this world,
Let me entrust my body and soul to you,
  and love Aeyangwŏn with all my heart, O Lord.
Amen.

Even for these leprosy patients, there were some happy days in the year; picnic day was one of them. Each year in the autumn, the primary students of Sŏngsan Elementary School, a school affiliated with Aeyangwŏn, went on a school picnic. It was the only day in the year they were allowed to see the outside world. While singing the song of their *alma mater*, the little school children marched across town, led by their teachers and my father, who was the school principal. Some of the boys and girls had severely disfigured faces, others were limping, and others were missing limbs. It was quite a spectacle for the townspeople. Young and old alike stopped what they were doing and stared scornfully at the children passing by. Nevertheless, the children continued to sing "What a Beautiful World God has Created" as they followed their teachers. Occasionally, the children turned their heads to make sure my father was still behind them. To them, their most beloved principal was the essential part of their picnic day fun because he never failed to entertain them with so much to laugh about.

One time while he was standing underneath a chestnut tree without his hat, a thorny chestnut burr fell on his head. He clutched his head and jumped up and down, feigning injury.

"Ouch! Ouch! My head, my head!" he cried with a

feigned grimace. All of the children burst into laughter. He always seemed to come up with funny ideas to make them laugh and enjoy their time surrounded by the beauty of God's natural creation. The children prayed in earnest before the anticipated picnic day that my father wouldn't have any problems that would hinder him from attending their picnic. Many of the little ones were orphans; some were abandoned by their parents because of their disease, and some were orphaned by the death of their own leprous parents at Aeyangwŏn.

One girl named Ye-sun came to Aeyangwŏn with her mother when she was only four years old. Because of her mother's disease, Ye-sun's father had abandoned both of them. Her mother died not long after. And although Ye-sun did not have leprosy, her father did not want her, choosing rather to remarry and forget about her. She remained at Aeyangwŏn for eight years. Whenever she felt lonely, she would sing a song that she wrote:

> When the sun sinks into the far, far, far away sea,
> Children gathering shells go away to their own homes.
> Young seagulls dancing above the water also fly far away,
> Far into their nests on the island.
>
> The night wind at the seashore feels forlorn.
> The beautiful crescent moon also seems to have its home.
> But as for me, it's been eight years since I left home,
> And I wonder when I will be able to return to my home.

There were many lonely children like Ye-sun at Aeyangwŏn. This is why Father tried his best to make them laugh and experience the love of God through his loving care and gentle touch. After he said grace for the meal, the children scattered about to eat their lunch. Then Father looked at them and asked, "My, I didn't bring my lunch. Who will share with me?" But strangely, none of them offered him their lunches. Yet it was not due to selfishness. They were more than willing to give their whole lunch to their beloved Pastor Son, but ever mindful of their disease, they were afraid to share their food and drink, lest he might contract leprosy.

My father knew their hearts well, but since everyone was reluctant, he approached the child with the most severe symptoms of leprosy. Though the child would refuse to share with him for my father's protection, Father would finally win and eat together with him and drink from the same cup.

"My goodness, what if our pastor gets leprosy from it?" some gasped with concern.

"That's nothing! I saw him touching the oozing sores of the most severely sick patients in the Intensive Care Unit (ICU) and praying with them," others whispered.

As they ate with Father, they all felt content and happy, knowing they were truly loved and accepted just as they were. They felt grateful for the freedom their disease brought in praising God, especially since no one wanted to get near enough to stop them from singing the many great hymns that were prohibited by the Japanese.

Each day, my father spent most of his time with the leprosy patients. Every chance he had, he visited them from house to house. He understood their pain and wanted to relieve their sufferings with the love of Christ that He himself demonstrated.

Naturally, he neglected his own family. Time was always scarce for my father to have any friendly, intimate talks with us.

As young children, we always felt a void in our hearts, but none of our family members, not even Mother, ever complained or expressed resentment because of it.

Mother was also enthusiastic about taking care of the leprosy patients. People say that a couple grows to resemble one another. Indeed, her desire to care for the lepers was no less than my father's love for them. From time to time, she would prepare special dishes, such as rice cakes and bread, and would take them with her when she visited the patients in Room 14 of the ICU.

This ward was home to the most severe leprosy patients. These patients suffered disfigurement far beyond anyone's imagination. Many had lost fingers and their faces were distorted beyond recognition. It was truly a miserable sight.

Some of them had dense red lumps like red beans from head to toe, and others had running sores that soaked not only their under garments but also their outer clothes. The stench, therefore, was extremely foul. Nevertheless, Father would pour out more of his attention and affection on these patients in Room 14. Though they refused, for fear that he might contract the disease, he held their hands and ate meals with them.

Some time ago, I received the following account by Elder Il-hong Paek, who was one of the lepers in charge of nursing the patients in Room 14:

> During that time, our building consisted of seventeen rooms. Rooms 1 to 10 were for the relatively healthy persons; Rooms 11 to 13 were reserved for those with light symptoms; and Room 14 was for patients with severe, well-advanced cases. It was often too miserable to look at them, and their severely disfigured faces showed well their

horrific battle with their disease. Among them, Mr. Pong-hwan Kim and Mr. Ch'ang-sik Pak were in especially severe conditions. Mr. Pak was a highly educated, erudite young man whose nickname was "Mr. Know-It-All."

It took at least two to three hours in order to treat these patients' wounds, even with two nurses working together. Because this room was littered with bodily discharge, bloodstains, and sweat, they constantly had to place newspapers on the floor to use as stepping stones to reach the patients and treat them. You can't imagine how miserable their circumstances were in those days! It was a time when not only food but also medicine was scarce. Moreover, those in Room 14 had to endure a miserable life.

Try to imagine the hearts of these people who were nearly mummified in gauze that quickly became soaked in blood and pus. I myself witnessed one episode at that time, one in which I will never forget.

The nurses, Mr. O-jae Kim and Mr. Bae, opened the door of Room 14 to treat the patients one day. They frowned because of the stench, so they covered their noses with handkerchiefs. They placed newspapers on the floor that was covered with blood and pus and were just about to enter the room, when all of a sudden, Mr. Pak stood up, kicked away the newspapers, and yelled, "You son of a bitch! Aren't you also lepers?"

Scowling indignantly at them with his contorted eyes, he threw his wooden pillow in rage. It struck Nurse Kim's head so hard that he suffered for several months before he was called to heaven. I suppose the lepers were only left with rage! Just then, Pastor Son came to visit Room 14 and saw what had happened. He quickly ran into the room in his *bare feet and held Mr. Pak's hand, comforting him with prayer to endure all things by faith and to forgive others out of love.*

In those days when lepers approached, everyone nearby would point at them and say, "Look, a leper is coming over here," and then turn away with grimace on their faces.

It was a difficult time wherein everyone ate bread that was drenched in tears, but only Pastor Son touched us and comforted us out of love. Whenever I think about him, I often stop what I am doing and look up into the vacant sky, reminiscing deeply for hours.

My father visited Room 14 regularly. Although there were strict regulations for non-leprous persons entering the room to wear masks, gloves, and rubber boots, my father chose to disregard these rules completely. He held their oozing, bloody hands without fear, while he talked to them for long periods. When he learned that a person's saliva could be good medicine for the running sores of leprosy patients, he often sucked out their pus and blood with his own mouth. At first, the patients were rather shocked and bewildered as they jumped to their feet, took a giant step back, and gazed cautiously at him.

There were some who stared suspiciously at my father, wondering why this young man would come to a place like Aeyangwŏn and show such kindness. How could they think otherwise? It was so common in their experience that everyone—even their own flesh and blood, even their wives or husbands who had vowed to spend the rest of their lives with them, and even their own children whom they reared—considered them unclean and fearful, chasing them away from their presence. So why would a total stranger, let alone a young pastor, consider them neither frightening nor unclean? How could he accept their disease-inflicted bodies so openly, even to the point of putting his own mouth on their running sores? It was no wonder they had a difficult time accepting my father's kindness without suspicion.

Even after my father's intentions were proven genuine to their hearts, they still refused his touch, although the reason for their refusal was quite different from before.

What if Pastor Son contracts our leprosy? they would reason. They were determined to avoid any physical contact with my father. Since he mingled with the lepers without taking any precautions, a rumor had spread that Father had finally contracted leprosy. To this, Father smiled and replied, "Oh, how wonderful it would be if I actually had leprosy! If I did, then none of the patients would step away from me or insist that I keep away. I could then laugh, talk, play, and have fellowship with them always." When the rumor reached the hospital, everyone wondered, *What if?* and persuaded my father to get a blood test. Though he declined at first, he agreed to take a blood test. When the lab results came back, they discovered that his blood was actually much cleaner than most healthy adults. Father responded to the test results in a rather disinterested voice: "Is that so? Still negative for leprosy, huh? What a pity."

6. Memories of Aeyangwŏn

Each year at Aeyangwŏn, a feast was held in honor of the elderly. The young people prepared food and planned joyous entertainment for this special function. Though it only lasted a day, the elderly were able to enjoy an assortment of delicacies atop a table that literally groaned under the weight of the food. Through such an event, they were able to find relief from their present worries and feel happy for a change. Though their bodies were disfigured because of leprosy, and though they were ostracized by the world, these elderly people looked forward to this day more than any other day throughout the year, which gave Father all the more reason to try his best to bring them joy on this occasion.

For the event, Father saved special grains and pumpkins. The young people under forty years of age collected a special offering to buy groceries in nearby Sunch'ŏn. Everyone clapped their disfigured hands, sang songs with their deformed mouths, and danced in a festive mood.

My father loved this festival very much. Sitting among them, he used to say, "Mothers and fathers, let's not put on the devil's face for having spent a lot of money; let's put on angel faces...it doesn't cost a penny." He would put on a smile the entire time while spoon-feeding those who had lost their eyesight or hands because of their illness.

Although Father loved all the patients at Aeyangwŏn as his own family, because he had deep filial affection for his own parents, his heart was especially attentive to the elderly. Apart from this feast for the aged, there were other annual functions at Aeyangwŏn, such as boating in the summer, an Olympic-like sports day in the autumn, and a game called *yut*[6] in the winter.

These festive days began when my father went to Aeyangwŏn. Perhaps he planned them in order to fulfill the filial duties he could no longer perform for his own parents. Early in 1935, Father lost his mother and had since deeply missed his mother's affection. Mrs. Ch'oe, a seventy-year-old patient, resembled his mother so much that he visited her quite frequently. She treated him as her own son. Mrs. Ch'oe always looked forward to the feast for the aged, but unfortunately, she died just two weeks before the next feast while my father was away leading a revival meeting.

As she was dying, she gasped for air and spoke deliriously: "Where is Pastor Son? When will he come? How can I close my eyes before I see him? Please send someone quickly to get him. I can't die without seeing him, I just can't..." Then she breathed her last breath.

When my father returned home later that day, he cried in remorse, wiping away his tears, and said, "If only she could have lived three more weeks, then she could have attended the festival."

My father spoke of another elderly patient in Room 14. The man had to have a tracheotomy and intubations because his leprosy had spread, clogging his trachea and esophagus. He was barely alive, breathing through a hole in his neck. And being fed through a tube, he waited only for death. He used to mutter, "I want to go to heaven, but why is this miserable life of mine being prolonged?" Then one day, he urgently asked for my father. "I want to close my eyes with my pastor here. Go and get Pastor Son...quickly, quickly!"

My father ran immediately to this man whose body was just as good as dead. As his life ebbed away, his hoarse voice whispered weakly between gasps, "Pastor, I'd like to have a sip of soda!" My father held his hand and sent someone out to get the soda. How thirsty must he have been to ask for a soda as his last wish!

In order to buy soda, one had to travel to Sunch'ŏn City. Though Father told his helpers to hurry, they just didn't have enough time. By the time they arrived with the drink, the old man had died. My father regretted not having been able to bring him the soda in time.

"How wonderful it would have been if he had died after drinking a refreshing, cold soda!" my father cried out in regret. Even after many years, Father thought of the old man whenever he saw a bottle of soda. He never ceased to forget that day. He told me the story many times, and each time, his eyes watered. He sighed heavily at the thought of the old man and never forgot to admonish me: "Even doing good is possible only when God allows for it; so when you can do good for others, do it, however small or large it may be." Like these two elderly patients, all the others at Aeyangwŏn asked for my father when they were dying.

Many patients were pleased with this loving man and responded well to him. However, some were displeased with Father and often criticized him. Conspirators are present in every organization and society, and Aeyangwŏn was not an exception. At Aeyangwŏn, there was a man full of hate and complaints, Mr. Sang-jip Kwŏn. The man heckled my father during his sermons, attacking every word he spoke and whispering criticisms to his group of friends.

From my father's sermons, many lepers received grace

and were filled with joy and praise. But these messages made Mr. Kwŏn's heart feel uneasy. Although he considered my father honest and rational at times, Mr. Kwŏn found the sermons to be so powerful and revealing of his conscience that he felt they were being directed at him. Unfortunately, he completely closed the door of his heart to my father. Perhaps it was because he was jealous that Father expressed more care and concern for those with severe leprosy than for those with lighter symptoms as he.

"Listen to what he's saying. Such judgmental remarks... Hah! It sounds like he's trying to speak against me! What a horrid thing to say! I won't tolerate it if he speaks like that ever again! I'll ruin him!"

Then one day, Mr. Kwŏn devised a malicious scheme to humiliate and destroy my father. He and several others plotted to force Father down from the pulpit in hopes of taking away his courage to preach ever again.

Fortunately, my father went to Samch'ŏnp'o for a revival meeting and was so buffeted by wind and waves on his way home that he arrived later than anticipated, barely making it in time for the worship service on Sunday morning. Without eating or washing, my father hurried off to the church where the worship service had already started. As soon as he entered the building, he walked toward the pulpit to preach. Right then, Mr. Kwŏn and the other young men kept an eye on him, waiting for their opportunity to pounce on him and bring him down by force. But God, indeed, works in amazing ways!

As God's word of grace flowed, their hardened hearts began to shatter into pieces. Tears of repentance began to pour from their eyes. Until this moment, they listened to my father's sermons with hearts full of scorn and malice, but on that day, in that hour and at that place, their ears were opened to hear a voice from heaven. Years later, I heard this very story from one of the men who plotted to bring my father down.

Although I have many memories that are entangled with Aeyangwŏn, I can never forget my childhood friends who grew up with me. On November 22, 1991, I attended the groundbreaking ceremony for the memorial center that was built in honor of my father. It was there that I met my old friend, T'ae-su. Since we had not been in touch with one another for many years, I didn't know how he was doing. Even now, whenever I think of him, a vague vision obscures my sight with a faint longing.

When I think about T'ae-su, I can't forget his harmonica playing. Aeyangwŏn had a much-treasured harmonica orchestra that made music like the sound of heaven. The music was beautiful and moving. The members of this orchestra consisted of posterior blind persons, those whose sights were taken by leprosy. T'ae-su was one of them. Though each of them bore the painful scars of the leprosy eating away at their optic nerves, thus requiring their eyes to be removed, they never ceased to give their thanks and praises to God. Why the harmonica? It was because they could not play the guitar or the piano with their deformed hands or fingerless stumps.

Because their vision was impaired, their sense of hearing developed greatly, thus enhancing their musical abilities. When they played their harmonicas during the groundbreaking ceremony, their music of praise was so impressive that the audience was stunned—their jaws dropped in amazement. As I watched T'ae-su play his harmonica again, I felt my heart burst with sorrow. He could not see me watching him play with all his heart, holding the instrument with his deformed hands. But he looked as if to say, *So glad to see you, Tong-hŭi! I know you are there. How does my harmonica sound?*

As I listened to him play the harmonica, my mind naturally pictured my childhood friends at Aeyangwŏn. In the blue waters of the Pacific Ocean, we lost all sense of time as we played, splashing the water. Oh, how we used to roll around and play all day long on that white sandy beach! My precious friends: Yŏng-ch'ŏl, Sun-ok, and T'ae-su.

Yŏng-ch'ŏl was my first love. He was a quiet boy and his face always carried a dark shadow. But he was handsome and so musically talented that he was always put in charge of conducting the church choir or playing the piano. I too loved music. Perhaps it was because we shared a common interest in music that we used to walk along the beach together until late at night, talking about music. Little by little, love grew between us. Even the horrible disease he carried could not hinder us; we loved each other to death.

Barbed wire fences surrounded the Aeyangwŏn compound and no one dared to go outside. But when it grew dark, we would sneak out and spend time together at the seashore. With the passage of time, our love for one another matured, but time also taught us the fact that there was an impenetrable wall between us that we could not overcome.

Yŏng-ch'ŏl often deplored his circumstances and moaned for our hopeless love that could not last. I later heard from T'ae-su that Yŏng-ch'ŏl cursed his circumstances and lost all hope for life. He committed suicide before reaching the age of forty. Even though he is no longer beside me, he remains in my heart as a sparkling star.

As for T'ae-su, he became blind with the sudden onset of leprosy at the age of thirty. He tried to commit suicide many times but failed with each attempt. When I heard this, I was so fretful and sad that the whole world looked pitch black, just like it was for him. How could this be? *How could he have lost his sparkling eyes?* It was a terrible shock to me. Living with an undeserved disease was unfair enough, but now that treacherous leprosy robbed him of his sight. Such bright eyes he had, but now...I squeezed his hand tightly. But the T'ae-su I met that day was resolute.

He took me to his home. I held his hand firmly and said, "T'ae-su, our journey in this world is temporary. We'll soon be going to our heavenly home. There, you can see me with your bright star-like eyes. Let's look forward to that day and continue to walk faithfully on our pilgrimage."

"Tong-hŭi, don't worry about me. I'm rather thankful to God for my circumstances. Now, you see, my hearing was spared so that I would be able to hear what you just said, and I was not made mute so that I would be able to respond. How thankful I should be for these gifts!"

Listening to him, I felt like collapsing to the floor and crying endlessly. Compared to his faith, my faith seemed so small, like a mere grain of sand. Discovering myself anew – healthy and wholesome on the outside but empty on the inside – I was somewhat ashamed, yet envious of his faith. I gazed at his sunken eyes with complete admiration.

PART TWO

God's Blessings from a Prison Cell

Romans 8:31-39

[31] What, then, shall we say in response to this? If God is for us, who can be against us? [32] He who did not spare his own Son, but gave him up for us all—how will he not also, along with him, graciously give us all things? [33] Who will bring any charge against those whom God has chosen? It is God who justifies. [34] Who is he that condemns? Christ Jesus, who died—more than that, who was raised to life—is at the right hand of God and is also interceding for us. [35] Who shall separate us from the love of Christ? Shall trouble or hardship or persecution or famine or nakedness or danger or sword? [36] As it is written:

> "For your sake we face death all day long;
> we are considered as sheep to be slaughtered."

[37] No, in all these things we are more than conquerors through him who loved us. [38] For I am convinced that neither death nor life, neither angels nor demons, neither the present nor the future, nor any powers, [39] neither height nor depth, nor anything else in all creation, will be able to separate us from the love of God that is in Christ Jesus our Lord.

7. Lord, I'm Your Servant

Wednesday, September 25, 1940, the unbearably hot summer season passed and autumn was already ripening. The golden rice plants of the fields were gently swaying. Rich red and orange hues began to seep into the leaves as the trees began to change colors. The beautifully clothed dragonflies soared leisurely into the endless sky. All was peaceful and serene.

Despite the serenity of the outdoors, this particular day was grim and darkened by the storm clouds that began to gather above Aeyangwŏn. My family finally stepped onto the path of suffering on that unforgettable day.

Until this day, Aeyangwŏn had enjoyed greater freedom from persecution than any of the other churches in Korea. Japan's demand for Shinto worship was less severe here and we felt less of its control. Because of the unique circumstances of the leprosarium, the Japanese authorities closed their eyes to minor violations.

Even then, the harsh Japanese police did not completely forget my father, who openly opposed Shinto worship in his sermons. Whenever and wherever he preached, he declared that worship at Shinto shrines was idolatry and thus a direct violation of God's commandments.

Faithful believers gathered everywhere, and whenever they gathered, my father would unashamedly preach against this sin of idolatry. But the Japanese were not about to tolerate my father's preaching.

The delicate cosmos flowers were swaying gently in the

direction of the breeze, when suddenly two detectives from the Yŏsu Police Station came trampling through them. As soon as they arrived at my house, they began to search for my father.

"Is Pastor Son home?" The uninvited guests' insolent voices startled Mother.

"Who are you?" she asked with a trembling voice.

"We're detectives from Yŏsu Police Station. We have come to arrest Pastor Yang-wŏn Son!"

My father had not yet come home from the three-day worship services at Aeyangwŏn Church. Only Mother had come home early. When she told them that he was not home, they made themselves at home and surveyed us with haughty eyes.

We could vaguely assume the purpose of their visit, but still we couldn't calm our anxious hearts. My father was the pillar not only for our family but also for Aeyangwŏn. We thought, *What will happen to us all if they take him away?* Just then, Father entered through the front gate. The two detectives sprang up like bullets to seize him, and before we knew it, they were dragging him outside. My father, as though he had already anticipated the event, quietly followed them without argument or physical resistance. He turned momentarily to face Mother, who stood pale like a corpse.

"Don't worry," he said to her. "Just pray for me."

Since that day until the day of our country's liberation from Japan, Father spent five long years in prison. Later, we discovered that my father had been imprisoned for refusing to worship the Shinto gods and for admonishing others to refuse as well. Father never had any reason to fear such "crimes." The sin he truly feared was breaking God's law.

Ten anxious months passed without any news of him.

There was no way of knowing whether he would be released or convicted, or whether he would have to serve time in prison. Time passed in anxious suspense. My mother's heart weighed down most, more than the people at Aeyangwŏn and his children combined. Without notice, she had become the head of the family, but she was unable to put her hands to any task. We could do nothing but pray everyday that our father would return to us safely. A single day seemed to be longer than a year for us during those months. We knew that anyone arrested by the Japanese police would suffer all kinds of torture. We wondered many times if our father was being tortured, whether he was healthy, and how much time would have to pass before he could be released.

Mother was obviously very much concerned about Father's physical well-being, but more than anything, she was deeply praying that he maintain his loyalty to God under the pressures of cruel Japanese torture. She had already heard many stories about other pastors who were arrested and tortured, and who eventually renounced their opposition to Shinto worship in order to be set free. Though she knew that her husband would never compromise, she was still concerned that there may be a slight chance that he might foolishly renounce his faith in a moment of weakness. One day, Mother couldn't bear the anxiety any longer and took a train to Yŏsu City, carrying my younger sister Tong-nim on her back.

When Mother arrived at Yŏsu, she went to every possible place to see if anyone could help her find information on my father's whereabouts and whether he would be released. Through an acquaintance, she was able to meet someone who worked as a cook at the prison.

"The court concluded that Pastor Son will leave Yŏsu Police

Station today or tomorrow," the cook replied when my mother asked him.

Mother realized that she would find out the next day whether Father would be released or not. Early the following morning, my mother took all of us on the train to Yŏsu and we waited in front of Yŏsu Police Station with no particular plan.

In anticipation of seeing my father's long-missed face, our hearts throbbed with great expectation. The moment when the gate of the police station opened, my oldest brother spotted our father.

"There he is!" Matthew cried out. We all stood still, staring in his direction, but something was wrong. Father's head was completely shaved and he walked under close guard. It was obvious that he would not be released. Though my mother's heart was crushed, she rushed over to him when the detectives weren't paying attention.

"Where are you going?" she asked him.

"To Kwangju City..." Before Father finished his sentence, Mother quickly opened the Bible she had smuggled in and pointed to a familiar passage: "Be faithful, even to the point of death, and I will give you the crown of life." (Revelations 2:10) With a tearful voice she whispered, "Dear, you know these words, don't you? If you compromise and accept Shinto worship, you are not my husband. Your soul won't be saved, either."

"Don't worry," he replied. "Just pray for me." His face was haggard and thin. There was only a momentary reunion before the detective took him away, marking the beginning of yet another long separation.

At that time, I was too young to fully understand our circumstances, but now when I look back, I feel deep respect for my mother. Her primary concern was not her husband's physical well-being nor the suffering he had to endure, but rather his faith that would be constantly tempted to fall to idolatrous compromise.

Father was thirty-eight when he was first taken to Yŏsu Police Station. While he was imprisoned there for ten months, he was summoned many times for interrogation by the detectives and by the prosecuting judge. They threatened him, sometimes all night long, sometimes using various methods of torture.

"Look, Pastor Son! All the other pastors and professors, even those with Ph.D.'s in theology, have yielded and bowed down before Shinto shrines. Why are you the only one who insists on worshipping Jesus?" they demanded, striking him across the face.

"Actually," my father replied, "Christianity is not a religion based on knowledge but rather on faith; it is not based on emotions but on experiences. The ignorant, poor and old experience what cannot be understood by the most learned and educated. Therefore, some things, though not all, can be shared between the realms of knowledge and faith. Christianity is a supernatural religion."

"Pastor Son, I can see that you are a difficult person. But I tell you, you won't see the light of day until you worship before the Shinto shrine!"

And so they questioned him many times about his Christian beliefs, especially concerning the end of the world and emperor worship. They tried to trap him each time, but my father's answers were always clear and consistent, and without fear of entrapment. They could imprison his body but never his faith.

One day, Detective Pae asked him again about the Bible. My father spoke of all sixty-six books of the Bible, from Genesis to Revelation, in a simplified manner so the detective would see that the focal point of the entire Bible is Jesus Christ; that He fulfilled the prophecies and revealed to us how we ought to live; and that in Him alone was the hope of resurrection to eternal life in heaven. He explained that God is a triune God—the Father, the Son, and the Holy Spirit.

Though he was imprisoned, he responded to every question as a pastor talking to a nonbeliever, not as a prisoner who was guilty of a crime.

"Now then, who exactly is God to you Christians?" the detective continued in a chilling tone. Father once again explained to him step by step.

"God is love. God is righteousness. God is light. God is Spirit. God is the Creator of the universe. God is the Sovereign Lord. God is the Supreme Judge of all the people in the world."

"What does all that mean?"

"I'll explain it to you one by one. First, God is love. This means that men are condemned to die because of sin. But in order to save us from sin and death, God sent His only Son, Jesus, to this world to die on the cross in our place. Jesus Christ died in our place to pay the penalty of our sins. Secondly, God is righteousness. This means that God is the One who will expose all the righteousness and wickedness of men, and that He will be the One who will reward the righteous and punish the wicked. Righteousness refers to what is right according to the Bible—God's Word, which is the Holy Scripture. God's Word is completely righteous and true."

"So, is the Japanese educational policy righteous or unrighteous?" Detective Pae interrupted.

"If the policy does not violate biblical principles, then it is righteous, but if it does, then it is unrighteous."

"You insolent fool!" Detective Pae suddenly slammed his fist against the desk and burst into rage.

Despite Mr. Pae's outburst, my father calmly continued. "Thirdly, God is light. This means that God gave light to men who had no awareness of sin so that they might know sin, acknowledge the existence of heaven and hell, and prepare for the Coming Day of Judgment. Thus, men can know who the true God is. Fourth, God is Spirit. He cannot be seen with our eyes. God dwells in our hearts. God is omnipresent and almighty. This means that He is everywhere and that nothing is impossible for Him. Fifth, God is the Creator of the entire universe. There is nothing that exists which He has not created. In Genesis 1:1, it is written: 'In the beginning, God created the heavens and the earth.' "

"If, as you say, God created the universe and everything in it, does it mean then that the nation of Japan was also created by Him?" the detective interjected, hoping to trap him with his own words.

"Of course, the Lord God created not only Japan but also every single nation on earth. They all move and develop according to His will because the world and all men are under His sovereign control."

Detective Pae could barely suppress his rage. "You Jesus freaks speak so well!" he said sarcastically.

"Sixth, God is our Sovereign Lord. This means that everything that happens in the world, including the birth and death of man, is all in God's hand. Even the emperor receives his breath and life, territory and people, and position and authority from God. Finally," my father continued, "God is the

Supreme Judge over all men. At the end of the world, after the 1,000 years of His earthly reign, all nonbelievers will suffer severe punishment and be cast into hell. Only true believers will spend eternity in heaven where there will be no more tears, suffering, disease or death. We will live in true happiness. Concerning the end of the world, all is written in detail in the book of Revelation in the Bible. All that I have said is just a brief explanation of what Christians know about God."

"The Japanese government does not forbid your belief in Christianity. You are allowed to believe what you would like, but only as long as you worship our emperor as god, too. Only then will our government let you live well."

"Christianity did not originate from Japan but from God. Therefore, if Christians conform to Japanese styles of worship, they are no longer Christians. How can you force the God of the universe under the small Japanese god? It would be like trying to fit a large vat into a small bowl."

In spite of the interrogator's rage and intimidation, Father maintained consistency in his answers about his belief, without fear or hesitation. He was also questioned many times about Shinto worship. Even at these times, he boldly voiced his personal convictions. From the beginning, he put aside any thoughts about freedom from his hellish imprisonment. No matter what the circumstances, he focused only on spreading the Gospel and did his best to use every opportunity to do so.

One time, he was called to the prosecutor's office for an intense interrogation.

"Did you know that it was announced at the 1938 Korean Christian Conference in Kurye that they would worship at Shinto shrines?" Prosecutor Yoda asked my father.

"Yes, I am aware."

"The Sunch'ŏn Mission opposed the decision and separated itself from the larger body. Did you know that, too?"

"Yes, I heard."

"Then, did Aeyangwŏn separate also?"

"Yes, it did," my father spoke candidly.

Prosecutor Yoda bit his lip and began to intensely question my father's beliefs. "What do you think about God?"

My father did not hesitate to respond. "The Lord God is the only true God who is eternal and almighty. He is the Creator of the universe and He is in charge of it."

"Is there a god other than the Lord God?"

"There are gods. But none are higher than the Lord God. It is written in the Old Testament."

"All right, then, what's your opinion on Shinto worship?"

As if he had been anticipating the question, Father strongly emphasized the wrongs of Shinto worship, just as he had always done whenever he was invited to preach at other churches. " 'You shall have no other gods before me. You shall not make for yourselves any graven image.' Though the god of Shinto is a god, it is not our God, and since it is merely an idol, it is wrong to worship it. If we bow down to idols and then try to worship God, He will not accept such worship."

"Look, Pastor Son, our emperor is god incarnate, the son of god. Not only do I believe it but the hundred million citizens of our nation believe it to be true also. Then why do you alone insist on disbelieving?" Yoda asked with his penetrating stare.

"Even if all the people in my country believe it to be so, I will not because Jesus Christ is the only Son of God; He is the only incarnate God, and the Japanese emperor is a mere human being. If you give me evidence that your emperor is the son of god, the incarnated god, then I will give you evidence that Jesus

Christ is the Son of God, the only incarnated God."

Of course, Yoda couldn't give any evidence for his statement, so he began to question my father. "Pastor Son, explain the basis for insisting that Jesus Christ is the Son of God."

"First of all, the birth of Christ on earth was prophesied 4,000 years ago. Tell me, has the birth of your emperor ever been prophesied? Second, Jesus Christ was conceived by the Holy Spirit and was born of a virgin. Your emperor, however, was born between two human beings. Third, for thirty-three years, Jesus Christ performed many wonders and miracles during his earthly ministry, but I have never heard of your emperor's making of any miracles. Fourth, Jesus Christ died on the cross for the sins of all humanity, but your emperor never hung upon a cross on behalf of anyone's sins. Fifth, Jesus Christ resurrected from the dead on the third day, but is there any evidence that any of Japan's emperors were resurrected from the dead? Sixth, Jesus Christ spent forty days with His disciples after He was raised from the dead, and then He ascended to heaven. All these facts prove that Jesus Christ is the Son of God. But where is the proof for your claim that your emperor is the Son of God?"

Prosecutor Yoda sat amazed and dismayed, unable to speak a word. My father was harassed in the same way for ten months at Yŏsu Police Station, and finally, his health deteriorated so much that his life was at risk. When he was summoned to the prosecutor's office, he didn't even have the strength to walk, so they had to carry him on a stretcher. Although some prisoners had been released because of poor health, they would not allow my father to go because he refused to compromise his convictions. Their hearts became more hardened toward him until finally, the detectives composed a 500-page report of their interrogation of my father and submitted it to the higher court.

On July 21, 1941, Father was transferred from Yŏsu Police Station to Kwangju Prison, where he was put on trial. On November 4 that same year, he was sentenced to eighteen months in prison at Kwangju Prison. On the last day of his term, May 17, 1943, however, my father was not released because he had refused to compromise his faith all throughout his time behind bars. Therefore, the prosecutor's office held court all day and concluded that if Pastor Son were to be released from jail, he would openly oppose Shinto worship. So they sent him to the detention center. Because of his refusal to accept Shinto worship, Father was sentenced to life in prison. The circumstances at that time are clearly outlined in a letter Father sent to Grandfather on June 8 that same year:

May 17th – the day you looked forward to most – oh, how you must have been thrilled but also worried? With what word can your unworthy son Yang-wŏn comfort you? I only wish for you to receive comfort and blessings with a firm foundation of faith like that of Abraham and Job. I was sentenced to life at the detention center on May 20 because I refused to compromise my belief in God. So I requested an appeal to a higher court for June 20. The reason for my appeal is not an attempt to avoid persecution but to further testify about the biblical doctrines. Perhaps if I'm sent to Taegu on the 20th of this month, the appeal will be over by August and I'll be sent to Kyŏngsŏng (Seoul) Detention Center at West Gate Prison. I heard that prisoners at the detention center are permitted monthly letters and visits from family. Don't worry about me. I heard that prisoners

at the detention center can move freely within the confines
of the facilities. I want you to visit me on your way to my
younger brother's house in Manchuria...

Whenever I read the following poem that my father wrote
on September 9, just after he was sentenced to life in prison, I
can feel the sentiment he held at that time:

When autumn comes, many flocks of crows fly
All in due course of time;
The swallows that had come on March 3rd
Flew away to their southern home near the Yangtze River.
But for this solitary traveler, so far from home,
The way home is still vague and indefinably dim.
Each morning and evening the cold wind tells
The news of the approaching autumn –
The season of high skies and plump horses,
The season of chilling breezes and cold moon.
The ever-falling leaves also return back
To where they came from.
It has been more than three years since I left home,
But as for me, the way home is still dim.
It seems like all the signs of the universe are announcing
The autumn of humanity.
And all the sins of the billions of people hasten
The Lord of judgment.
But as for this unprepared, mortal body,
The road to my heavenly home is still vague.

8. *Oh Suffering, If You Must Come, Come*

My father's life in prison, which began at Yŏsu Police Station, took him from place to place–to Kwangju Detention Center, to Kwangju Prison, to Kyŏngsŏng Detention Center, and then finally, in November 1943, to Ch'ŏngju Probation Center. He was transferred five times, and it was at the Ch'ŏngju Probation Center that he spent the remainder of his term in prison until his release. For nearly five years, he had been separated from his family and suffered a lonely, painful imprisonment. During those years, he experienced and learned many great lessons.

One day at Kyŏngsŏng Detention Center, the supervisor confiscated my father's Bible and hymnal and then brought before him an armful of Buddhist books to read. This was one of the many strategies that the authorities used to persuade my father to compromise his beliefs.

Once Father finished reading all of the books, the warden, the inspector-general, the press secretary, and the most famous Japanese Buddhist priest of that day came and sat before him. The prison officials wanted to persuade my father through debate with their famous priest. Thus, a fervent debate ensued between the two.

For several hours, the debate continued with neither yielding to the other. From the beginning, the Buddhist monk looked down on Christianity as an inferior religion. The debate between the two grew hotter. But as time passed, the monk was dumbstruck.

At the climax of their exchange, the Japanese monk asked as a last resort, "Now then, has anyone ever seen God?"

"We cannot see God with our eyes. If it is so awesome to see a great king on earth, how much more awesome would it be if we, mere mortals, got to meet God who is King of Kings? God dwells in great light. If we were to look directly at Him, even for a second, we would instantly be blinded. More important, if we behold God in our physical, sinful state, we would instantly perish."

Still, the monk demanded that my father reveal God to him.

"If you insist, you show me your Buddhist god and I'll show you the God in whom I believe," my father concluded.

Realizing that he, the most highly regarded Buddhist monk, was losing the spiritual debate to this insignificant prisoner, he became furious. He jumped to his feet and, without warning, struck my father across the face.

"How dare you challenge me!"

But my father calmly responded to the infuriated priest. "Though a follower of Avalokitesvara of Great Love and Great Mercy strike the cheek of a poor prisoner like me, I, a faithful child of God, will still follow the teachings of Jesus Christ. Jesus instructed us, 'If someone strikes you on the right cheek, turn to him the other also.' So now, strike this side as well."

"How dare you try to win?" The Japanese priest went out of his mind and lost all self-control. He jumped up and down in rage and attacked my father, kicking him with his feet and punching him with his fists. The unforeseen uproar surprised the prison guards, and they escorted the priest out of the room lest something unpleasant should happen.

The priest couldn't win the debate, so he tried to win

through violence. Thus, in truth he lost. The police at Ch'ŏngju Probation Center invited another man, one who was very knowledgeable about Christianity, in order to persuade my father to compromise his beliefs. This man had graduated from a Christian school and college, and he had claimed to be a Christian once in the past. He assured the prison officials that he could persuade my father within a month.

"Pastor Son," the man began, "the Korean church is facing a great time of trial right now. In spite of such difficult circumstances, the shepherd must keep his flock, don't you think? Should you be so stubborn and remain locked up in this place? Don't you think you are just like the Apostle Peter who left his flock in Rome because of Nero's persecution?"

My father was dumbfounded. "Yes, these are difficult days for the Korean church. We cannot freely witness the Truth, and everyone who tries to preach the Truth is imprisoned like me. In such repressive circumstances, should I kill my flock by feeding them poisoned grass just to save myself, or should I preach through my imprisonment for the sake of the Truth? Just as a lotus flower blossoms and scatters its fragrance in the midst of a muddy pond, so now is the time for Christians to reveal the Truth."

From that day on, they punished my father by giving him only half of his food ration. The reason for such treatment was not only because of his stubborn refusal to compromise his own beliefs but also for witnessing to the other prisoners. Then they halved his daily food ration again to an amount barely enough to keep him alive.

Reduction of food wasn't the only punishment. The officials ordered my father to read Buddhist books every day and to submit a reading report each day. This was the obvious workings of the humiliated Buddhist monk, who was now seeking revenge against my father.

One day, Father wrote the following in his report:

How can there be two suns in the sky, two kings in a nation? How can there be two lords of the universe? Where can salvation be apart from the way of the cross?

There are many lords and gods in the world, but to me there is no other than Jehovah. Buddha is famous, Confucius is also a great man, but Jesus Christ alone is my Savior. Therefore, how can I serve two gods? Who else is redeemer but Jesus? What would I not give for my God? Where would I go if I abandon my Lord?

Father was growing increasingly weak. His young body needed more nourishment, but after he ate, he became even hungrier and could barely stand on his two feet. He was becoming nothing more than a living skeleton. His eyesight was growing dim and his handwriting in the letters he sent home became larger and shakier, resembling the writing of a young child. In his letter to Tŏk-sun Hwang, his sister in the Lord, he wrote: "Tŏk-sun, I am becoming blinder with each day."

Miss Hwang worked at a clothing factory. When she received his letter, she bought two big bottles of cod liver oil and sent them to him. He kept one and sent the other bottle to Mother. Each day thereafter, my father's eyesight was gradually restored.

Life in prison was always cold, hungry, and lonely. Regardless of how many years might have passed, it was never easy to adjust. Because of the lack of food and heat in the cell, and because of the yearning for freedom, most of the inmates gradually became more lethargic and weak-minded. But my father, always armored with faith, was an exception. Though his physical body was perishing, his spirit was always being renewed. He sang hymns with a lively voice and testified of God's Word to both prison guards and fellow inmates.

An exception among the guards was a Korean man who sympathized with my father and respected him. He thought highly of my father's faith and tried to help him in many ways. On one occasion, the guard tried to make a false report that my father had bowed down at a Shinto shrine.

"Pastor Son participates in Shinto worship these days and his behavior is excellent," he reported to Yoda.

He came to my father with great sympathy and said: "Pastor Son, you are a great man, a rare find in this world. That's why you should seek to be released so that you can do many good works, rather than be imprisoned here like this. Your crime is merely refusal to bow down to Shinto. Let's do this. You don't actually have to bow down, just place your thumbprint here to say that you did. Then you can be released immediately." The paper he presented to my father was a written pledge to participate in Shinto worship because it was a national ceremony.

"No, I cannot," Father rejected the offer flatly. "I thank you for your concerns, but this is a very important matter. How can I say I did something when I really didn't? How can I lie that I will do something that I know I will never do?" Among the many essays Father wrote, the one on this incident expresses his strong conviction especially well.

In prison were all kinds of people—some who were caught stealing and some caught in fist fights—but there were others who were caught fighting against Japan for our nation's independence. In my father's cell were also patriots and freedom fighters. They were summoned daily at midnight. Soon, everyone could hear the agonizing cries of the tortured and the angry shouts of the torturers.

"Name the ones who conspired with you! You know where they are hiding, don't you? They're working for the independence movement, aren't they? Tell me where they are at once...How dare you keep silent!"

The voice of the torturer was bloodthirsty, but from the mouths of the independence fighters came only moans of intense agony. If they could no longer bear the suffering alone, they would rather die than betray their friends. They were subject to bamboo torture, a form of torture in which sharply cut bamboo knives were forced underneath each of their fingernails. When this failed to make them talk, they were hung upside down, and hot water mixed with chili pepper powder was poured into their nostrils to bring them to the point of suffocation. At times, electric shock torture was also used. When the continuous torture became too unbearable for the freedom fighters, many of them chose to bite off their own tongues rather than release any information.

As Father saw how faithful these men remained to their love for Korea, he became even stronger in his own faith. He thought to himself, *Look at them, they are more than willing to give their own lives for our country. How much more I need to be willing to sacrifice my life for God? How can I say this suffering is too difficult to bear?*

My father's faith was strengthened all the more by the example of the Korean patriots and their deep love for the nation. And through his first-hand experience with brutal

Japanese torture, he was convinced of Japan's defeat. Japan was destined to be routed. God would surely destroy this idolatrous nation. He would surely punish these people who were eager to do as much evil as humanly possible.

It was at Ch'ŏngju Probation Center that my father suffered the most. Every morning when he awoke, he would witness to the other prisoners until night. This continued until finally the prison officials decided to put him into solitary confinement because they felt he was "too noisy."

Loneliness was of secondary concern in comparison to bitter coldness. The bone-chilling winter temperatures that fell below 10 degrees penetrated his thin body, which went without a blanket to shield it from the cold. It was, indeed, a difficult season for him to endure. Solitary confinement was even more difficult to bear since he couldn't feel the warmth of the other prisoners' bodies. Because of the cold weather, Father's hands and feet were frequently frostbitten. Eventually, his fingernails and toenails became gangrenous and fell off.

Whenever he suffered from extreme cold, my father would write letters to the family or write poems that expressed his steadfast faith in God:

As I am alone in this empty cell,
Overwhelming loneliness sweeps over me.
But since the Father, the Son, and the Holy Spirit
Are here with me,
Now there are four of us here together.
Oh, you suffering of every kind, if you must come,
Then come in order that I may experience
All the truth hidden in the midst of suffering.

Far away from home and in prison,
The night is deep and
This prison is deep.
The concerns of my heart are also deep.

Though the night is deep,
Though the prison is deep,
Though the worries of my heart are also deep,
Since I abide in the Lord, my joy is complete.

Though the four years of suffering in prison
Are made up of long, long days,
Since my Lord abides with me, each year feels like a day.
During these past four years,
My Lord has protected me with peace.
I'm convinced He will do the same in the future.

However, writing letters and poems couldn't keep him warm in the room without heating. Once, Father froze curled up in the fetal position in the corner of that solitary room. He could neither stand up nor lie down. Against his will, his body was constricted beyond restricting bodily functions and to the point of death.

On this particular night, the weather was unusually cold. My father, suffering from malnutrition as well as a bad flu, struggled with a high fever and a severe headache. His mind became hazy and delirious, and finally he lost consciousness. In the early morning, the guard found his stiff body. He thought my father was dead, so he had his body transferred to the morgue. He didn't even appear to be breathing.

On the following morning, Father regained consciousness

and looked around to see where he had been taken. *God must have revived me!* he thought. Bowing down in worship, he began to sing a hymn. Then the guard came over and said, "Humph! I thought this wretch was dead." He yelled at my father to be quiet and poured a bucket of cold water over him. But my father couldn't stop singing praises to God.

The long, severe winter finally passed and spring came, and with it also came a watery discharge from Father's ears. I suppose prison is an unparalleled training ground. If he had not endured such a brutal time of suffering, how could he have developed a faith that did not fear death?

Later in Kwangju near the end of his prison term, he still would not compromise his faith. The prison officials tried all forms of torture to break him, but he refused to bend. Once, the authorities decided to write to Grandfather in an effort to manipulate him into changing his son's mind: "Your son's health is weak and he is near death. So write to him now and tell him to bend his stubborn will. He must bow down to Shinto in order to be released." Opposite to their intentions, Grandfather replied: "If you perish, you perish. If you bow down to the Shinto gods, you are not my son!"

"What an ingrate!" the prison warden said as he read my grandfather's letter. Despite his letter, the warden approached Father and outright lied to him. "Your father sent a letter and said that your family is in deep trouble. He urged you to bend your stubborn will so that you may go home to help your loved ones."

"Is that so? It was because of my father's teaching that I have come this far. My father would never say such a thing. Let me see his letter."

"Where on the earth would you find such a venomous

father as yours!" the warden shouted in rage. "Like father, like son," he yelled and threw the letter down before walking out.

I heard this story later from Reverend Sang-gŏn Pak, who read that same letter at my grandfather's funeral in Manchuria. In a letter to my oldest brother, dated August 13, 1942, Father admonished: "I heard that you are sending home 20 wŏn out of your monthly income of 23 wŏn. How then are you managing to eat and clothe yourself? Do not overstrain yourself financially. You are at the age now that requires much nourishment to grow and develop. Eat as much as you can and maintain your health. Act wisely and within reason."

Father also wrote to ask us to make sure we continue our studies at home since we could no longer go to school:

December 10, 1942

Dear Matthew (Tong-in) and John (Tong-sin),

Although you cannot go to school, you can still acquire as much knowledge as you would like. Knowledge stems from an understanding of objects and principles; therefore, you can gain understanding and thus acquire knowledge wherever and so long as objects and principles exist. Who would have guessed that Joseph, a boy who was thrown into a pit by his own brothers, would later become the prime minister of Egypt! Who would have guessed that Moses, abandoned and set afloat down the River Nile, would later become the deliverer of Israel! Though now you work at a container factory, who knows what your future holds? Therefore, always conduct yourselves with good behavior and only focus on building up your character. Exert yourselves to attend to your studies and do good deeds with diligence. Set healthy, high goals and persistently persevere to the end. The God who was with Joseph of old will be with you. So trust Him and wholly depend upon Him. Pursue holiness for the completion of your character.

So my two older brothers read books everyday after work at the factory. They taught all of us younger siblings how to read and write Korean since the Japanese forbid the use of the Korean language. And at times, Father wrote about how he wondered how much we had grown. He asked that all of our heights be measured and be sent to him. Matthew would line us up against the wall to measure us and would report our heights in our letters to Father.

The following is an excerpt from one of Father's letters to Mother:

October 14, 1942

It is so strange...you never fail to send me a letter each month, but since your letter is late in coming, I wonder if perhaps something has happened at home. Is someone sick? Did something happen? Anyhow, if you are faced with circumstances that hinder you from coming to see me, please write me a letter so that I no longer wonder and worry. Please let me hear from you soon. Each night, I see you in my dreams and you look worried and unsure.

Perhaps you have fallen ill under the weight of your concerns. But you need not worry or fret. Worrying is the worst disease among all diseases—the sin of all sins. We usually consider only physical infirmities as diseases, but the wise know that worrying is also a disease. We consider stealing and murder sins, but few consider worrying a sin.

Don't you think that the biggest sin is unbelief? I believe there is no greater sin than this. God promised to care for us if we cast all our cares upon Him. So if we keep our cares in our hearts, this is an act of disobedience, right? Fleshly thoughts give birth to worries and worrying becomes a disease. But spiritual thoughts give birth to a contented heart and contentment leads to spiritual riches.

Worrying is the disease of all diseases—the sin of all sins. A contented life is far better than life as a rich man.

As I have always said, suffering is truly a great blessing. Receive it gladly as though it were sweet honey. If we patiently endure, we will someday realize that there is no other blessing greater than this.

Rich men, scholars, and saints are all products of suffering, don't you agree? Suffering is the mother of success; suffering is the seed of the harvest of blessing. When we are in the midst of suffering, we recognize all of our past wrongs and sins, and this enables us to receive His grace of forgiveness. And for those who have become friends to this world and have fallen into sin, suffering becomes the rod of discipline that enables them to draw near to God.

Physical and spiritual worries are like rocky soil and thorny bushes that suppress the growth of our faith. Therefore, these worries and anxieties rob the joy of our salvation and blind our eyes from seeing the heavenly glory of the future.

In ancient days, the Israelites were glad to sacrifice their firstborn to Molek. How much more must have been the joy of Abraham to offer his only son Isaac to God! Therefore, Abraham became the father of faith and the example for us to follow today.

Please, do not worry at all about me. One handful of rice and one cup of salt water tastes like the food of fairies and the cakes of angels. Dear, you worry that I suffer in the freezing cold, but will not He who feeds the birds in the sky and clothes the lilies of the field also feed me, His child and servant?

As I've always eaten small portions anyway, I am content with the food here. Since I'm short, my clothes are long enough to cover my feet. I am content.

Our Lord often said, "O you of little faith! Why did you doubt?" The only thing I sigh about is the fact that we lack faith. That's why I continue to pray. Please be at ease.

My father's letters were always filled with encouraging words and hopes for us to be content, patient, and thankful.

9. As Sheep without a Shepherd

After my father was taken into custody, Dr. Wilson and Missionary "Wŏngari" left Korea weeping when the Japanese started a war with the United States. Aeyangwŏn was no longer a peaceful place where the sound of beautiful prayers could be heard. As soon as Director Andō arrived, he ordered our family out of our private residence. He said that the family members of a political prisoner could not stay in that house. We had no place to go, but even if we were asked to stay, we would not have because Andō demanded Shinto worship.

My family left Aeyangwŏn and went to Kwangju first. It was spring of 1941, and at the time of our departure, the leprosy patients held a secret meeting and gathered 700 wŏn as a gift for us. Since my father was held prisoner in Kwangju and since we were allowed to visit him once a month, we decided to move there to be near him.

But even that once-a-month visit was a luxury for us. Though we wanted to see Father, we couldn't come up with the required fee for the visit. In order for us to survive, somebody in the family had to get a job, but doing so wasn't easy. After much effort, Matthew and John managed to find a job at a factory that made wooden containers. Deacon Sin-ch'ul Pak owned the business. Pastor Ki-ch'ŏl Chu's third son Yŏng-hae introduced my brothers to Deacon Pak. However, the factory was not in Kwangju but down in Pusan.

My brothers lived in lodges and worked at the factory. Each month when they received their wages, they paid for their room and board and then sent the rest home to us. But that money was not nearly enough to feed all of us. When Deacon Pak learned of our circumstances, he suggested that the entire family move to Pusan and live together in order to save money on housing. It was a good idea, so we moved into a makeshift shack on top of Pŏmnaetkol Mountain.

Our new house was a wretched hovel. At night, we could look up at the night sky through our roof. In the summer, bedbugs infested the house so badly that we had a hard time falling asleep. When it rained, my younger siblings and I took shelter in the corner of the one-room house, while my two older brothers took turns keeping rainwater out.

My brothers worked hard to feed our family of seven. Whenever they had to work overtime during the night, they took soybean gruel with them. And when they returned home, they often climbed up the steep stone steps carrying big sacks full of sawdust from the factory. The sawdust was a good source of fuel.

Since Pastor Ki-ch'ŏl Chu was also imprisoned for his faith, his son Yŏng-hae took refuge in our home. He knew no one else in Pusan, so whenever he was lonely or needed some help, he always came to us.

My mother went out to Tadaep'o Sea in Pusan and gathered edible seaweeds. On the mountain, she often found young leaves of mugworts, shepherd's purse, and other plants to gather for food. It was usually dark when she returned home. These plants and leaves not only filled our hungry stomachs but they also provided us with the necessary nutrients.

My chore was to go to the village nearby and draw water from the "Hunchback Fountain," as it was called. My brother made a water pot for me to carry on my head and also a dipper made from a gourd that floated on top of the water. The dipper prevented the water from overflowing as I walked. It bothered me as a young child when passing adults told me to stand still as they took a drink with the dipper. I became so upset that I got rid of the dipper at one point.

Occasionally, my mother sighed as she looked at my petite stature, even years later when I had become an adult. She believed that the heavy water pot I carried on my head each day had hindered my growth. At that time, I was at the age when children have their growth spurts, but with such poor nutrition, how could I grow tall? I can still hear the villagers call me *Multongi*, which means "water pot." Despite the difficulties we endured because of our poverty, our love and care for one another and for our imprisoned father never wavered. In the midst of all our suffering, our faith was strengthened ever more and our love deepened.

On one stuffy, hot summer day when I came home from playing outside, I heard Mother and Matthew arguing with each other. They had never argued before and I thought it odd. As I listened in on their argument, I noticed that my brother was about to tear down the old, dirty wallpaper that was smeared with dead bedbugs, in order to put up new wallpaper.

"What's the big deal about living with bedbugs? Your father is suffering far more in prison!" Mother angrily said.

"Do you think Father has wallpaper in prison?" Matthew responded.

I knew that deep within her heart, Mother would feel ashamed of having clean, new wallpaper while my father had no choice but to live in deplorable conditions in prison. But my brother thought it would be better to live in a more clean and orderly environment, especially during the hard times, in order

The wooden tub factory where my two brothers used to work.

not to be seen as needy.

"Think about it, Mother," he argued. "What do you think Father would prefer? A clean and organized room or one that is dirty and foul? Surely you don't believe Father would be offended by us cleaning up this place!"

"Even so, it is not right," Mother retorted. "No matter what your father's opinion might be, we who are not in prison ought to share the pain and suffering of those who are in prison for their faith."

Who could side with either of them? My mother's reasoning had its own logic, and my brother made sense, too. What was clear, though, was that both of them spoke out of their profound love for Father and our family.

Personally, I agreed with Matthew. I didn't think Father would have wanted us to live in such squalid conditions. However, Mother ordered Matthew to take down the new piece of wallpaper, leaving the old, soiled paper exposed once again. Apart from Mother's reasoning, the truth of the matter was that new wallpaper might have seemed too luxurious for us at that time.

Each Sunday, our family fasted all day. Even my youngest sister, though very young, was not excused. Mother's friends, who were of kindred spirit, would gather in our small, one-room house and worship together. The admonishment of Father that "our faith in Christ will be all the more strengthened through suffering" deeply compelled us not to be lazy with our spiritual lives.

My two brothers were also diligent in their witnessing to coworkers at the factory. Since we could not go to any church that engaged in Shinto worship nor invite more than a few to our house, we held worship services up on the mountain in the summer, breathing in the fresh summer air. There we studied the Bible and worshipped. The factory workers who didn't pay much attention at first were moved by the fervent zeal of my two brothers. One by one, they began to believe in the true God.

Even in such difficult circumstances, there was a day of joy. Even in the midst of poverty and suffering, Christmas came to even the shabby container factory. Is there any place where the joy of Christmas cannot reach? Wasn't the birthplace of Jesus also a shabby manger?

On Christmas Eve, we held onto Mother's hands and climbed down the steep stone steps to the container factory to celebrate Christmas. Inside the factory, my two brothers and Yŏng-hae were practicing the carol "It Came Upon a Midnight Clear." About twenty people attended the worship service.

The day was so cold that when they practiced the hymn,

you could see white clouds of cold air coming from their mouths. In spite of the cold, the people who gathered there were all in high spirits and filled with joy. They constantly blew their warm breaths into their hands to keep them from getting frostbites. It was the day on which our Savior came to earth. Filled with great delight, such spirits were more than enough to endure the freezing temperature.

We made a bonfire in the middle to keep ourselves warm as we laughed and tapped blocks of wood to the beat of the music, creating a cheerful harmony to fit their music. Though clad in soiled work clothes and their faces thin and pale, we created beautiful, heavenly sounds.

My brothers loved music since their childhood. They sang very well. Whenever it was Christmas or some other special occasion, it seemed to me as though all the pain and suffering in the world were simply washed away through music.

I was overjoyed in the jubilant environment, almost as though baby Jesus were right in front of our eyes. Suddenly, I thought of my father whose freedom had been stolen away. *He is struggling with the cold and spending Christmas night all alone! He has no one to share this joyful day with*, I thought. Yet somehow I knew he would be singing praises to God even if he was alone. My father, who was rather joyful and grateful for the sufferings he endured in that dark, narrow prison cell, would by now be opening heaven's door with his prayers and spending Christmas with God.

10. *The Seven Angels Expelled from Aeyangwŏn*

After my father's arrest and our eviction from Aeyangwŏn, the lepers who remained became like sheep without a shepherd. Since they no longer had a spiritual center, the harmony they previously possessed was nowhere to be found among them. Without a spiritual leader, they had no choice but to wander. What's more, the newly appointed Japanese director, Andō, was like a wolf and so seized the occasion of the shepherd's absence to attack the sheep. Confusing and disorderly days continued without respite.

First, Andō urged the lepers to participate in Shinto worship. So far, Aeyangwŏn had been untouched by the storms of Shinto worship, but the whirlwind of idolatry blew even to Aeyangwŏn. Since they all had heard many times through Father's sermons that Shinto worship is a dreadful sin against God, Andō's forceful demands for Shinto worship were unbearable and intolerable.

Most of the people at Aeyangwŏn prayed all night long in order to guard their faith from this immoral oppression. But among them were cunning ones who entered into an unholy alliance with Andō and persecuted their fellow patients. One of them was Mr. Sang-jip Kwŏn, a man who hated my father and had previously planned to bring him down from the pulpit by force. He failed, however, to carry out his initial plans because he was convicted by his own conscience.

We thought he was born again, but as the old proverb says,

"a man cannot give his own habits to a dog." Soon, Mr. Kwŏn surrendered again to temptation. He formed a group and tried to flatter the Japanese, pledging their loyalty to Director Andō. They not only pressed the leprosy patients to worship Shinto but also observed their actions to make note of anyone who refused to bow down before the idol. Violators were ordered out of Aeyangwŏn. Soon, Aeyangwŏn came under the domination of Sang-jip Kwŏn, who began to exert his power without impunity. Though his symptoms were not severe, Mr. Kwŏn was also a leprosy patient. Rather than sharing in the pains of other patients or comforting them, he unscrupulously oppressed them.

The lepers at Aeyangwŏn feared Mr. Kwŏn more than Director Andō. Consequently, their hatred focused far more on Mr. Kwŏn than on Andō. Therefore, when liberation came in 1945, Mr. Kwŏn ran away. The leprosy patients, however, chased him down and brought him back. They put him into a large sack and stoned him to death. How ironic? He died at the hands of the Aeyangwŏn lepers whom he had persecuted.

Aeyangwŏn lost the freedom of faith and instead became a place where the unrestrained forces of evil took over. Fortunately, there were very few who were like Mr. Kwŏn at Aeyangwŏn. I cannot fail to mention that most of the leprosy patients, though they couldn't openly rebel, worshipped God in secret and kindled the flame of faith.

There were also patients who concluded that they could no longer keep their fidelity of faith in such an environment and decided to leave Aeyangwŏn. Even if they had to wander around as beggars, they knew they could not continuously sin against God. They knew that remaining at Aeyangwŏn would relieve them of their worries about food, clothes, and shelter, but it also meant that they would be forced to bow down to Shinto gods. This was more serious than a matter of meeting or foregoing basic necessities.

In fact, leaving Aeyangwŏn wasn't the major problem, begging from house to house was. Most were unwilling to open their doors to lepers. Yet the patients put their heads together and decided to leave Aeyangwŏn anyhow.

Miss Tŏk-sun Hwang, Miss Chŏm-sun Sŏng, Miss Chu-sim Kim, Miss Su-nam Kim, Miss Mu-yŏn Sim, and Mr. and Mrs. Kil-su Sin all left in search of Namgang Bridge without any definite plans. There were known to be about a hundred lepers who were already camped out underneath the bridge, surviving only by begging. Except for Mr. and Mrs. Sin, of course, the rest of them were all single at that time.

The clan of leprous beggars was quite exclusive. No one dared to invade their territory. If other "unauthorized" beggars were caught there, the word "survival" took on a completely different meaning for the intruders. The group of leprous beggars under the bridge lived by strict rules in order to maintain a systematic, orderly life. They were very hostile toward outsiders.

The seven from Aeyangwŏn went to this bloodthirsty colony of lepers without any particular plans and without any protection. The only absolute thing they held onto was their faith in God. However, they faced a challenge–who would be able to soften the heart of Kyŏng-dol, the ringleader of the leper band who was notorious for his violent temper?

The seven from Aeyangwŏn went to see Kyŏng-dol with a fearful heart and told him their predicament. They explained that they had to leave Aeyangwŏn because they were being forced to participate in Shinto worship against their will. Then, strangely enough, this tough leader welcomed them with warm greetings. Perhaps he believed in the solidarity of lepers or perhaps he held Aeyangwŏn in high esteem. The miracles of grace didn't end there.

Explaining the current situation at Aeyangwŏn, Miss Hwang and her group were able to witness to the beggars. They testified of God's Word and even taught Kyŏng-dol a hymn. God began to move this man's heart. By the power of the Holy Spirit, Kyŏng-dol rounded up all the beggars and had everyone kneel down. In a firm voice he said, "From this day on, these lepers from Aeyangwŏn are members of our group. They will each be issued a beggar's permit. From now on, they will lead us in worship and witness the Gospel among you. You must absolutely obey their words. Finally, no one must touch them. If anyone does, he will surely die!"

The group frightened Miss Hwang and the other four young, single women. Here before them were so many young men who had not been with a woman for a long time. Although their leader warned the men, the young women were still apprehensive about what might happen to them. So after they received their "beggar's permits," the seven of them moved to Sugokmyŏn, which was a short distance away from Namgang Bridge. Later, they built a hut at Pukpangni, Okchongmyŏn with the money the other lepers at Aeyangwŏn gave them. Whenever they were afraid and in desperate need of His protection, the women fervently prayed to God. Just as God changed the hard, violent heart of Kyŏng-dol, He took charge of the other hundred leprous beggars. And the five single women were free from further anxiety.

During each worship service, the number of people who desired to accept Christ into their lives increased. Kyŏng-dol especially shed many tears each service and prayed, "Oh God, thank you for sending these seven angels from Aeyangwŏn." God demonstrated His amazing power through Mr. Sin and these obedient women.

One day, Miss Hwang told Kyŏng-dol the details about my father's arrest and imprisonment, and that his family was suffering from severe hunger. Miss Hwang wanted to help us in some way, but she didn't know how. She poured out my father's story to Kyŏng-dol in tears. Now as a born-again believer, Kyŏng-dol immediately gathered all the beggars together and suggested that they set aside a tenth of all the grain they received from begging in order to take care of my family.

Although they lived in humble circumstances beneath a bridge and survived only by begging, not one of them opposed this suggestion. All of them gladly agreed to do so with a sense of deep compassion for our family. They were grateful for the opportunity to help someone else in need. Their bodies may have been disfigured, but their hearts were as pure as the morning dew.

Cautious of the Japanese police, Miss Hwang would carry one or two bushels of rice in a container on her head all the way to our little hut in Pŏmnaetkol, Pusan. Sometimes she would put the rice in a water pot and cover the top with smelly fermented soybean paste in order to avoid the suspicion of the Japanese police. With her face dripping with sweat, she would come into our house and hold our hands firmly with red-rimmed eyes that filled up with tears at the sudden recollection of the sweet old days at Aeyangwŏn. Miss Hwang was to us as the ravens that brought bread and meat were to Elijah.

Whenever Miss Hwang came with rice, Mother embraced the sack of rice and cried, "Oh, how thankful I am! Had you not come, I would have had to cover my face with a towel and go down to the village to beg tomorrow."

The grains that Miss Hwang brought us were not all from the leprous beggars who lived under Namgang Bridge. The families remaining at Aeyangwŏn too gathered one or two handfuls of grain from each of their rations. Miss Hwang would sneak pass the barbed wire fence surrounding Aeyangwŏn in the middle of the night and knock on the doors. Then each household would give her a handful of rice. If caught, Director Andō would have ordered unimaginable punishment for her, but Miss Hwang wasn't afraid of taking the risk. With her sacrificial acts, she saved our family of seven.

It was a happy day for us children whenever Miss Hwang came to our home. Normally, we only had soybean gruel to eat. However, when she came, we had white rice, a true treat and joy-giver. Besides the food, there was joy in hearing the latest news about the dear people at Aeyangwŏn with whom we no longer had direct contact.

Naturally, on such nights, the entire family would stay up all night talking with Miss Hwang. Our conversations were filled with truth and love, two things that were hard to find anywhere in the world back then. Oftentimes, our fellowship with her was greeted by the light of dawn.

Miss Hwang was not related to us, but since she was a sister in the Lord to my father, we children considered her our aunt. In fact, we called every female patient our "aunt." But in her case, it carried a very special meaning.

Aunt Hwang currently lives in Nonsan and remains single. Her character is upright like a bamboo. Her zeal for the Lord is hot like fire. To me, she's a hero. She never compromises the truth in the face of injustice. She has never been arrogant before

God. She is a true woman of faith, always ready to die for the cause of Christ.

I gathered most of the material for this book from her. She knows far more about my family's affairs than I do. She came to Aeyangwŏn at the age of eighteen and was the pianist for the choir. Not only was she exceptional in music but talented in writing as well.

Later, after Korea liberated from Japanese colonial rule, Father heard how the lepers under the bridge helped our family during his imprisonment. He immediately went to visit them. He met John on the way and together they went to Namgang Bridge.

The lepers were overjoyed to finally meet my father face to face, especially since they had heard so much about him. When everyone gathered, Father expressed his profound appreciation and prayed earnestly for their souls.

The worship service continued with prayer and praises to God, and naturally, a revival meeting was held underneath the bridge. The leprosy patients clapped their hands, sang hymns at the top of their lungs, gave thanks to the Lord, and received the word of grace in their hearts.

After the revival meeting, many of them came to live at Aeyangwŏn. And some time later, several of them became elders and deacons.

11. Lord, How Much Longer?

Among the pastors who took the lead for Shinto worship was Reverend Kil-ch'ang Kim, who was very close to our family and even reared like a son by my grandfather. Though he was grounded in the Word of God, he began preaching a different gospel during the Japanese occupation.

"Do you know what I see whenever I bow down before the Shinto shrine? A vision of Jesus receiving my worship from behind the shrine," Reverend Kil-ch'ang Kim declared one day. "Romans 13:1-2 reads, 'everyone must submit himself to the governing authorities, for there is no authority except that which God has established. The authorities that exist have been established by God. Consequently, he who rebels against the authorities is rebelling against what God has instituted, and those who do so will bring judgment on themselves.' God has blessed Japan now in such a way that He has given authority to Japan to conquer the world. You saints here in this place must surrender to this power. Do not pray for the saints in prison. They are foolish and senselessly stubborn."

Reverend Kil-ch'ang Kim, therefore, insisted that whenever we Christians bow down before Shinto, we must bow down low enough that our noses touch the ground in expression of our highest respect for the established authorities.

Did he really think that Japan's rule would continue for 10,000 years? Did he really think that everything would be okay; that his needs would be met, as long as he flattered the Japanese?

Reverend Kim was well-taught in the Scriptures and should have known that God would not tolerate this idolatry. *How could he have said such a thing? Did he believe that Japan's power was so great that he could forget about God's existence?* It was hard for me to understand what was going on in his mind. Not only Pastor Kim but many other pastors who participated in Shinto worship confused the saints with their strange logic. After liberation from the Japanese, these same pastors quibbled with another kind of logic.

"All the pastors were one by one arrested and all the churches in this country were about to close their doors, so we at least had to remain free in order to revive the church, even if it meant we had to take part in Shinto worship. If it weren't for us, who else would have led the church? Therefore, condemning us as pawns of Shinto worship is unfair." They were still good at making excuses and denied all association with past pro-Shinto teachings. In a way, they were admitting that their previous teachings were false. They were hypocrites!

One day, Reverend Kil-ch'ang Kim visited our home. As he entered our humble dwelling, he handed a white envelope of money to my mother with an arrogant attitude, as if he were doing us a favor out of pure kindness and sympathy.

Mother was not one to accept such tainted money. Even if we all had to die of hunger, she wasn't about to accept such dirty, corrupt money that was given out of cheap sympathy. She trembled with indignation and threw down the envelope.

"Pastor Kim, we won't die of hunger without this money. Take it back! Feed yourself and live well!"

Mother held me in her arms and cried sorrowfully. I too was so sad and indignant that I burst out into tears and cried with her until sorrow completely engulfed me like a shroud.

Even the sky seemed to be like-minded with my heart. Thick, heavy clouds gathered as if they were about to pour down. The humiliated Pastor Kim could not speak a word. In a moment, he dropped his head and walked out the door.

It is said that the greatest sorrow of all is the sorrow of hunger. Our family was, indeed, sorrowfully hungry, and in order to fill our hungry stomachs, we all worked very hard. But in those days, my true distress lay elsewhere. More than hunger, more than the lack of clothing, the greatest sorrow I felt was the fact that the other children who got to go to school wouldn't play with me. Whenever they played jump rope or hopscotch, they always played among themselves. I could only watch them play from a distance. I was envious of those who could go to school. I longed to play with them. They excluded me all the time. Even when we met, they weren't friendly toward me, pretending they didn't know me. And so I felt bitter towards them. Although I somehow already knew that my request would be denied, I felt so sore inside that I begged my mother to send me to school.

"Mother, please send me to school...please!"

"No! If you go to school, you will have to bow down to the idol."

"It will be okay as long as I don't bow down, won't it?"

"You know very well already that that's not possible. Think about your brothers. Don't you remember how Matthew was nearly kicked out of primary school and barely managed to graduate? John refused to bow down in the third grade and was expelled as a consequence."

Mother always gave me the same answer. I resented the fact that all the other children could go to school, whereas all of us at home couldn't. At times, I also resented my mother for giving me the same answer over and over again. Although her answer was always a definite "no," I couldn't help but want to go to school.

One day, with no particular plan in mind, I followed the other children into the school. I could hardly bear the curiosity of knowing what kind of place school was and what they learned there. The children lined up in the schoolyard to listen to the principal's morning message, and after that, they went in to their classrooms.

I didn't mean to, but I followed them surreptitiously, although I didn't dare enter their classroom. The sounds of the children's voices drifted out the windows. Standing on my tiptoes, I peered into the classroom through the gap in the window. All of the children looked so happy. All of them had bright, innocent faces. The boys were like princes; the girls were like princesses.

I was so absorbed in watching them with furtive eyes that I fell into a fanciful daydream. Indulging in a reverie, I also became a princess, so happily talking and laughing with the other school children. In my dream, no one hated me or rejected me. I was their best friend. While I was lost in my daydream, someone kicked me very hard on my bottom.

"Ouch!" I screamed, feeling a sudden sharp pain. When I turned around, I saw an adult who appeared to be a schoolteacher looking down at me.

"Who are you? How on earth did a beggar come into the schoolyard?"

In a split second, I had become a beggar. I ran out of there as fast as I could, forgetting the pain I felt on my backside. Once I got home, I discovered a big black-and-blue bruise on my bottom.

I thought about why such things had to happen. *It's because we, the people, are so weak that we lost our country... it's because of the Japanese and their brutal oppression and demands for idol worship...it's because of my father who was sent to prison.* Feelings of sorrow overwhelmed my young heart.

My mother endured many bitter experiences she cannot bear to share with others. One time on her way home from washing clothes at the village stream, she felt so hungry that it felt as though the skin of her abdomen was touching her spine. She wished so much to eat a bowl of warm rice. We survived only on soybean gruel at that time, and so a vivid image of white rice was always before our eyes.

As she walked a little farther, her eyes suddenly caught a glimpse of a cross. It was a cross of a church. *It's a church... surely they'll give some rice to a hungry person*, she thought. She was so hungry that she began moving mindlessly toward the church.

A man was sweeping the church yard with a long besom. My mother approached him and asked, "Excuse me, may I have some cold rice to eat?" But he pretended not to hear her and began to sweep the dust and dirt more vigorously toward my mother as if to say, "Get out of here, you beggar!" Humiliated, Mother simply turned around to leave, but then she thought she might as well go inside and pray since she was already there. So she went in, avoiding the dirt being swept toward her. Just then, someone ran toward her.

"Ah! Mrs. Son!" a familiar voice shouted out. It was an acquaintance from the past. She was the pastor's wife. Mother was taken aback and felt embarrassed. She told the woman rather ambiguously that she had just stopped by on her way from washing some clothes.

The pastor's wife led my mother into a room where there was a table of food and steaming hot rice. Mother's mouth began to water. She began to think, *Should I ask if I could eat with her? No. Even if I were to starve to death, I couldn't ask such a thing!* Her mind began to battle back and forth many times.

Whether it was a misfortune, Mother did not know, but the pastor's wife never even bothered to ask if she had eaten or if Mother would care to join her at the table. While the woman ate alone, my mother couldn't help but feel disappointed at the fact that she had not even been asked to share the meal. Mother was so hungry that she would have been quite satisfied eating the burnt rice at the bottom of the pot. All this happened just four months before liberation from Japan.

After our nation was freed, that same lady came and apologized to my mother for the incident. "Mrs. Son, I was wrong. I knew very well that you had come because you were hungry, but I pretended not to notice."

The pastor's wife never told us why she didn't share the food with Mother. She might have wanted to save my mother's face or simply save her rice, I don't know. I guess it doesn't matter since she was warm and hospitable afterwards. Even after many years, my mother would say she'd never be able to forget that day.

On another day, Mother packed her lunch and went out to the levee of a rice paddy to gather mugwort leaves; she picked them all day long. Although she had already eaten her lunch, it wasn't enough to fill her stomach, let alone sustain her. She felt extreme hunger pains, the same pains she felt the day she went to the church. Her stomach was so empty that she barely had enough strength to walk.

Mother kneeled down for a long time on a hill and prayed to God. What a pleasant surprise! She opened her eyes and saw that the ground in front of her was covered with fresh, plump red strawberries! As God had given manna to the children of Israel in the wilderness, she could only reason that He had prepared this fruit just for her. She ate and ate until she was full, and then she filled her empty lunch box with strawberries and came home.

I suppose my mother's life can be summed up in one phrase: "a life of patience and sacrifice." All her life, she remained poorly clothed and lived in constant hunger, but she always thought of others before herself. While battling with unbearably difficult afflictions, she was never discouraged, nor did she complain of her fate.

During my father's imprisonment, Mother was allowed to visit him once a month. Whenever she did, she made sure to memorize a verse of Scripture and share it with him.

"If you take part in Shinto worship, you are not my husband!" Mother would tell Father in order to encourage him to remain faithful to God in prison.

My mother often worked at the home of a wealthy family, the Changs, in Pusan. After working all day long, she would come home with food wrapped in the folds of her long skirt. To this day, I still vividly remember what she told us as she placed the food in front of us.

"They gave this food for me to eat, but I couldn't eat it because I thought of you. I hid it to bring to you. Help yourselves!"

Because of malnutrition, Mother often fainted and showed symptoms of severe anemia during work in the family's kitchen. In spite of this, she didn't eat the portion of food given to her and instead brought it to us. Even after our period of hunger had ended, we struggled with poverty year after year, though no one knew.

Nevertheless, we gave thanks to God for everything and lived positively. Yet still I couldn't hide a dark shadow that was somewhere in my mind. In the midst of such sufferings, Father sent us a letter every month, which was a great comfort to us all. Sometimes it was addressed to my oldest brother, Matthew, and sometimes to Grandfather or to Mother. Every member of the family took turns reading it, and as we did, we were assured that his faith was ever more strengthened.

When it was about time for a letter from my father to arrive, Grandfather would crouch down by the stone fence and wait for the mail carrier to arrive. When the mail carrier handed him the letter, he would come quickly into the house.

My grandfather's hands were always shaking when he opened the letters. Out of his mouth came his ceaseless lament, "My son, Yang-wŏn! My son, Yang-wŏn!" Once he finished reading the letter, he would call out my father's name and stretch his arms and legs out in front of him, singing hymns of joy.

12. Life Sentence

The day of my father's release had finally arrived–May 17, 1943! Time had, indeed, been passing throughout our sufferings. We had longed for this day since November 17, 1941, when my father was sentenced to 18 months in prison at Kwangju. It had nearly been three years since September 25, 1940, when my father was arrested and taken to Yŏsu Police Station.

This day was more special than any holiday. How long the days had been for my mother who longed to see her husband, for us who longed to see our father, and for my grandfather who longed to see his son! How long we all had anxiously waited for this day! We even marked it on the calendar! Our family in the Lord at Aeyangwŏn looked forward to this day together with us.

Mother could not sleep the night before Father's release. She rose early at dawn, took a bath, and fixed her hair as best as she could. She moved busily about the house. She was thirty-six years old at the time. During the past three years without her husband, she had suffered unspeakable pain and sorrow, struggling to survive against the rough blows of this world. But now, since her husband was returning home, she felt as though all the suffering she endured in the past seemed so insignificant. I could sense the overwhelming happiness Mother felt inside. She also changed the five of us into a clean change of clothes and made sure to pack the new set of clothes and shoes she had prepared for Father.

Mixed with tears and joy, she sang the Hallelujah Chorus and laughed, unable to contain her joy. In some ways, she looked half-crazy. For the five of us children, our joy also matched that of our mother's. The day we thought would never come finally did and soon we would be able to see our father. I was so happy that I felt as though I could fly up to the sky.

We held hands as we walked toward the prison in Kwangju. When we visited before, the prison fences looked frightening to me, but they looked almost friendly to me on that day. We sat down at the gate of the prison and each of us fell into our imaginations of a sweet reunion. I imagined my father hugging me and rubbing my cheeks with his stubbly face, speaking to me with eyes wide open saying, "Oh how tall my Tong-hŭi is already!"

But the tightly shut steel gate seemed as if it would never open. We were all hungry and thirsty, so Mother bought some food and brought it to us. As we sat there eating the delicious food, anticipating our reunion with Father, we totally disregarded the open stares of passersby. We were neither ashamed nor envious of anyone. Our hearts throbbed with a sweet anticipation that could not be expressed with words.

Time passed and it was already midday. My father did not appear. *What's going on?* we all thought. Anxiety slowly began to creep into our hearts. Lost between anticipation and hope, for some reason an unknown anxiety suddenly gripped our stomachs. Someone spoke out, "Mother, will Father be able to come out today?"

"Your father's prison term is over. He should rightfully be released today. Let's be patient and wait a little bit longer. He will come out for sure." Although my mother tried to reassure us, she too could not hide her anxiety. She couldn't sit still and instead paced back and forth with a worried countenance.

The sun soon began to set as though it were mocking our expectant hearts. We couldn't just sit around and wait any longer, so Mother went inside to talk to the officer in charge.

After nearly an hour, the door of the office reopened and Mother walked out with a pale face. Father was nowhere to be seen. Matthew ran to support my mother who staggered with faltering steps, shaking her head from side to side. We all looked up at her with an intense gaze, waiting for her to open her mouth.

But our hearts were already crumbling down with disappointment. Mother's vacant look gave us a far clearer answer than a hundred words. We could already guess that the situation was grim. But still we hung on to hope and tried to suppress our assumptions. Mother finally collapsed on the street, and shaking her pale face from side to side, she began to sob uncontrollably. She squeezed tight her eyes as the tears flowed down continuously.

How could I even begin to express in words the bitter sorrow I saw in my mother at that time? Who could understand my mother's despair? What could ever fill the vast emptiness she felt because of such a big disappointment?

As we listened to her sobbing, all hope disappeared from our hearts. It was clear that Father would not be released from prison in spite of all our hopes and prayers. With great disappointment, we all collapsed to the ground with our mother as if the sky were falling. Finally, Mother began to speak with a hoarse voice. "Today, your father was sentenced to life in prison."

What a bolt from the blue! Life in prison? What great transgression had he committed that he could no longer see the outside world? Oh how long we had looked forward to the end of his prison term. The news came to us like a thunderbolt. It felt like the hope that had been building up in our hearts had crumbled down all at once. Life in prison, this meant we could no longer see him. Even Matthew, who tried to comfort us, had tears running down his face. No one could stop our tears from falling.

On the way home, our steps were no different from those of a defeated army. There could be no strength in the steps of the hopeless, only dark despair all around.

Once we reached our shabby hut on top of Pŏmnaetkol Mountain, we embraced each other and burst into tears again. In spite of much suffering during all these years, we had always expected to see our father return to us, but now, no such hope remained. It was futile to continue marking the calendar. I could no longer dream of playing with my father or of even holding his hand.

Even though Father twice served a full prison term, the Japanese did not release him because he refused to renounce his loyalty to God both times. He was transferred to Kyŏngsŏng (Seoul) Prison.

Shortly after receiving his new sentence, my father expressed his emotions about this sudden change of events in a letter he sent to us. He was not worried or fretful but rather full of joy and gratitude. My father, who to the end refused to worship the Japanese emperor or to take part in other Shinto rites, kept his faith despite constant threats and coercion at Kwangju Prison. He considered all these trials, including his life sentence, an expression of God's great love. Immediately after hearing about his new sentence, Father responded in a letter:

All right, while I am in prison, I'll live with Jesus. When I'm released, I'll still live with Jesus. It doesn't matter where I am. If I am imprisoned, it is my gain, for it is also a blessing from God. God's will be done. If this is for His glory, I'll follow gladly. Although it may seem better for me to be free sooner than later, I can learn more in prison, so I am grateful.

His letter revealed his personal view that Christian faith is strengthened through suffering. My father also said, "Japan will be ruined. No matter what they might try, they will face destruction. History reveals that all nations that worship idols eventually perish."

Although Father was placed in circumstances that others considered misfortunate, he remained a contented person, always considering each situation a work of God's blessings, grace, and sovereign hand. He penned the following poem after he received his life sentence:

O, suffering that strikes me,
Strike me with all your might.
I'll taste the truth of God's unfathomable love
That is hidden deep inside severe suffering.

13. *Scattered Family*

In January, 1944, after Father was sentenced to life in prison, Matthew went to Ch'ŏngju Probation Center to visit him. Until then, they had exchanged news only through letters, so it was the first time in a long, long time that my brother, who was nineteen at the time, was able to see Father.

Seized by such a strong desire to see Father, Matthew put all other matters aside and traveled the long distance to Ch'ŏngju. His heart was beating hard with expectation and he struggled to calm himself down as he requested a visit. Upon hearing his request, the Chief of Public Information at the prison summoned my brother. The man smiled slyly and then asked my brother, "Will you bow down before the Shinto shrine?" Matthew shook his head from side to side and replied that he would not.

Although the man did not seem to be particularly angry at my brother's refusal, he began to lecture Matthew for a long time in order to change his mind. While speaking, the man's smile oddly never left his face. But for some reason, just looking at the chief's snakelike face sent chills down his spine, and so he turned his head away.

"How can a young man like you have such a closed mind? It is quite understandable that your father could be stubborn as he is an old-fashioned person. Look at the other Korean church leaders. Do you think they lack education or faith compared to your father? Do you know what the difference between them and your father is? They are wise and realistic, much more than your father. Think for yourself. How can Shinto worship be a religious ceremony? If it is religious in nature, why then doesn't the Ministry of Internal Affairs direct it instead of the Ministry of Education?" The chief continued in his attempt to persuade Matthew, "As you can see, Shinto worship is only a national ceremony. Refusing to participate in this national ceremony indicates one's disinterest against Japan and suggests one's intentions to see Korea as being independent. Your father's rebellious actions stem from his foolishness. He does not understand the true meaning of our 'assimilation policy'," which stated that every Korean must become Japanese from the inside out. "He who can't see the situation as it really is and attempts to foster a national movement under the mask of religion can never be forgiven. He is a political offender before being a religious man. You, however, are not at fault, for you have been improperly educated by your father. Deep thought is unnecessary. What need is there for deep thought in bowing down before the Shinto shrine? Thinking too deeply itself is a problem. Think of it more as a simple action or slight tilt of your head. Well, now try it, just once." At this, Matthew didn't reply.

The chief utilized all types of methods, using threats as well as gentle persuasion. Matthew wanted to refute in order to dismantle the man's dark scheme that was hidden behind a veil of false logic, but he thought it would not help to do so at the moment. He just wanted to see Father, that's all he wanted. In order to see Father, he felt that listening in silence would be the best policy. This wasn't the place to argue philosophy or religion. My brother felt he could endure anything, even listening to such false syllogism, if it meant he'd be able to see Father.

However, Matthew underestimated the director. The

snakelike man could clearly see through my brother's desperate hope to see his father. He knew it was my brother's weakness. That's why he put on such a good-natured face and spoke to my brother again.

"Shame on you! Do you still not understand? All I'm asking of you is to bow down just once. If you insist on refusing, I'll also insist on refusing your request to visit your father. So, take it or leave it. You scratch my back and I'll scratch yours."

His words came to my brother like a thunderbolt. He had traveled such a long distance to see Father and had waited so long for the opportunity. If it didn't happen today, he didn't know when or if he would ever be able to see Father again. Even if he could try to visit some other time, that didn't comfort him as he knew that no one in the family would ever be allowed to visit Father without first bowing down before the Shinto god, or for as long as this man held his position as Chief of Public Information.

Numerous conflicting thoughts passed through Matthew's mind. *What should I do? Should I commit this unrighteous act just once in order to see Father, or remain clean and return home without fulfilling my purpose?* His Christian conscience would only permit him to turn around, but the vivid image of Father's face was too strong before him. He knew idol worship was the very first violation of God's law. But since the day of our father's arrest, Matthew had not been allowed to see Father's face, not even once. He simply missed Father too much.

Finally, the desire to see Father before returning home overcame all of his other thoughts. *It's only a formality. God who sees the heart will understand my heart.*

Matthew followed the chief to the Shinto shrine, and while the chief wasn't paying attention, Matthew turned around and walked out without bowing his head. My brother didn't know whether the chief had seen him not bowing down, but since nothing was said, he was safe. Then my brother was led into the chief's office and was asked to put his thumbprint on an affidavit that confirmed his participation in Shinto worship. Only after Matthew stamped his thumbprint would the chief allow my brother to visit Father. In an act of desperation, Matthew did as ordered. All of this happened in a matter of seconds. Having set his course, feeling that there was no alternative, my brother gave in, trusting that God would understand and forgive him.

As soon as Matthew saw Father in the visitation room, he cried out, "Father!"

"Don't cry, Matthew," Father comforted him. "Even if we don't see each other here on earth, we can still see each other later at the foot of God's throne." Our father looked so pale and thin, practically just skin and bones, but his penetrating eyes were still the same. Although his physical body was weakened beyond its limits, his soul was ever more strengthened.

It was too short a time. When time was up, Father secretly passed Matthew a letter he had previously written. With that letter securely gripped in his hands, my brother caught a train home. On the train, he read the letter that contained these words of admonition:

Because emperor worship and Shinto worship are sins before God and violations against God's first and second commandments, do not participate in them under any circumstance. Keep the Lord's Day holy and do not skip daily family worship or early morning prayers. Be diligent in Scripture reading, practice tithing, take good care of your grandfather, and obey God's Word.

As Matthew read the letter, his hands trembled. He realized for the first time how foolish he had been, and before he knew it, tears of remorse began to run down his cheeks. Obedience to God's laws was the very reason for all their suffering, but in order to see Father, he had participated in Shinto worship, the very thing Father had refused to do even at the cost of his very life. *Although I was able to avoid actually bowing my head before the Shinto shrine, what is there to be proud of? I gave them my word that I had done so? What if they show the paper to Father? Oh, how much pain the news would cause his heart?* Matthew thought. Suddenly, as though he had awoken from his sleep, he became sober.

Matthew's heart was torn with remorse. The images of the chief's sly smile, along with Father's grieving face, replayed in my brother's mind. My brother couldn't help but admit that he had given into Satan's temptation, and though his sin lasted but a moment, a sin was a sin. Matthew admitted to committing a shameful act before God.

He didn't know how he would face God, and everything turned black before his eyes. He began to shake uncontrollably. God's Word passed through his head like lightning.

"Oh, God!" my brother cried out with his eyes closed.

Everything became clear now. He knew he should have refused to participate in Shinto worship no matter how badly he wanted to see Father. Even if it meant he would never see Father again, he should have kept God's commandments. This was not only the will of God but also the admonition of our father. How foolish it was of him to want God to understand.

The train was racing fast. Looking out through the window at the beauty of nature, it seemed as though the birds and trees were staring sharply at him with condemnation. Matthew didn't even bother to wipe away his tears. He began to pray to God in repentance:

Lord, I am a foolish, foolish, foolish sinner. I am a sinner. I fell into Satan's temptation and committed idolatry. I shamelessly expected Your understanding of my unrighteous acts. I don't know what came over me... something must've blinded me. Please open my eyes to see clearly. Please help me to make better choices that are more pleasing to You. Please help me to live according to Your righteousness, Your will, and Your sovereignty.

Matthew's prayer of repentance was full of tears and it drew the attention of the transit officer who approached him to ask why he was crying. Matthew sat down and began to tell the officer that he was on his way home from visiting his father at Ch'ŏngju Probation Center.

"Is that so? Then why do you cry?" the Japanese officer probed, as if he were genuinely interested in the story. My brother wiped away the tears that welled up in his eyes and began to openly explain why Father had been imprisoned. He also admitted to the officer that he had "participated" in Shinto worship in order to visit Father, and that his tears were of remorse for going against his father's faith. There was no reason for my brother not to be bold at this time.

"Nonsense! Your father obviously has no idea what the current situation is like. How else could he dare to continue to oppose Shinto worship? He deserves to suffer in prison. Boy, you must see the current situation realistically and meet the demands of the day, otherwise, you yourself will fall into the same fate as your father."

However, Matthew felt that God had heard his prayers and had accepted his heart of repentance for the foolish sin he committed. Matthew thought that God had now provided him with this opportunity to speak boldly against Shinto worship.

"Shinto worship is a sin. It is not a national ceremony but rather a religious one. It goes against God's commandments, and therefore, it is blasphemy to participate in it. No matter how hard Japan tries to rationalize Shinto worship, the truth cannot be hidden."

Only then did Matthew feel relieved from his guilty conscience. He should have said this earlier to the chief. I guess the more we try to avoid fear, the bigger it gets. As father had always done so boldly and fearlessly, it would have been best if Matthew had confronted the sin sooner. But because his desire to see Father was so strong, the crafty Japanese chief was able to trick him into wrongdoing.

The transit officer stared sharply at my brother for a long time as if he were saying, "How dare you!" He immediately demanded to know my brother's name, age, as well as his home address. Matthew was no longer afraid, not even of being dragged before the judge or forced into prison like Father.

My brother told the transit officer about everything that had happened during his visit at the prison, and the officer made a record of it in his notepad. Without saying a word, the transit officer left. It was this encounter that caused my family to be scattered later, something my brother didn't foresee at the time.

Not long after Matthew returned from Ch'ŏngju, a draft

notice arrived for him, requiring him to be examined for conscription into the army. We all assumed that the notice was the work of the Japanese transit officer who might have thought that the most convenient way to deal with this young teen was to send him off to war, where he would be required to perform Shinto worship every day at the military base. That draft notice dropped on us like a bomb and eventually shattered our family.

If he were to be drafted, who knows when he would return home? There was no guarantee of returning alive either. But more than anything, what feared Matthew most was the thought of having to bow down to the Japanese emperor and to the Shinto gods. How would he escape this time?

My brother, of course, passed his physical exam for conscription. This was a time when it would have been more fortunate not to be healthy. It would have been much better to be a disabled person than to be healthy and forced into Shinto worship. Therefore, my mother gathered all of us everyday and prayed. "Dear God, if my son Matthew is drafted into the army, he will be forced to commit idolatry. Please help him to avoid committing such a sin, even if it means he'd have to become a leper."

Days passed with worry and concern. Draft evasion meant death on the spot. In fact, Matthew even considered suicide, but he knew suicide was also a sin against God. He thought of running away, but he couldn't dare to because he knew what kind of suffering the entire family would have to endure on his behalf.

Finally, in true desperation, he decided to leave everything to God and began to fast and pray with Mother and Grandfather for God's answer. John also joined them in fasting and prayer. After several days, their eyes were deeply sunken and their cheeks were hollow. They had no strength left and looked like ghosts. Tears still fill my eyes every time I try to describe their physical conditions at that time. Because food was already scarce for us—most of the time eating only soybean gruel—their fasting multiplied their physical weakness. Unless one had been there to witness their miserable state, there is no way one could understand the extent of their pain. Oh, how painful my brother must have felt inside!

One day, Matthew, his body thin beyond recognition and having received an answer from God, shared with us his final decision. "Mother, I can't join the Japanese army, even if my life is at stake. No matter what, I cannot perform Shinto worship, because it is blasphemy against God and our father. So..."

Matthew couldn't continue. He dropped his head. I believe this was the fruit of his repentance. No one spoke a word. Heavy silence filled the room. Only the tender sound of my brother weeping filled the room.

"Mother...?"

"It's all right, son. Tell us your decision." Mother broke the silence first. But Matthew didn't reply for a long time.

"Speak up, son. Is there anything you can't tell your mother?" Worry and tension filled the already heavy atmosphere in the room. Mother seemed to know what God's answer to Matthew's prayers was, so she finally spoke up.

"I know, son. You want to tell me that our family must scatter for safety."

It seemed like Mother had also received the same answer as Matthew. Since the two had prayed together, it was quite natural for them to receive the same answer from God. Since Matthew could not accept the draft or commit suicide, scattering the family was our only choice. Each of us would have to run away and hide from the Japanese. There was no other option. No matter how hard we tried to look for alternatives, we came to the same conclusion—to scatter about.

It had not been long since we had left Aeyangwŏn, which was a home and paradise to me, and settled into a shabby hut on Pŏmnaetkol Mountain. With another threat looming against us, we were being forced to leave our home again. Through the years of poverty and suffering without Father, we had become a refuge for one another and persevered without complaint. Yet how could we possibly endure separation when even the thought of being separated was too much to handle? Though we lived a poor, empty life without Father, we remained faithful to God and kept our conduct blameless. But now what would happen to us?

No one knew how long this separation would have to last. Perhaps we wouldn't see each other ever again. Mother concluded that even if we wouldn't see each other again on earth, it would be far better than surrendering our brother to the Japanese army. Matthew agreed. Though he had been tempted once, he was determined not to fall to it a second time. It hurt him deeply that his family would suffer, but he believed it was ultimately for the good of the family.

I was just a little girl at the time. Although I didn't clearly understand why we had come to the conclusion that it would be best to separate, I now know that it was the fruit of their great faith, a faith that no one can emulate. Clearly, it wasn't an easy decision for them to make, but it would've been impossible without faith.

We didn't know when the notice for Matthew's enlistment would arrive, but we knew it wouldn't be long. Mother began to look for places for us to hide, and as circumstances allowed, she decided for each of us where we would go.

As for my grandfather, it was decided that he would go to his second son Mun-jun, who was in Harbin, Manchuria. My uncle had settled down there because the Japanese police constantly chased him and kept close watch on him, especially because of Grandfather's imprisonment for participation in the March First Movement and also because all of Grandfather's other sons were in prison. My uncle later became a pastor. Once it was decided that Grandfather would go to my uncle's house, Mother and the youngest of us decided to go to the house of Mr. Chang for whom my mother used to work. John went to the hut in Pukpangni Okchongmyŏn, where the seven lepers who were forced to leave Aeyangwŏn lived together. Matthew went to hide deep in the forest near Namhae. My younger brother and I were sent to an orphanage called Aerinwŏn, which was located in Kup'o, Pusan.

In reflection, it was an exceedingly difficult situation. Though the five of us children weren't orphans, we were forced to become like orphans and scatter about. I can only imagine the aching hearts of my mother, brother, and grandfather! The atmosphere of our home was filled with darkness. Even the ticking of the clock seemed to hasten us. We gave up eating and drinking while the hour for our separation drew ever closer. Our separation was inevitable and could not be reversed. There was no time for wallowing in sentiments. We had now reached a dead end.

14. Brother, What Do You Mean 'Orphanage'?

In July 1944, my younger brother Tong-jang and I had no idea we were going to be sent to an orphanage until it happened. Mother loved us dearly, so she didn't tell us in advance, because she didn't want us to have to go through a long anxious wait.

At dawn on the day of our departure, we found out about our fate through Matthew. He stroked my hair gently and spoke in a soft voice. His face was gaunt and haggard. His eyes were full of tears.

"I'm sorry Tong-hŭi, you and Tong-jang will have to live at the orphanage for a while."

"Brother, what do you mean 'orphanage'? Why the orphanage? Why do I have to go there? I'm not an orphan!" I yelled in resentment. *Why would I go to the orphanage?* It didn't make any sense. Both my parents were still alive.

"There's just nothing else we can do. Our circumstances are grave. You understand our intentions, don't you? Later, God will make it up to you for all that's about to happen."

Only then did I vaguely understand the endlessly depressed atmosphere in our home, the fasting and praying, the heavy silence of the day when they decided to hide, the sobbing of my two older brothers, and the occasional heavy sigh of my mother. But I just couldn't accept the fact that I had to go to the orphanage.

"Brother, I like the way it is now. I'm okay with being

hungry. I can handle it as long as I live with Mother and my brothers. Please, I beg you! Don't send me to the orphanage, please!" But the dice had already been cast; the arrow had already left the bow. It was a decision they made after strenuous fasting and praying. It was a fate that was inescapable.

Mother was weeping with crushing sorrow at the imminent separation from her children. How hopeless, how broken her heart must have been! I could not understand at the time how she could willingly tear her family and own heart into pieces, and scatter them into the unknown.

Although our home was only a shabby hut on top of a mountain, our family had lived in a close bond of love. But now we had to bid farewell. *Why do unfortunate things keep happening to us, one after another?* I thought to myself. *Good-bye steep hill, I will always remember climbing up with heavy water pots; good-bye Hunchback's Water Fountain; all of you... so long. I have to leave you behind and keep you only in my memories. Tong-jang and I are leaving forever...good-bye.*

Mother took out her Bible and hymnal. We gathered under the sparkling lamplight for our last family worship. Since there were no guarantees that we would ever meet each other again, our throats choked and an ocean of tears flowed down our faces.

"Perhaps we will only see each other again in heaven," Mother said briefly before she began to sing a hymn. All of us followed and we sang the hymn together.

> *God be with you till we meet again;*
> *Neath His wings protecting hide you;*
> *Daily manna still provide you;*
> *God be with you till we meet again.*

Till we meet, till we meet,
Till we meet at Jesus' feet;
Till we meet, till we meet,
God be with you till we meet again.

We embraced each other and cried so much that we could barely worship. From the hut of Pŏmnaetkol Mountain, the sound of sobbing burst out deep into the night and carried a sad story. No one came to comfort us. Though we lived poor, we were happy living together with our mother and our siblings!

We left our home early the following morning in order to avoid the watchful eyes of the neighbors. We all went our separate ways, speeding through the thick morning fog, soon after we said our red-eyed good-byes to our beloved family. Matthew placed Tong-jang and me on his rented bicycle and sped down the steep hill. I held on tightly to his waist, constantly looking back at our home. My mind was filled with empty thoughts and sadness. I couldn't control my tears. Even in the midst of all that sorrow, I found comfort in smelling the familiar scent of my big brother and leaning against his back.

The chilling morning air scraped at our faces mercilessly. Mother's face became more and more faint and distant. On the way to the orphanage, no one spoke a word. We were all depressed at the ominous thought that we might not see each other ever again.

Finally, we arrived at the orphanage. Matthew lifted us off the bike and began to cry with his face buried in his arms. His shoulders were shaking. Gazing at us for a long time, he said, "I believe that since the two of you are very patient, you can endure the separation even though you may miss the rest of us, right? After all, aren't we the children of a great father?"

The orphanage was located in Kup'o, Pusan, and was called Aerinwŏn. It was established on May 15, 1938, by Reverend Chŏng-gyo Han in the spirit of Christ's love and ministry. At the time of its founding, Su-ok Cho, a deaconess who had been released from prison, helped out at the orphanage and helped many other Christians who were being chased by the Japanese police because of their refusal to take part in Shinto worship. Aerinwŏn became a hiding place for many. But this wasn't at all a place for a young girl like me to call home. Only the unfamiliar faces of orphans passed by us. After entrusting us to the care of Reverend Han, Matthew forced himself to turn around and walk away. Tong-jang and I endlessly looked at the back of our brother's head as he rode farther and farther away until he became a disappearing, hazy dot on the horizon. We stood speechless, hopelessly gazing down the road like one who had just missed his only ride home. We felt all alone, stripped of our identities and as if we had been cast out naked into the wilderness. We felt abandoned in a world where we could not depend on anyone. I was twelve years old; Tong-jang was just nine. And together we lived at the orphanage until our country gained independence from Japan.

What lives we had to live, lives full of hardship! Though our parents were still alive, we had to live in an orphanage. It was widely known that our older brother Matthew had escaped from the Japanese authorities who tried to force him into the army. Reverend Han and the elders thought it would be best to change our names. I became "Hŭi-ya" and Tong-jang became "Chang-ŭn." If that wasn't enough, we were instructed to act like we weren't brother and sister. *What is happening to us? Which commandment of God has put our beloved father in prison and us in this orphanage? Why does our loving family have to be scattered?* I kept asking myself these questions.

At Aerinwŏn, there also lived two boys, Yŏng-jin and Yŏng-hae, who were the sons of the famous martyr, Reverend Ki-ch'ŏl Chu. They were older than us, but our situations were very similar. Their father was also martyred because of his refusal to take part in Shinto worship. *What made them confront Japanese imperialism in spite of imprisonment and separation from their family? Is it okay to sacrifice your family for the sake of obeying God?* I began to resent my parents. I couldn't understand them. I didn't even want to try to understand. *Why do my parents believe in this eccentric Jesus so much that we have to live as orphans?* I thought.

From that time on, I found myself gradually transforming into an impulsive and impatient person. I couldn't control the violent anger that boiled over from within. Alive in my mind was the desire to destroy anything that came within my hand's reach.

I gradually withdrew myself and became silent. Even when someone tried to force me to speak, I closed my mouth tightly and refused to reply. I was sick and tired of everything. If one of the children asked, "Are you mute?" I would just shake my head. And if I was asked, "Are you ill?" I would shake my head again. I was tired of the quiet gazes of other adults who thought I behaved this way because I missed my mother. I think I was much less irritated with the indifference of other children.

I even began to reject God in my heart. *Where is God anyway? It's all a lie! If He really exists, why did He make me an orphan when my parents and brothers are still alive?* Whenever such thoughts crept into my mind, tears would wet my cheeks. Though I cried, no one was there to comfort me. A strange, unexplainable, rebellious spirit took over my heart. Whenever it began to take control, I shook my head forcefully and told myself firmly, "No, you must not cry. Don't cry, Tong-hŭi! You must learn to stand alone in this world. It is now your duty to take care of Tong-jang. Be strong!"

Tong-jang was too young to understand the situation. He often grabbed the hem of my skirt and throw a hissy fit.

"Sister, where is Mother? Where did our brothers go? Why don't they come back? I miss them..."

"Don't cry, Tong-jang. You still have your big sister. I'll do anything for you." Several times a day, I had to hold Tong-jang in my arms and comfort him.

About two weeks after we were dropped off at Aerinwŏn, some of our belongings arrived from our home on Pŏmnaetkol Mountain. Reverend Han must have suggested it. When I saw the familiar objects my family had touched, I was suddenly overcome with homesickness and missed that shabby little hut more than ever. More than that, I missed my brothers and my mother. At the thought of my mother, I swept my hand across the dresser that had my mother's fingerprints. I could no longer suppress my emotions and began to cry uncontrollably. Looking at so many familiar things from home, I could see my mother's warm smile in my mind's eye. I wept with a longing that was much more sorrowful than bitter. *Is there any better word than 'mother' in the entire world?* I thought.

To this day, when I reminisce upon my days at Aerinwŏn, though I don't care to remember it much, my mind draws an image of another unforgettable face. His name was Kap-chu Yi. Physically, he was nothing out of the ordinary, somewhat short and chubby, but his personality was twisted and violent. He especially enjoyed picking on me, and to this day, I don't know why.

He knew I lived in constant fear, so he would purposely make a ferocious face to scare me and then push me to the ground. Whenever he did, I resisted the tears and instead burst out into laughter, "Ha ha ha!" Sometimes he would say, "There's a dragon fly on your head," then strike my head with a fly swatter and run away. He would then hide and try to get me into trouble. I could hardly endure this ill-natured boy's pranks, nor could I understand him. So, I developed a habit of watching for his whereabouts, and if he were near, I would run away from him unnoticed. I can look back with a thin smile now, but back then, his constant harassment added additional misery to my already sorrowful life.

Mealtime at Aerinwŏn always began with the ring of a bell. We were given corn porridge three times a day, every day. It was the food ration from the government. We always sat in a large circle eating corn porridge, while Reverend Chŏng-gyo Han always sat in the middle eating corn porridge with us. I liked Reverend Han very much. Even in my childish mind, I considered him a truly great man. He was a true father to orphans and looked after us with a sincere love.

Whenever I had a face-to-face encounter with him, I could see my father through Reverend Han's gentle and quiet disposition. His quiet and gentle spirit reminded me of my father and it made me miss him even more. Reverend Han often said, "Hŭi-ya, bring your younger brother and come by my room."

When we entered his room, there would be two cups of goat's milk from the goats they raised at the orphanage, and sliced tomatoes that he himself picked from the garden behind the orphanage. He specially prepared all of these things for my brother and me. On each occasion, my heart was filled with gratitude, but at the same time, I had difficulties holding back my yearning for my own family.

Biting into the ripe tomato, I could feel Father's deep love. Eating tomatoes was not easy because our throats often choked with tears. I felt a strong impulse to call Reverend Han "Father" and throw myself into his arms. Tong-jang felt the same way. So many times, we wished so much that Reverend Han would hold us tightly against his warm chest, even for just a moment.

At Aerinwŏn, we had worship service every morning. Reverend Ki-ch'ŏl Chu's son Yŏng-hae taught Bible to the children, and shortly all of us were able to recite 1 Corinthians chapter 13 from memory.

I slowly adjusted to life at the orphanage. By then, the anger and bitterness I felt when I first arrived mostly disappeared. I used to be a loner, insisting on keeping my heart closed, but I eventually opened up my heart. Little by little, I returned to being a normal young girl who liked to chitchat.

Around this time, as I was beginning to gain a sense of security, Matthew unexpectedly visited Aerinwŏn. Since he was a draft dodger and was still being pursued by the Japanese police, he had been wandering through the forest. His face looked deeply tanned and his body was far gaunter than ever before. Even the clothing he was wearing was heavily soiled and torn here and there. Regardless, Tong-jang and I were overjoyed to see him.

"Tong-hŭi, Tong-jang, I have come!" Matthew said as he handed us a bag of cookies. He opened the bag and placed a cookie in each of our hands, and then, as if he could no longer restrain his overwhelming emotions, he took us both into his arms and began to weep uncontrollably.

"Oh, how you must have suffered because of me!" Matthew cried out, repeatedly blaming himself.

"It's okay, Brother. It wasn't as difficult as you think."

"Tong-hŭi, Tong-jang, I made you orphans. You hate me, don't you?"

"No, it's okay, really. Your friend Yŏng-hae is here with us; we feel safe and secure. And Reverend Han loves us very much."

Matthew felt extremely sorry for separating us from our family. It was not, in fact, my brother's fault, but still he continued to blame himself for our situation.

That night, Matthew delivered a message from the Bible to the thirty orphans. He spoke sincerely from his heart:

> *I have fought the good fight, I have finished the race, I have kept the faith. Now there is in store for me the crown of righteousness, which the Lord, the righteous Judge, will award to me on that day—not only to me, but also to all who have longed for his appearing.*   *(2 Timothy 4:7-8)*

What a joy it was for the three of us to be together once again. But too soon, the night broke into dawn. It seemed that morning had arrived much earlier than usual. Matthew had to leave us again. He left us with his promise to come back again for us in several days and a word of admonition not to fight with the other children.

I found out later that in order to avoid the Japanese military draft, Matthew was hiding in the forest and tamed his hunger with tree bark, wild berries, and herbs found in the mountain. For some time, he lived deep in the forest, wandering around Namhae, and he also stayed at the home of Mrs. Tŏk-nye Han, who was Mother's close friend of faith.

Her house was located in a Namhae village called Naesan. My brother put himself in charge of miscellaneous odds and ends for her family as he felt guilty about depending upon them for food when they were themselves already poor. He emptied the septic tank, fertilized the vegetable field, gathered the pine tree branches and fallen leaves to dry them for fuel, and tended to the fire for heat in their rooms. He didn't even mind carrying Mrs. Han's two-year-old daughter on his back to rock her to sleep.

I was told that he never stopped singing praises to God in spite of all kinds of hardship he endured. Even when he walked down the mountain, carrying heavy loads of wood on his back, he sang praises to God. (Mrs. Chŏm-sun An, the oldest daughter of Mrs. Tŏk-nye Han, told me this later.)

My mother also briefly stayed at their house with our youngest brother. Fortunately, there happened to be a small room in the house that the family set aside for fasting and prayer, and it was there where my mother and our youngest brother prayed deep into the night, and at times until daybreak.

My second oldest brother John was living on a desolate mountain in a shabby dugout among lepers. The seven lepers who had left Aeyangwŏn because of their refusal to consent to Shinto worship had built this place.

Before our family was scattered about, I too spent two months there. All of them went out to beg, and we lived on the rice that was gathered from begging. The day our family scattered, Aunt Hwang (Miss Tŏk-sun Hwang) took John to her dugout, and the lepers gladly welcomed him as they would have greeted my imprisoned father. They were truly faithful believers and our true family in the Lord!

In spite of their difficult circumstances, the lepers held a daily prayer meeting, and after prayer, they didn't just go to bed but read the Bible under the flickering lamplight. Some of them prayed all night long, while others studied the Bible in depth.

Although the lepers were rejected and despised by the world because of their diseased bodies, they possessed a powerful strength, at least in their faith, that most people were unable to obtain. All of them were influenced by my father's faith. Father loved and cared about the lepers far more than he cared for his own brothers and children, so the lepers trusted and respected Father, next to God. Their faith was never shaken. They firmly believed that though my father was in prison, he would surely return to them. They were glad to have at least John among them.

It was early morning when Aunt Hwang was jerked awake at some strange premonition she had while sleeping. She didn't know what time it was, but it was still dark. She felt an empty space at her side. When she turned the light on, John, who was supposed to be asleep, wasn't there. Aunt Hwang got up and went out to look for him.

It was an unusually bright and starry night. John was nowhere to be seen. Aunt Hwang took the mountain road behind the dugout house and called out my brother's name, thinking that perhaps he might have gone up that road to the mountain. "John?" she called out and then quietly listened. Again she called out, "John?" Suddenly, she heard an indistinct mumbling mingled with the sound of grasshoppers. To Aunt Hwang, who had led a faithful prayer life for many years, that sound was unmistakably the sound of prayer.

Realizing that John had woken up early in the morning to go deep into the forest to pray, she approached him quietly in order not to disturb his prayer time. John was praying in tears:

Heavenly Father, give this weak heart of mine courage. It is said, 'happy is he who suffers because of his faith.' Give me boldness, too. Like father, like mother, like my older brother Matthew...give me a strong and uncompromising courage, too. Though my family is now scattered, I know this also is an expression of Your great love and blessings. Heavenly Father, help us to persevere without dismay. I'll carry the cross that is given to me without refusing. Now I'm living with lepers for whom my father used to serve and care. I don't know how long I will be here, but don't let me be a burden to them; rather, help me to be their helper in faith. I don't mind becoming a leper while living among them. The only thing I seek from You is strong faith so that I may help them even in the slightest way.

John often went deep into the forest to pray aloud for our imprisoned father's health and release; for the well-being of his two orphaned younger siblings; for the welfare of our mother and the youngest child; for Grandfather, who had left on the long journey to a foreign land; and for our oldest brother Matthew, who was out in the wilderness, being chased by the Japanese police. When morning came, everyone else went out to beg here and there. Since they had to travel far, once they left home, they sometimes didn't return for a week.

One day, John suddenly said to Aunt Hwang, "Auntie, I'll shave my eyebrows and go beg with you."

When he insisted on going, Aunt Hwang held him back

and said, "No, I won't let you become a beggar. You stay home."

While he stayed home alone all day, and at times all week, John would go up to the mountain to gather fallen leaves for fuel and carry them down on his back. Sometimes he would gather green pine tree branches to dry them and use them to heat the rooms. At times, he helped clean the house. He did everything he could to help his loving hosts.

15. *Japan Surrenders*

It was a very hot summer day. The air at the orphanage felt somewhat strange. Excitement lingered on the previously morose faces of the adults. Several members of the church stood in a circle around Reverend Han under the shade of a tree and worshipped God out loud. Since coming to the orphanage, I had never seen such an exuberant worship service. The adults raised their hands toward the sky and cried aloud, "Oh God, thank you! Hallelujah!" They sang hymns powerfully and prayed in teary voices. A deep sense of gratitude overflowed on their faces.

Instinctively, I knew something good must have happened. But because I was only a young girl of thirteen, I couldn't figure out what exactly the good news was. I had no other choice but to wait anxiously until the worship service was over. Finally, the loud, enthusiastic worship service ended. Spotting me, Reverend Han ran toward me. His countenance was bright and he was wearing a suit. My heart was beating hard with anticipation.

"Hŭi-ya," he said as he gazed into my eyes and held my hand, "you truly suffered all these years, but from this day on, you and your brothers' hardships will perish. Today, our country won liberation from Japanese colonial rule. We are free from the Japanese. Your father will soon be released from prison."

"What? Liberation?"

"Yes. Liberation! Japan was struck by an atomic bomb and

they have surrendered."

"My father will be released from prison?"

"Yes. That is exactly correct. Japan has been defeated."

Who would have guessed? It was the last thing I expected to hear. At first, I couldn't quite understand what he was saying. It was obviously good news, but I suddenly felt as if I had traveled back to the day in 1943 when our family waited anxiously for Father's release. My emotions became a muddle.

It seemed like just yesterday we were waiting outside the prison gates in anticipation of seeing Father again. And it seemed like just yesterday when we were crying because our hopes and efforts had all been in vain since Father had been sentenced to life in prison. I remember how Mother collapsed to the floor and cried aloud to us, "Do not expect to see your father ever again."

But now Reverend Han was saying that our father would be released from prison. I thought I would never see him again, but now, Father was probably on his way to the orphanage to pick me and my brother up! I couldn't believe it! It just couldn't be real! Japan was now defeated, my father was going to be released from prison, and our family was now going to live together once again.

I had been living under the assumption that my future would be a wretched and gloomy one, and that I would be stuck at the orphanage forever. But now, there was hope.

The possibility that my father was going to come for me seemed like a miracle, almost as if a dead person were coming back to life. And this time, Father was, indeed, returning. The people at Aerinwŏn Orphanage, and the entire nation, were engulfed by a deep sense of gratitude for our newly obtained freedom.

While intensifying her oppression of Korea, Japan was engaged in a series of military conquests that plunged her into World War II and that finally resulted in her defeat.

In 1940, Japan made a military alliance with Germany and Italy. At the end of 1941, frustrated by the United States and the United Kingdom's imposition of an oil and scrap-metal boycott, by the freezing of Japanese assets and by the closing of the Panama Canal to Japanese shipping, Japan provoked America to war by attacking Pearl Harbor in Hawaii on December 7, 1941. At first, the Japanese badly crippled the U.S. Navy and drove the Americans out of Guam and the Philippines, taking over the British strongholds of Hong Kong and Singapore. But with the battle of Midway Island in June 1942, the tide began to turn and Japanese expansion in the Pacific was curtailed. Meanwhile, the Italian fascist dictator, Benito Mussolini, was overthrown in Europe, and Italy surrendered to the Allies.

With the invasion of Normandy in 1944, Hitler's mad pursuits in Europe came to an end. Germany surrendered in May of 1945 and the Allied Powers turned their full attention to the war with Japan in Asia. On July 26, the leaders of the US, Great Britain, the Soviet Union, and China met at Potsdam and issued the Potsdam Declaration, demanding the unconditional surrender of Japan. However, Japan refused, determined to fight to the end.

On August 6, the first atomic bomb destroyed Hiroshima, and on August 9, another fell on Nagasaki. Russia declared war on Japan on that same day and was in full control of northeastern Manchuria and the northern part of Korea within the next five days. Japan was driven back from all her Pacific territorial conquests and her cities were pounded by the tremendous destruction of the atomic bombs. Terrified, the Japanese emperor hid in the underground bunker that had been prepared inside his palace and he held an urgent meeting on August 14. Finally, on August 15, 1945, Emperor Hirohito announced Japan's complete surrender to the Allied Powers. At the end, the emperor added in a teary voice, "I'm not a god, just a person." After thirty-six years of struggling against Japan's oppression, Korea was finally free.

At noon on August 15, the Posingak Liberty Bell on Chongro Street in Seoul rang thirty-three times. The Korean people ran out into the streets and jumped up and down in a state of jubilant confusion, fully enjoying the freedom that was restored after nearly four decades. They burst into tears of gratitude. For thirty-five years, they had been forced to be mute and were humiliated as people without a nation. They silently endured all kinds of persecution and oppression under Japan. How persistently our people fought for freedom and how patiently we had endured with a dauntless spirit!

Among them were those whose sentiments of freedom were particularly special. They were the independence fighters and Christians who had suffered imprisonment. The patriots considered the nation's independence more valuable than their very lives. The imprisoned Christians were ready to die in order to keep their faith. Many of their families stood by them and encouraged their great, lofty determination. The liberation of our people must be credited to those who cried out for freedom.

God had answered the desperate, tearful prayers of the Koreans just as He had answered the prayers of the Israelites during the Exodus. This demonstrated to the world that God does not remain silent, for He is just.

The streets of every town and city were filled with the

joyful cries of the people chanting, "Long live Korea!" Men, women, young and old alike, waved the national flag and cried out, "*Mansei!*" until their voices were hoarse. The wave of independence spread throughout the nation; it also reached the prison where my father was locked up. Though Liberation Day arrived on August 15, the gates of the prison actually opened two days later at 11:00 p.m.

Some years before in 1936, a notoriously cruel Japanese general, Minami Jirō, had been appointed governor-general. At an imperial meeting, he had to report on the current situation in Korea. When a delegate asked him, "How are things going in controlling Korea?" Minami Jirō answered, "Well, right now in Korea, there are 40,000 soldiers who are not afraid of death and nearly all of them are Christians."

Since 1937 when the notorious "assimilation policy" was put into effect, all educational institutions, as well as all religious institutions, were placed entirely under the control of Japan. All Koreans were ordered to use the Japanese language exclusively and change their names to Japanese ones in order to obliterate their very identity as Koreans. All meetings and ceremonies in Korea began with an oath of allegiance to Emperor Hirohito, and every Korean was compelled to worship at Japanese Shinto shrines. Many Christians who refused to worship the Shinto gods were arrested and brutally tortured or even put to death.

As the strain on the Japanese war machine reached the breaking point and defeat loomed on the horizon, the actions of the Japanese government in Korea became increasingly cruel and desperate. It became clear to everyone, even to many Japanese, that the defeat of Japan was inevitable. It was only a matter of time.

The Japanese believed that Korean Christians might join the forces of the Allied Powers when Americans and Russians began to enter Korea to push the Japanese out, so the Japanese authorities planned a scheme to uproot Korean Christians. They began to organize a full-scale holocaust—they prepared a huge cave, about 80 square yards, where they would kill all the Korean Christians with swords and bamboo spears. They set the date of the slaughter to August 17, 1945. But just two days before this date, Korea became an independent nation. Who else would have accomplished this deliverance but the wondrous sovereignty of God? In my young mind, I thought this happened because God wanted our family to reunite with Father.

"Father!" I thought I would never be able to utter this word again. Though my parents and siblings were all alive, they were too far away. I never imagined my life outside the orphanage as I had earlier accepted the fact that I could very well spend the rest of my life at this place. Intentionally, I had tried to forget my father and was, in fact, gradually doing so. But now, having been told that we would be reunited with him, I felt as wonderful as Jesus' disciples must've felt when the resurrected Jesus came to visit them. My head swam with joy. To me, the return of my father was far more exciting than the liberation of our nation. *Oh, God, is this for real or just my imagination?* I thought. God heard the prayers of His children and vindicated His people who had for so long been mercilessly trampled on.

Tong-jang didn't know anything yet, so as soon as I found him, I told him the good news. "Tong-jang, Father will be released from prison. He will come get us soon."

"Sister, is that true?"

I had expected this response from Tong-jang as the news had made my own heart thump with such anticipation. I thought it would excite young Tong-jang much more, but his words were surprisingly calm. It was all too sudden and so unexpected that it appeared surreal to him. His face was more perplexed than excited.

Several minutes later, Tong-jang held my hand tightly and asked in a teary voice, "Does this mean we won't have to live at the orphanage from now on? Will we live together with Father, Mother, Matthew, and John?"

"That's right, Tong-jang. Reverend Han told me. It has to be true. Let's have faith and wait."

"Sister, is it really true? It's not a lie, right? It won't be like before, will it?"

"It is true, Tong-jang."

"Is it really, really true? Perhaps you are teasing me Sister."

Like Tong-jang, even in the midst of excitement and expectation, I myself couldn't believe my ears. Always living in adversity, I had grown accustom to disappointment and lived with the skepticism that great blessings could never come to me.

Our father barely made it to the orphanage. One evening, he appeared before us as though he had resurrected from the dead. His appearance was as one of the most wretched beggars.

He was still dressed in his blue prison uniform and looked so shabby that I had to turn my face away. His beard was long and flowed down below his chin; his complexion was pale like that of a terminally ill tuberculosis patient; his eyes were deeply sunken and hollow; his body was merely a sack of bones that looked like a corpse which stood upright; and his skin literally clung to his bones. But from his deep sunken eyes, an indescribable beam shined through.

On August 17 when my father was released from prison, no one stood outside to greet him. Although the other prisoners were greeted by their families and were brought a clean change of shoes and clothes, our family was scattered so far apart in the most remote areas that none of us had heard the news of independence or of Father's release until later.

Two weeks later, Mother, as well as Matthew and John, finally discovered that our nation was liberated. Who could have gone to greet Father? Who could have prepared new shoes and clothing for him to change into? None of us. Father only received a quiet welcome from God.

Father took off his slippers and blue prison clothing at the orphanage and he changed into something more suitable. Unfortunately, we had not prepared anything for him, so what he borrowed did not fit him at all. Wearing the loose clothing on his emaciated body made him look like a scarecrow hanging loose out in the field.

"Look at that man!" the children at the orphanage said as they gathered around my father.

Even passersby stopped for a moment and stared at my father, as if observing a rare animal at the zoo. It didn't matter how filthy and unworthy of attention Father might have appeared. To Tong-jang and me, his presence was priceless. With the joy of reunion, my little head was dancing. It was the most amazing fantasy that had ever come true.

"Let me look at you, my precious children. Oh, how much you must've suffered all these years!" Father embraced us both. We cried out only one word, "Daddy!" and threw ourselves into his arms. The moment we were in his arms, the sorrows that had accumulated over the years began to disappear all at once.

It wasn't a dream. This was very real! Even in our father's eyes were tears. Could there be a happier day than this?

But on the day when all the people in our nation rejoiced and in the midst of uncontrollable joy, there was one person who was left in anguish, Yŏng-hae Chu. The Japanese had murdered his father, Reverend Ki-ch'ŏl Chu. Even on this joyful day, no one visited Yŏng-hae.

Soon, Yŏng-hae ran toward my father, gasping for air as he cried out, "Pastor!" He couldn't speak further; he simply embraced my father tightly before bursting into tears. Yŏng-hae didn't pay any attention to the stares of others as he cried aloud.

"I'm Yŏng-hae Chu, the son of Reverend Ki-ch'ŏl Chu."

"Oh, you are the son of Reverend Ki-ch'ŏl Chu, the man who was martyred in prison and whom I respected most. Looking at you, I see your father."

Father's heart sank, not knowing with what words he could comfort this poor boy. The two of them just embraced each other. Father deeply respected Reverend Ki-ch'ŏl Chu and had called him "big brother" as the reverend was five years older.

When Father met his friend's son, his eyes moistened with tears at the thought of his martyred friend. Suddenly, Yŏng-hae wiped away his tears with his fist, grabbed an ax from the corner, and ran outside the orphanage. The children at the orphanage ran after Yŏng-hae. They thought something serious was about to happen since he ran out with an ax in his hands and a scowling face.

"Look! Yŏng-hae is running outside with an ax!" one child yelled.

"What's going on? Why is Yŏng-hae running out like he is out of his mind?" the others asked.

Each of them screamed and ran after Yŏng-hae. Yŏng-hae ran toward the big park that the Japanese had erected a *kamidana*[7] idol. Koreans had been forced to bow down before it whenever they passed by. With a tear-stained face, Yŏng-hae shattered the idol with one blow. Without looking back, he disappeared. How heartbroken he must've been, knowing his father couldn't taste the joy of independence on this day nor see the bright light of day outside his prison cell before passing away.

Thinking back, Yŏng-hae Chu had a truly deep relationship with my family. When Matthew and John worked at the container factory in Pusan, Yŏng-hae worked there also. At one point in time, our home was the only place of refuge in this world for Yŏng-hae. He shared in our joys and sorrows and walked through the dark, rough times with us. He was the first person to deliver the sad news of his father's martyrdom to my family.

Rarely did he become angry, always acting according to God's words and maintaining his composure. He was gentle and positive in all things, but on that particular day when he saw everyone else but his father being released from prison, I suppose he could no longer keep his anger locked up in his heart. We all understood.

16. *Release from Prison*

"**I**'ve come to see Pastor Yang-wŏn Son. I've learned that he's just been released from prison," said the man standing before him.

"I'm Yang-wŏn Son," my father said as he greeted the visitor who had been searching for him at the orphanage. Tong-jang and I were still clinging onto Father. We had been reunited for only several hours and we weren't about to let go of him any time soon.

"Pastor Son, how do you do?" the visitor began. "I came to ask a favor. Our church is planning to have a special worship service tonight to celebrate our country's liberation. We would like you to preach for us."

"Yes, of course." My father gladly replied. He was never one to turn down an opportunity to preach God's Word. Holding our father's hands, the three of us went to the church. I cannot recall the exact location of the church, but I'm sure it wasn't far from the orphanage.

Supper was provided at someone's house, but it was poorly prepared. On the table, there were only three lumps of cold rice and a murky, thin soup with dried turnip tops. How could they treat my father like this? My father was the pastor who came to preach the Gospel. In my mind, though still a young child, it was an obvious display of their disrespect for this poorly clad preacher who came to speak to them. Otherwise, how could they present a table fit only for a beggar? But we were simply too hungry to say this and that about the food. My father probably didn't care much about it anyway since, to him, the meal was far better than prison food. It is said that "a good appetite is a good sauce," and though it was cold rice and thin vegetable soup, it tasted quite good.

Once we put our spoons down and looked around, we noticed that several people were watching us eat. It felt quite strange to be stared at. On their faces, I could see their feelings of disdain. They looked as though they were watching hungry dogs lick empty bowls. They might not have thought so, but that's how I felt. I wanted to say, "Father, let's stop eating and just get out of here," but I didn't. Being treated for so long as mere orphans, I guess I got used to such treatment.

Looking back now, I can somewhat understand their curiosity. Perhaps they had high expectations, especially having heard that the pastor who was going to preach to them was quite famous. Perhaps they imagined a person with an appearance like Jesus. But the preacher who appeared to them was far from their expectations or wildest imaginations and was dressed like a miserable beggar with two ragged children clinging on both sides.

Although Father was wearing ill-fitting clothing, Tong-jang and I were also dressed quite shabbily. I admit it must've been quite natural for them to give us such pitiful stares. But my father's countenance remained calm and he didn't seem to care how the others felt about him.

When service began, Father walked slowly up to the pulpit. Just when he was about to open his Bible to preach, his gentle smile suddenly disappeared from his face. He looked extremely furious. My father's eyes glared at the *kamidana* idol that was still standing at the pulpit. Even after liberation, the congregation was unable to truly experience freedom because it failed to get rid of the idol. My father's face became distorted with anger. He looked around once before he knocked the idol over with his hands. With an unusually loud smash, the lingering fragments of Japanese imperialism fell to the floor. And the eyes of the entire congregation widened with astonishment.

Everyone sitting in the pews focused on my father in alarm. Until that moment, the people had continued to bow down to the idol before beginning every service. They worshipped the idol first before God. They considered it natural. Then a poor, emaciated pastor came and smashed the revered idol without hesitation. They could not help but be astonished. They were a weak and foolish congregation.

The idol was the shape of a small house carved out of wood, and inside were four clearly written Chinese characters that read: "GREAT GOD WHO CREATED HEAVEN." During the period of Japanese colonialism, no church could conduct a worship service unless they first bowed down to this idol. If anyone refused to do so, he would be dragged into prison like my father. Korean Christians were more afraid of Japanese laws than God's commandments. But now our nation was set free! What more were they so afraid of that they could not throw away such an abominable idol? As the Scripture reads, "Therefore, my dear friends, flee from idolatry." (1 Corinthians 10:14)

They were not the only ones to be blamed; they might have had the wrong spiritual leader or a false shepherd. In 1938, the 27th General Assembly of the Korean Presbyterian Church decided to participate in Shinto worship as they believed it was not a religious act but a patriotic national rite. Their leaders set the example by going to the Shinto shrine at

P'yŏngyang. They wanted the lay people to believe and follow their teachings. How could we condemn these ignorant people? The blame had rest solely on the pastors who agreed and actively participated in Shinto worship, and who insisted that the first and second commandments applied only during the Old Testament times.

Some years ago, Father said that because the Korean church was so corrupt and because it had committed a great sin against God, He revealed His wrath and allowed our nation to be divided along the 38th parallel. Liberation was granted as a result of the faithful testimonies of Christian martyrs and prisoners who refused to bow before the Shinto god, and who faithfully obeyed God's commandments. But the 38th parallel that divides our nation to this day represents the consequence of the sins of the church leaders who enticed the innocent people of God onto the wrong path and sold themselves to Japan.

The truth of the matter is that during oppressive, torturous Japanese occupation, refusal to worship the Shinto gods was extremely costly. It was a matter of life and death. Resistance was possible only when one was absolutely confident in his belief and not afraid of death. Many churches and Christian schools that refused to accept Shinto worship were forced to close down. Many Christians were imprisoned and suffered extreme torture, hunger, exposure, and sickness. But the majority of the churches followed the decision of the General Assembly, leaving the most humiliating stain on the history of Christianity in Korea. Only after liberation did the General Assembly hold another meeting and finally acknowledge that Shinto worship was a sin against God.

Father's sermon began aggressively, reflecting back to the circumstances of the past. He scolded the people's weak faith with a thundering voice. It was his very first sermon after his release from prison. Perhaps it was because of the five years of accumulated lament over the church that his extremely fervent and fiery faith cried out boldly, "Repent!" His voice burst out like thunder from a blue sky. His sermon was like that of John the Baptist crying out in the wilderness. It was just like how Jesus spoke out when he scolded the merchants who tainted the holy temple of God.

For a moment, a deathly silence fell over the church, and then sudden cries of repentance broke out here and there. Soon it became a sea of wailing. Some beat their chests in repentance, jumping up and down in anguish; some mumbled tearful prayers; and still others hugged the person next to them and sang praises with loud voices. Indeed, it was this hour of grace that fully opened heaven's gate. Since these Christians were for so long deprived of true teachings from God's Word, it seemed as though they were being drenched with God's living water that showered down from heaven through His Word. Their eyes were now newly opened to the Truth. Their parched souls absorbed the nutrients of my father's sermon and they finally began to revive. Only a few hours ago, they treated my father like a beggar. But now, they were shaken by the electrifying spiritual shock of faith that came from this man they had looked down upon.

Even now as I reflect back to that evening, I am amazed at how such a great and powerful voice could burst forth from such an emaciated body. I remember looking up at my father in awe and wonder. Although his physical appearance was rather unattractive, similar to the shape and form of a withered autumn leaf, his spirit was so enriched each day that he became a person of light who could move heaven and shake the Earth.

Though I do not remember the contents of his sermon in detail, his cries that day for the people to repent was deeply embedded in my heart and remain vividly in my memory.

I remember another incident. It had something to do with the red bean gruel that the church members made us. In the middle of his sermon, Father casually shared a story about red bean gruel.[8]

"None of us in prison had winter clothes to protect ourselves from the bone-chilling cold. Prisoners sentenced to life received no special treatment, not even when it was a special holiday like the winter solstice. Sitting on the cold floor, we grieved about our fate and wondered how we could pass safely through this unbearably cold winter. But then it was strange. Obviously, there was no reason to expect red bean gruel in prison. Strangely enough, the smell of red bean gruel passed through the air, gently touching my nose. All of a sudden, I wished so much to eat a bowl of hot red bean gruel. We didn't even get enough rice, so it was highly unlikely that we'd ever get a taste of red bean gruel. In fact, it was absolutely absurd to even imagine it. I would've been quite satisfied with eating just one marble-sized ball of rice cake in the red bean gruel."

On the following morning, the church members, who were so blessed by Father's sermon, brought red bean gruel and we had a party. Truly, human nature is fickle. Only one day before had they tossed a bowl of cold rice in front of us as though they were feeding dogs. But now we were eating as much warm red bean gruel as we wanted. After that day, Father traveled to many places and preached.

Fortunately for us, since Tong-jang and I were at the orphanage, we met our father right away after liberation, but the rest of my family did not. They were scattered about in hiding and were forced to constantly search for one another, crossing paths at different times.

Two weeks after liberation, John, who was living in a hut deep in the mountain with lepers, said to Aunt Hwang, "I will be back. I have some business with Mr. Sin-ch'ul Pak." When John arrived at Mr. Pak's house, he learned of the defeat of Japan and Korea's liberation.

Fortunately, Father also went to see Deacon Sin-ch'ul Pak, with whom he exchanged correspondence while in prison. He wanted to find out the whereabouts of his family. In God's providence, he and John were reunited. John told Father about the leper beggars who lived under the Namgang Bridge and who helped our family. Father suggested that the two of them visit the lepers first. He expressed his gratitude and preached to them.

Afterwards, John and Father left for Pukpangni Okchongmyŏn to meet Aunt Hwang. In the meantime, she also learned of our country's liberation and went to Deacon Sin-ch'ul Pak's house in Pusan in hopes of meeting my father. Aunt Hwang was too late. But she was advised by Deacon Pak to go see the lepers who lived under the Namgang Bridge. But again, Father wasn't there.

"Alas, Miss Hwang, you're only a step behind. Pastor Son and John just left for Pukpangni to meet you," the leader of the lepers told her.

She quickly returned to Pukpangni Okchongmyŏn and there she had a reunion with my father. The three of them agreed with one another to go to Aeyangwŏn first instead of wandering about in search for the rest of the family. They decided that the best thing to do was to wait for the family to join them at Aeyangwŏn.

Holding hands with one another, Father, John, and Aunt

Hwang returned to Aeyangwŏn. All the lepers gathered together like a cloud along a long oceanside road, waiting for my father.

"Our Pastor Son has returned. Hallelujah!"

"Look! Our shepherd has overcome his trials."

"Oh, God, thank you...thank you again."

All the lepers at Aeyangwŏn surrounded Father and welcomed him with a loud, joyful cry. My father hugged them and reached out to each leper's hand. He wiped the tears away from their eyes as he asked them how they had been doing all those years.

Quite some time after Liberation Day and after a long search, someone finally informed us of the whereabouts of my mother and older brother Matthew. A person from Aeyangwŏn was sent off to bring them back. They were still hiding deep in the forest near Namhae. After nearly five years since we were forced out of Aeyangwŏn, we all returned to our old sweet home. Father was able to minister once again as pastor and renew his relationship with the lepers.

Finally, all of us were gathered in one place again. It was like a dream come true. How could I have dared to dream that such a day would come? God didn't abandon our family. He freed our nation from the oppression of Imperial Japan and gathered our family into one place once again. The reunion didn't stop with my family. The lepers who left Aeyangwŏn and lived in remote dugouts at Pukpangni for the freedom of their faith also returned. The leper beggars who used to live in tents under the Namgang Bridge also came to Aeyangwŏn. God preserved us all throughout the rough times and did not allow a single strand of hair to be harmed. When His time came, He led us safely back to Aeyangwŏn.

It was a shame that my grandfather couldn't share this great joy with us. Despite his old age of seventy-five, he always worried about his imprisoned son and never stopped writing letters of encouragement to him. Grandfather was the root of our faith and he never stopped praying for his children's futures. However, four months before liberation, without getting to see the joy of this day, Grandfather closed his eyes and breathed his last breath in a foreign land.

On the day he died, Grandfather, who was strong like an eagle and gentle like a dove, enjoyed the sunshine of spring as he played with his grandchildren at my uncle's house. When evening came, Grandfather said, "I'm going to pray now, so keep the room warm." Then he entered his room and began to pray. He died in that position, praying until the very moment before going to heaven. He died while praying for my imprisoned father, for us children who became orphans, and for our scattered family. Ever since he first received Jesus Christ as his Savior, he kept his faith alive throughout his life. He was the beginning, the central point, the foundation of our family's faith. His death caused us much grief, especially Father who was well known for his deep filial love for his father.

While he was alive, Grandfather always used to say, "I want to be buried in my hometown." Later, Matthew brought back Grandfather's remains from Manchuria, China, and buried him in our ancestral burial place on the mountain in Ch'irwŏn.

Andō, the cruel Japanese director who was posted at Aeyangwŏn, was soon chased out. And Dr. Wilson and Reverend Unger, both of whom had left Korea in tears during the war, returned. It was a free world now and no one tried to intrude. I was happy like a bird that had just been set free to fly about in the sky. We were brought back to life.

17. Oh Spring, Why Must You Leave So Soon?

Summer at Aeyangwŏn that year was full of life. Though the ocean remained the same, it looked somewhat different after liberation. As if it had been newly adorned, it looked limitlessly blue and clear. Even in the passing breeze, I felt a great vigor. The lepers were more beautiful than ever to my eyes. They did not look like pariahs with distorted faces and disfigured hands. Heaven and earth, even the leaves and stones, each and everything seemed lovelier. Everything looked as though they were praising God for His great grace. We were reborn like new buds that spring up on a brittle twig.

Aeyangwŏn reclaimed its peace when my father resumed his ministry as pastor to the lepers. Whenever Father lay down to rest after preparing his sermon, Tong-jang and I would pounce on the chance to be next to him and used his arms as pillows, constantly turning his face toward ours. Father would turn his face back and forth between Tong-jang and me. At times, he would ask us, "Tong-hŭi, Tong-jang, while I was in prison, what was Grandfather doing each day?" It seemed like my father had terrible guilt about not being able to be by his father's bedside at his last moment on earth. We would tell him whatever we could remember.

"Grandfather used to go around trying to catch mountain cats," we told him, "because he wanted to eat some meat. But he could never catch any, not even one. Instead, he searched the trash cans of wealthy homes and gathered tripe for Mother to make some soup with."

"Whenever we received a letter from you, Grandfather always cried. His hands shook so much that he could barely open the letter. He would call out, 'Yang-wŏn! Oh, my son Yang-wŏn!' Then he would bend down, press his face into the dirt, and cry. Once he finished reading the letter, he would hold the paper tightly in his hands and cry out, 'Yang-wŏn, my poor son Yang-wŏn!'"

We were much too young to realize at all how our words would so terribly crush our father's heart. We were hardly thoughtful enough to realize that our words would become a sharp knife that deeply penetrated his heart. His unfulfilled filial love tore him to pieces. All we thought about was which one of us could win over Father's attention with the most stories.

Father pushed us away and buried his face in his arms. His shoulders were shaking. Only then did we realize what we had done. We didn't consider how our father's heart would ache as we chattered away needlessly. Yet on the following day when our father asked us to tell him more, we would make the same mistake again.

My mother and brothers never opened their mouths about how we had suffered during those years. When asked, they only replied, "With God's protection and provision, we were able to get by without serious problems for the five years." They didn't want to hurt him.

Father replied in the same way. When we asked, "Father, we heard that Reverend Ki-ch'ŏl Chu and Reverend Sang-dong Han suffered severe torture while in prison. How were you treated?" He only responded, "I was fine. While in prison, I rested well without much suffering."

Words were not necessary. Conversations of the heart were far more precious than spoken words. Father, Mother, and my two older brothers were already exchanging conversations from their hearts. But I was much too young to understand the depth of their heart-to-heart conversations.

Father used to say that the Christian faith is strengthened through suffering. In a letter to Mother from prison, dated August 18, 1943, he wrote:

My dearest,

To me, Job's suffering is more precious than Solomon's wealth and prosperity; Job's patience is far more beautiful than Solomon's wisdom. Solomon's wealth and prosperity later became the means to corruption, while Job's suffering and patience became glorious in the end. The glory of man will be determined in the end, and true wisdom is to shun evil. Since joy and a peaceful mind are the tonics for many diseases, cast all your cares on the Lord and please get well soon...The end of wealth and prosperity is always disappointing, but at the end of suffering stand comfort and joy. How much more comfort and joy there will be for those who suffer in the Lord?

Since my father considered suffering a prerequisite for glory, he wasn't one to tell every detail about the suffering he endured in prison.

With liberation came the freedom for us to enter school. Oh, how I wished to go to school all those years; oh, how I envied the other children! But now, I too could go to school. It was not lack of fervor and abilities or even poverty that kept me from going to school during the Japanese occupation. Only one thing kept me away from my studies – keeping God's commandment to refrain from idolatry. For this, we had to put aside our academic pursuits. When freedom for schooling came to us after liberation, my older brothers and I couldn't contain our joy.

But there was one problem – we were too old. Our absence from school had been too long. Matthew was expelled in the fourth grade because of his refusal to bow down before the Japanese emperor, but he later transferred to Ch'angsin Elementary School and just barely completed his elementary studies. John was also expelled for the same reason when he was in the third grade. In my case, Mother was so concerned about the sin of idol worship that she decided not to send me to school at all.

It was too late for me to register as a first grader. It wasn't easy for us to gain admission under our particular circumstances. The school told us that because we were too old, they could not enroll us in classes. Fortunately, Father's friend, Pastor Tŏk-hwan Na, took each of us to visit the school principals and explained the reason why we had not been able to go to school. Thanks to Pastor Na's insistence, the principals consented to our enrollment. Matthew entered the twelfth grade at Sunch'ŏn High School and John was placed in the eighth grade at Sunch'ŏn Middle School. As for me, I should have been in the sixth grade, but because I had received no previous schooling, they enrolled me in the fourth grade, and my younger brother Tong-jang was placed in the second grade.

It was very difficult for my two older brothers to catch up academically. Putting aside their studies for so long in order to work at the factory had brought about inevitable consequences. My older brothers studied hard, often past midnight. Whenever

I woke up in the middle of the night, I saw how deeply immersed they were in their studies, especially as they often had cotton balls stuffed in their nostrils to stop the nosebleeds. They seldom went to bed before midnight and only slept until 5 o'clock in the morning. In order to stay awake, they often dashed cold water on their faces. Sometimes, their noses would bleed from exhaustion and dizziness would overpower them.

Compared to my older brothers, it wasn't that difficult for me to catch up with the other elementary school children. Because I had desperately hoped to go to school for so long, each day at school was spent with pure joy. Not only the studies but also school life, as a whole, was exciting to me.

In fact, my grades gradually got higher and higher. By the end of my first year at school, I scored the highest in my class, so I skipped the fifth grade and went straight to the sixth grade. Back then, students who scored first or second in the class were allowed to skip a grade. I graduated from elementary school in just two years. Whenever my older brothers introduced me to their friends, they bragged, "My younger sister is a genius!"

The surrounding area near Aeyangwŏn was a remote mountainous village that had no schools. We had to go to the school in Sunch'ŏn, which was 50 miles away from Aeyangwŏn. Fortunately, Aeyangwŏn provided us with a place to stay in Sunch'ŏn. In the beginning, we temporarily stayed at Pastor Tŏk-hwan Na's house and walked to school from there. A month later, a house for us to live in was arranged. While we lived in Sunch'ŏn, my parents lived at Aeyangwŏn. I went to Aeyangwŏn every Saturday and spent my school breaks there.

In Sunch'ŏn, we attended Sŭngju Church, where Pastor Na was the minister. Both Matthew and John served as Sunday school teachers, and the older of the two served as the director of the church choir as well. Matthew had become famous for his singing ability. His voice was unusually fine and lovely and he possessed an exceptional musical talent, thus he led almost all the musical programs at the church. Matthew had many opportunities to sing solos and he enjoyed it very much. He especially loved to sing the hymn "Bright, Heavenly Way."

More than anything, Matthew loved sharing the Gospel with others. On one occasion, he spoke at a Christian student fellowship meeting about a true story of a Korean girl who had been killed during the persecution of Christians. The soldier who had been ordered to shoot her demanded that she give up her faith, but she stood firm, assuring him that she would go to heaven if she died, all the while urging him to repent. The soldier shot her, but he later became a Christian. The location of her death was honored with the construction of a church, which has come to flourish throughout the years. Many women served full-time in Christian ministries because of this girl's martyrdom. As Matthew told the girl's story, he pointed out that it was through her death that she bore much fruit. He urged his fellow students to take refuge in Jesus Christ so that even in death, they too, like the martyred girl, would safely make it to heaven. His sermon made a great impression on those who heard it.

At school, Matthew was quite popular. He was president of the school's Christian Student Society, he sang well, and on top of that, he was very handsome. His character was upright and gentle, holy and compassionate. During that time, he received free voice lessons from Kyŏng-sim O, a music teacher at Sunch'ŏn High School. Ms. O entered him into nearly every music contest, and he always managed to win first prize. The voice teacher suggested that he become a professional singer.

Because of his amazing talent, Matthew was very popular among the many teenage girls. I knew several of them. Whenever they saw me, they would greet me as happily as they greeted my brother and would ask me about him. Thanks to my brother, I received many expensive gifts and was often invited to the bakery or other special restaurants.

Matthew's love for me was truly special. Every now and then when I got into an argument with John, Matthew always took my side.

Matthew used to suggest that I study music. He tried very hard to provide me with opportunities. One day, he came to me smiling and said, "Tong-hŭi, I'll help you get piano lessons and later, you can accompany me on the piano when I sing. How about that?" A few days later, he actually found a woman, who was a foreign missionary and pianist, who was willing to teach me.

I was so happy I could hardly breathe. Wasn't it me who used to think that I would live out my childhood at the orphanage and that my brother, a draft dodger, would always have to hide deep in the forest? Now, an unprecedented event was happening. What a change of fate! I was not only able to go to school, my greatest dream, but I could also learn to play the piano. I felt as if I were on cloud nine. I was completely overjoyed, but at the same time, I was somewhat anxious and worried that all this happiness would be taken away from me any minute. It was my first encounter with the piano and also Matthew's last gift to me.

During summer break, we normally went home to Aeyangwŏn. We spent time with our long-missed parents and enjoyed the summer at the beach near the ocean behind our house. Mother would go up to the mountain and pray. John, so intent to go with her, would tie a string to Mother while she was sleeping so that he would wake up when she did and be able to follow her to pray. He kept up his daily prayers and sometimes spent all night praying in the church.

Matthew occasionally went fishing midday in the hot summer sun in order to rest his tired brain. He asked me to go with him every time he went.

"Tong-hŭi! My dear Tong-hŭi! Follow me."

"Where are you going?"

"I'm going fishing. If you follow me, I'll catch you some fish."

He wore a straw hat and carried a fishing rod on his shoulder. In one hand, he held a container of hot red pepper paste and in the other, my hand. As we walked toward the beach, he would sing beautifully with all his might as though competing with the sound of the crashing waves. His singing mingled with the sound of waves, spreading the happy music. Whenever I listened to him sing, I would think that his voice was truly a precious gift from God. There was an unexplainable power in his singing. His voice was deep, limitless, and impressive, moving like the deep, blue ocean. It flowed deep into my soul and left an unforgettable impression on my heart. I held my brother's hand and followed him. Matthew sang and I sang with him. If he ran, I would run with him. If he fell down on the sandy beach, I would fall down also. If he burst into laughter, I followed him and laughed aloud. The walk to the beach was always happy. Our favorite spot was by the turtle-shaped rock. Whenever Matthew caught a fish, he would make sashimi, dip it in seasoned red pepper paste, and put the first piece in my mouth.

Even several decades later, I can still taste the sweet

sashimi we ate together by the turtle-shaped rock. The countless stories we exchanged, warmly gazing upon each other, remain forever in my heart like precious pearls. The sound of singing and the warm talks we shared still live and breathe in that deep, blue ocean.

Memories of the winter breaks I spent with Matthew are full of joy. There were many icy roads at a place near Aeyangwŏn called Tangmŏri where Matthew always took me to go sledding. He used a hammer, nails, and some wood to make me a sled.

Matthew would call, "Tong-hŭi, my dear Tong-hŭi! Will you ride the sled with me?" Whenever he called, I would put aside everything else and run to him. When the temperature dropped below 10 degrees, the ice was perfect for sledding. Many children skated and sledded on the ice. Apple-cheeked and glowing with excitement, I would ride on the sled, imagining myself as Snow White, while Matthew ran through the wind, pulling the sled. Time passed as quick as running water. I would get off the sled and try to thaw my frozen cheeks with my hands. Matthew would take off his coat and put it over my small shoulders. I could feel the warmth of his heart from inside his coat. I would breathe in his scent as he held my hands in his and blew hot air from his mouth to melt away the chill.

Wearing my brother's coat, I felt just right—warm, sleepy, and hungry. Somehow, my brother always knew what I was thinking. He would lead me by the hand to one of the bonfires that the farmers had made in the area. I would sit down in between the farmers, while Matthew roasted a sweet potato over the fire. I had to blow on it because it was too hot to handle, but it was delicious.

On my right elbow is a mark that reminds me of Matthew's love for me—a noticeable scar. One day, I was on my way home from school when I tripped over a large rock on the road. My elbow struck hard against the rock and began to bleed profusely. The pain was unbearable, almost as if my bone had been fractured. It was too much to endure. This was the first time in my life that I'd been seriously injured. Pain shot through my body so sharply that I could hardly breathe. I squatted down for a long time on the side of the road and barely managed to stand up and walk home.

While holding onto my injured arm with my other hand, I cried aloud and said to Matthew, "Brother, I think I broke my arm." His face turned pale with concern. In tears, he carried me on his back and took me to get acupuncture. In spite of the treatment, the pain did not disappear. I wish I could have at least fallen asleep, but the pain was so excruciating that I could not sleep at all. Matthew carried me on his back, pacing back and forth around the house until finally, I managed to fall asleep. To this day, now past the age of sixty, whenever I see that scar on my right elbow, I am reminded of my oldest brother's tremendous love and become choked with emotions.

Reminiscing about Matthew, I am reminded of another incident. Matthew's school, Sunch'ŏn High School, caught on fire one day and the entire building burned down. The students gathered and discussed how they would help rebuild the school. They all agreed to hold a concert and use the proceeds from the concert, however little, towards constructing the new school building.

The program of the concert consisted of a play, a vocal quartet, and a solo by Matthew. Whenever he had to sing a solo, he ate a raw egg beforehand. I used to hold the egg tightly in my hand to warm it up for him. My brother sang Korean folk songs like "Come" and "The Herb-Gathering Girl," which were

My oldest brother Matthew (seated, third from the left) with his classmates three months before he was killed.

composed and written by Chae-myŏng Hyŏn. His voice teacher, Kyŏng-sim O, accompanied him on the piano.

Our whole family clapped our hands with all our might as we watched the performances. All the performers sang and played their roles to the best of their abilities. Matthew's solo was a display of his sheer talent. Many people praised him, saying his voice sounded like that of an angel. His singing ability was, indeed, truly amazing. Even now, I still seem to be able to hear the melodies of his songs in my head.

But did he know he would die so young? Matthew was only twenty-five and John was only nineteen when they died. Their short lives on earth were but a brief springtime.

The following is the poem that Matthew submitted to the school newspaper on June 19, only four months before he died.

Oh Spring, Why Must You Leave So Soon?

Oh spring, why must you leave so soon?
The north winds gust across the snow,
Freezing our ears and nose.
When the trees and plants were stripped
And beaten by the icy winds,
Who didn't long for you?
Oh spring, why then must you leave so soon?

My heart, while waiting for you, had many pleas.
I was looking forward to sharing
All sorts of tales underneath Nam Mountain.
Oh spring! Oh spring, why must you leave so soon?

I reminisce about the times when
Mother would sit by a fading lamplight
Sewing a red vest, piece by piece,
While telling stories of the heroes of yore
Like Mong-ju Chŏng and Admiral Sun-sin Yi.
Oh, how I miss my mother and our hometown.
Oh spring! Oh spring, why must you leave so soon?

Between the faraway mountain and sky,
A shimmer of heat is barely visible.
Gathered heat waves open the forsythias.
A lark soars, trilling sadly.
Leaving all these wonders behind,
Oh spring, why must you leave so soon?

If you go now, when shall I see you again?

If I row a boat across the Pacific Ocean, will I see you?
If I climb up Mt. Paektu or Mt. Halla, will I see you again?
No, only when I go up to heaven will I meet you.

The truly happy and blessed days passed by like a dream. Looking back, it was indeed the best year of my life. It was like living in paradise. My happiness reached its climax very soon. A fierce storm was gradually approaching our doorstep, but who would have guessed?

PART THREE

Endure with the Spirit of a Martyr!

Acts 7:54-60

⁵⁴When they heard this, they were furious and gnashed their teeth at him. ⁵⁵But Stephen, full of the Holy Spirit, looked up to heaven and saw the glory of God, and Jesus standing at the right hand of God. ⁵⁶"Look," he said, "I see heaven open and the Son of Man standing at the right hand of God." ⁵⁷At this they covered their ears and, yelling at the top of their voices, they all rushed at him, ⁵⁸dragged him out of the city and began to stone him. Meanwhile, the witnesses laid their clothes at the feet of a young man named Saul. ⁵⁹While they were stoning him, Stephen prayed, "Lord Jesus, receive my spirit." ⁶⁰Then he fell on his knees and cried out, "Lord, do not hold this sin against them." When he had said this, he fell asleep.

18. *God, What Are You Doing?*

It is now time to retrace my memory of that unforgettable, wretched day. I was unsure of whether my trembling hands could write about the day, but I persevered with the determination that if tears overflow, I would wipe them away; if my heart trembles in fear, I would calm it down; and if my hand won't write because of indignation, I would give it some rest before writing further. I felt a greater need to testify of the life and death of my two older brothers who were sacrificed in a brief moment of outrageous madness. The horrible event that tore my sixteen year-old heart into pieces was so haunting that I never wanted to look back upon it.

Although so many years have passed since then, the scars and memories have been so deeply etched in my heart that I remember it all vividly as though it happened just yesterday. As I begin to recall how Matthew and John died at the hands of their classmates, I can already feel my heart beginning to tremble with indignation and sorrow.

I remember perfectly the events of October 19, 1948. At that time, I was in my first year at Maesan Girls' Middle School in Sunch'ŏn. My heart was filled with expectations because it was the day of my school's autumn picnic. The sky was blue and clear, and the fields were golden with waves of ripened rice plants waiting to be harvested. No omen forewarned us of approaching death. That morning when I walked out the door, I felt as if I could fly up high into the sky.

"Tong-hŭi! Wait a minute," Matthew suddenly called out.

"Why, Brother?" I replied, thinking perhaps I had forgotten something. I stopped and turned around.

"Come here for a minute," he said, making a gesture with his hand. So I sat down on the wooden floor where he stood. "Let me take a look," he said, "since Mother isn't around, you probably didn't pack much for your school picnic, did you, Tong-hŭi?" He placed a bottle of milk and some cookies in my bag. How he got the money or found the time to buy them, I don't know, but he even put some spending money in my hands.

"Brother, thank you. I must go now," I said. "By the way, today after the picnic, I will go straight to Aeyangwŏn. Since tomorrow is a holiday, I will stay there over the weekend and go straight to school from Aeyangwŏn on Monday."

As I hurriedly ran out the door, my brother called me once more, "Tong-hŭi!"

"Why do you keep calling me? I don't have much time."

"Yes, I know. My dear Tong-hŭi, come here for a minute, please." Matthew opened my bag and searched the contents inside. He then held my hand tightly. Although I sensed that my brother was acting somewhat strange, my mind and heart were already at the picnic, running toward the mountain and clear water.

"Brother, you seem strange today. Why do you keep calling me?"

Matthew stood silently, smiling. I turned around to run out, but he called me for the third time. This time, I was annoyed. I didn't have much time left and if I didn't get to school soon, I would be late for sure.

"Good grief! I told you I really needed to hurry. What do you want?" I frowned as I walked toward him. For some reason, I thought he was playing a mischievous prank on his little sister whose heart was already at the picnic. But Matthew's facial expression was sober. He placed his hands on my shoulders and gazed deeply into my eyes for a long time.

"Nothing serious," he said, "I just wanted to tell you to have a good time at the picnic. That's why I called you."

That's silly! I thought. He wasn't acting anything like his usual self. I ran out the door without looking back, afraid he might call me again. And this was my last moments with my two older brothers.

While I was having fun at the picnic, walking on the autumn leaves, laughing and running, my two older brothers were facing imminent danger. The footsteps of death moved ever closer to them.

Because the following day was a holiday, I didn't return to Sunch'ŏn but instead went straight to Aeyangwŏn. I chatted about this and that with my family and was fully immersed in the warmth of my home after being away for so long. Like a child, I just wanted to chatter endlessly like a skylark. All day long, my heart felt unusually light and happy, and I hummed happy tunes spontaneously. After listening to my father's sermon, I met some old friends from Aeyangwŏn and enjoyed the sunset on the beach. Just like the previous day, this day passed without any gloomy foreboding.

On Monday morning, I walked to the Sinp'ung Train Station to catch a train to my school in Sunch'ŏn. But the train, which always arrived on time with a loud whistle, did not come. Instead, people stood around with worried faces. I was anxious to know what all the commotion was about. *What so great has happened that the train has not yet arrived and the people are whispering?* I thought.

I squeezed through a crowd of people to listen in on their conversations. They were saying strange things. They said that the Communists had risen up in revolt and were indiscriminately massacring innocent people in Yŏsu and Sunch'ŏn. They also said that the Communists had piled mountains of sacrificial corpses in the streets. The people's endless exchange of stories implied a gloomy foreboding. I was told that the reason for the train not coming was that the Communist insurrectionists had cut off the train tracks. The people added that this was rather a good thing since they would have otherwise unknowingly entered a war zone.

I couldn't help but plod back home. Mother's eyes were wide in surprise. "How come you didn't go to school?"

"The train didn't come. I was told that the Red Army had cut off the railroad. The people at the train station said that Sunch'ŏn has been turned into an ocean of fire."

"Is that so? Well, nothing can be done then. Stay one more day and go tomorrow."

"Good grief, I hate having to miss school..."

I was upset about missing one school day. Mother felt some anxiety, but she didn't seem to take the situation so seriously. The rumor quickly spread throughout the entire village of Sinp'ungni. Various other rumors, rumors that could not be confirmed, were spreading from person to person by word of mouth. People gathered in their own groups to exchange the rampant rumors and they stood about with anxious faces.

I heard that an unbelievable number of people were killed in Yŏsu and Sunch'ŏn. Even young students joined the insurrection army and fought against the National Army of the Republic of Korea (ROK). It seemed that a serious riot had broken out. As if to confirm such rumors, gunshots began to ring out in the distance. Only then did my mother's face turn pale with fear and concern for the safety of her four other children who remained in Sunch'ŏn.

"I'm worried about your brothers," my mother said with a troubled heart. Right then, Tong-jang, who was supposed to be in Sunch'ŏn, came trudging through the front gate. We were glad to see him, but also puzzled as to why he had come so suddenly. Mother asked him what had happened.

Tong-jang spoke in tears. "Matthew and John told me to go home since Father and Mother might worry. They said the world is in upheaval. When the insurrection army didn't allow me to pass, I begged them repeatedly, telling them I was on my way home. I barely managed to get through."

Tong-jang was only twelve at the time. At such a young age, he wrestled through a war zone where bullets rained down. He told us he was terrified because he had seen so many corpses on the streets. "After the morning worship service, Matthew and John stroked my head and told me to study hard and to obey Mother and Father's words. They also said that an unfortunate event might happen, and if it does, they said we would meet again in heaven."

To me, Tong-jang's words sounded strange. It was not like the usual admonition from my two older brothers. Only then did a dark foreboding penetrate sharply into my heart. I was truly anxious. It felt like something terrible was about to happen for sure. Mother couldn't put her hand to any useful task and she stood nervously about. We remained gripped with fear all day.

Despite the chaos, time passed and night fell. After supper, Mother was doing the dishes and Tong-jang and I were talking when suddenly, we heard the sound of a truck approaching from a distance. It was very rare to see vehicles in Sinp'ungni.

The truck was getting closer and the sound of the engine grew louder and louder. I listened carefully to make out the direction of the truck. It seemed to be heading toward our house. I prayed silently that the truck would pass us by. But ignoring my wish, the truck stopped right in front of our house. Inside the truck were many armed students. As soon as the truck stopped, they all jumped out. They kicked the gate open and burst into our house. Murder was written all over their faces. They were thirsty for blood. Judging from their insane expressions, it seemed impossible to expect any form of rational thinking from them.

"Is this the house of Pastor Son?" they shouted. "Pastor Son, come out right now!" Although they were all very boyish in appearance, their greasy faces beamed with a lust that revealed their loss of innocence. They had become bloodthirsty beasts.

Was it because the time wasn't right or because God already knew what was about to happen that He let Father escape? Fortunately, my father was not home at the moment. Undoubtedly, Father would not have been able to escape the calamity of that day if he had been there to face the young men.

The young men were merciless, cruel, insolent, and impertinent to us even though we were telling the truth that Father was out. Nevertheless, they didn't take our word and instead ran into the room with their shoes on, in search of Father. As if searching for lice, they used their bayonets and bamboo spears to poke through the ceilings and floors as they searched every inch and corner of the house. Their bloodshot eyes gleamed under the light. When they couldn't find Father, they walked out, clearly disappointed.

Mother was leaning against the door and trembling with fear, whereupon one of the students took a quick glance at her with a malicious smirk as he headed out the door. It was a vicious look, like that of a snake staring at its vulnerable prey.

"Did you know your two oldest sons were executed today?" the student asked Mother. How could such a young boy blurt out such horrible words so easily? His words pierced my mother's heart. He then glanced back with that same malicious smirk and disappeared. Even now after several decades, that young man's face remains so clear before my eyes.

"What on earth are you saying? What do you mean my sons are dead? For what? What are you talking about? My sons are not...Good heavens!" My mother fainted before she could even finish her sentence. Apparently, terrible things had, indeed, happened to her sons. Hearing the news, the entire church was thrown into utter confusion.

Shocked, some of the church members ran to our house. "Mrs. Son, Mrs. Son! Please calm down! How can we trust them? It probably isn't true. They just said that because they were upset about how they failed to capture Pastor Son, don't you agree? For what reason would the students kill other young students? It's probably just a lie."

The church members tried hard to offer comforting words to my mother, who was slowly regaining consciousness. But Mother was not the only one in need of comfort. My legs were shaking so much that I couldn't even stand up straight. It was only the day before yesterday that I had seen my brothers alive. There was no reason on earth for my brothers to be murdered. They were very faithful, polite, bright and joyful, and exemplary students. *What? My brothers are dead? It can't be!*

It's a lie! I thought. *The church members are right. The students said that Matthew and John were dead because they couldn't find Father!* I tried very hard to remain positive, but I couldn't keep my heart from crumbling down.

The shock to my heart felt as though a heavy rock had just crashed down inside. Then suddenly, a memory flashed through my head. "Ah-ha!" I blurted out. On that day, my picnic day, Matthew called me back three times. *That gentle, deep, and serious gaze...Was that an omen of some sort? Did he feel a vague sense that he might not see me again? Was that why he acted so out of character that morning? Is that why he repeatedly called out my name? What the students said must be true!* With these questions, a gloomy premonition passed through my mind.

My head was swimming and, stupefied by the shock, I gradually lost consciousness. I could not think anymore. Like a drug-induced hallucination, I gazed helplessly into space and finally collapsed to the floor.

"That's why...so that's why..." Out of my mouth leaked only broken thoughts and sentences.

But I couldn't just sit there. If I didn't do otherwise, I was sure to lose my mind. I had to see for myself whether my brothers were dead or alive. Otherwise, I would not believe a single word I heard. *Forget this ominous presentiment! I must go and see my brothers who are surely alive! It couldn't be possible! They couldn't be dead! All I've heard so far came from complete strangers. They have no proof!* I thought. I wasn't about to give up—not yet. Why should I believe that insurrectionist? For the time being, nothing was certain. I felt I had to go to Sunch'ŏn to see my brothers whom I was sure were still alive.

My mind was made up and my heart burned uncontrollably with determination. Unusual courage sprang out from within like a fountain. The authorities had forbidden any travel to Sunch'ŏn, so if I were to go, my very life would be at risk. Mother told me not to go because it was far too dangerous, but I shook myself loose from her grasp and began to run toward Sunch'ŏn.

The road from Aeyangwŏn to Sunch'ŏn was a ten-mile walk. Of course, the railroad had already been cut off, but even this couldn't stop me. I felt that there was no hurdle I could not overcome. Nothing and no one could stand in my way. I ran with one thought and one thought only—that I would soon see my brothers. I kept running towards Sunch'ŏn. The road between Yŏsu and Sunch'ŏn was very dangerous. Trucks passed by rapidly, cutting through the wind. More trucks, tanks, and artillery clattered down the road. Sunch'ŏn itself was dangerous. Many Communists were on a maddening rampage, marching about as though the whole world were theirs. The trucks full of young students who were brainwashed by the Bolsheviks paraded on the streets of Yŏsu and Sunch'ŏn. The road leading into Sunch'ŏn was violent and terrible. The rumbling sound of heavy gunfire filled me with apprehension, and though I possessed a great sense of determination, whenever I faced the Bolshevist soldiers, I couldn't help but get goose bumps all over my body. Honestly, I was terrified. I felt as if they would grab my neck at any moment. Whenever one of their trucks approached my way, I crouched down and walked on. I wanted them to see me simply as an innocent child.

It was nearly at dusk that I arrived at Sunch'ŏn. I could not bear to look at the brutal scene that lay before me. It was like hell. Although I had seen bodies lying here and there on the way, the sight that met my eyes at Sunch'ŏn was beyond anything I had seen before. Bodies were piled in great mounds on the streets. The dogs were devouring the corpses. Some of the dead were lying naked, face down, while others were tied to electric poles and charred black. The entire city reeked with the smell of blood. The terrible stench from the decaying corpses that mingled with the smell of blood made me feel like vomiting. Shameless people could be seen scavenging the pockets of the corpses to steal watches, money, and other valuables. I covered my nose with a handkerchief and hurried by the mounds of corpses.

What were the motives for these bloody riots in Yŏsu and Sunch'ŏn? On August 15, 1948—the third anniversary of our country's liberation from the Japanese—the newly formed Republic of Korea (ROK) was proclaimed to the world. It soon received diplomatic recognition from the United States, and about thirty-five other countries and the United Nations (UN) proclaimed the ROK the only legitimate government on the Korean Peninsula.

In the midst of all this progress, the last feeble gesture toward peaceful unification between North and South Korea ended in failure. Matters had gone too far for Korea to be united through negotiation. The North Koreans established the "North Korean Provisional People's Committee" as a step toward establishing a permanent Communist regime. The Russo-American agreements at the Moscow Conference were dissolved, and in defiance of the UN resolution, the so-called People's Democratic Republic of Korea was formed in North Korea in September, 1948. Almost immediately, the North began a series of guerrilla raids against the South, coupled with a Communist propaganda campaign. These fomented sporadic riots made it very difficult for the new government in the South to maintain public order.

These Communist-inspired strikes and bloody riots became more frequent. Early on the morning of October 19, 1948, when the army was ordered to transfer to Cheju Island, some forty soldiers—core members of the left—revolted against the order to quell the Communist-inspired riots that had caused a bloody slaughter of innocent civilians on the Island. With the sound of a trumpet as a sign, the revolting soldiers started another riot in Yŏsu by taking over the armory and killing their fellow soldiers who resisted their plan to overthrow the ROK government. Then the revolting soldiers began to broadcast their Communist propaganda: "The time for the People's Democratic Republic of Korea to arise has finally arrived! And at this moment, masses of North Korean troops are crossing the 38th parallel and taking control of the entire nation, all the way from Seoul to Cheju Island."

Soon Yŏsu and Sunch'ŏn became lawless Communist strongholds and were turned into cities with pitiable oceans of blood. The first gunshots by Communist rioters in Yŏsu killed many policemen and, joined by young Communist students, the revolting soldiers took over the town of Sunch'ŏn as well. The Communist students were put in charge of searching out reactionary elements. As a result, they began arresting and murdering without mercy the leading townspeople, educators, the wealthy, and well-known members of right-wing political parties. They also sought out and killed Christians. After killing them, the students left the bodies of the dead in the streets. Countless individuals were put to death for no apparent reason. It took a week for the ROK soldiers to bring down the Communist insurrectionists. In the meantime, Yŏsu and Sunch'ŏn were literally hell-like.

Waiting for a ripe opportunity, the young leftist students joined the Communist insurrectionists and aggressively helped them slaughter innocent people, which led to more crises. Only one day before were all these students sitting in the same classroom, but now they were divided into left and right, treating each other as enemies. Such conflicts between the two sides reached its highest focal point when the armed leftist students fired into the chests of their friends without hesitation, obviously seized by a madness and hatred toward something that they themselves didn't quite understand. They even killed classmates whom they thought would become potential enemies. A person's life was less valuable than that of a fly at that time. According to the report on casualties that was issued by the South Chŏlla Provincial Health and Welfare Department on November 1, 1948, during the week of the Yŏsu-Sunch'ŏn Mutiny, a total of 3,401 people died, 48,600 disappeared, and many more were injured.

As I witnessed these incidents, I realized that all the rumors I had heard in Sinp'ungni were true. My apprehension for Matthew and John grew. The rumors were nothing in comparison to the reality that stood before my eyes. I barely made it through chaotic Sunch'ŏn and to the house where I hoped my brothers would be. The gate was wide open as though welcoming me in. But in spite of my hurried, anxious heart, my legs would not move forward. I wanted to run far away. Since my brothers were innocent of any wrongdoing, I could not imagine why they would ever be anyone's targets. Yet an unexplainable fear of a possible tragedy made my feet freeze on the spot.

I felt a gloomy presence. Cold shivers traveled down my spine, preventing me from stepping inside the house. Finally, I poked my head through the door and peeked inside. It was quiet, perhaps too quiet. I felt as though my older brothers would jump out any moment and say, "Tong-hŭi, why aren't you coming in? Hurry in! Did you have fun at the picnic?"

I could actually hear their voices in my head. It seemed as though the wind had even withheld its breath. Everything stood still. Then, I saw Matthew's and John's books, school uniforms, school bags, pictures, and the scarves I knitted for them...all scattered about the front yard.

Then the vague omen proved itself true. My heart pounded with hope and fear. I tried my best to hang onto hopes. After all, I knew nothing. So I gathered all my courage and stepped slowly inside the house. I cried out to my brothers loudly, "Matthew! John!" However, there was no reply. A hush fell over the house. Then I saw a crimson pool of blood in the corner of the front yard that testified to the reality which I was trying so hard to deny.

Soon I realized I had all the facts right before my eyes. I could no longer deny them. I could not move, not even a finger. I could not cry or scream. My head reeled and became blank. Everything was still, even time. My anguish overwhelmed my body and spirit. For a long time, I stood fixed on that spot.

Suddenly, my younger sister Tong-nim ran in with a soiled face, full of fear. As soon as she saw me, she grabbed a hold of my skirt and began to cry.

"Sister!" Tong-nim began, "Matthew and John...they..." Tong-nim explained to me how many of our brothers' classmates came in, forced them to the ground, and beat them up mercilessly with a thick wooden bat. They dragged our brothers away and killed them. "Sister, what are we going to do?" Tong-nim asked.

I could not reply. I couldn't even shed a tear. My thoughts had seemed to stop. I just stood still in a daze. I couldn't even think about comforting my little sister Tong-nim who needed to be held. My whole body was stiff and I felt as if something was pressing down hard on me.

Not long after, Deacon Yang, who lived in the room next to ours as a tenant, came through the gate. "Good heavens! Tong-hŭi!"

But his voice didn't even register in my ears. Since he couldn't hear a reply from me, he shook my shoulders and I began to slowly regain my senses. The voice that seemed so far away finally seemed clear and audible.

"Deacon Yang?"

"Yes, Tong-hŭi. Your brothers...Matthew and John are..."

Deacon Yang turned his face away from me and ended his sentence vaguely. Even though he didn't say it, I knew what he was going to say, but I didn't want to hear it. I struggled to think straight.

"What happened to their bodies?"

"I found them and moved them."

"Please take me to the place where they are, Deacon."

In a ditch on a wide stretch of empty fields, there lay my two brothers on a straw bag. The early cold autumn winds were blowing through their baggy clothes. They must have suffered from severe blows to have so many purple bruises all over their bodies. Scattered carelessly across their chests and foreheads were crude bullet holes.

Only then did I feel tears flow down my cheeks. I finally woke up from my daze. I fell to the ground and held their bodies in my arms. With tears streaming down, I began to scream at the top of my lungs toward heaven: "Oh God! What were you doing at that moment? When my innocent brothers were dying, were you closing your eyes? Couldn't you have stopped the flying bullets from hitting them?"

Instead of cursing the leftist students who killed my brothers, I hurled complaints against God and said a lot of things I really didn't mean.

"If you were going to let them live only a short time and then take them away, for what reason did you send them to earth? Isn't it too cruel? God, why did you turn your face away from my brothers at the time of their deaths? Answer me! What were you doing at the time? Didn't you say that not even a sparrow would fall to the ground without your permission? Then why did you let my brothers die? Why? Since you're the all powerful God, couldn't you revive them again?"

I screamed out bitter complaints. I felt truly bitter against God. I resented Him for not protecting my brothers. I screamed at God, reproaching Him and attacking Him until finally, my voice became hoarse. All night long, I cried and screamed and finally reached a state of complete exhaustion. I looked vacantly at my brothers, and suddenly, I heard Matthew's voice, as clearly as though he were standing right next to me:

Don't cry, Tong-hŭi. I'm afraid our pretty Tong-hŭi's face will become ugly. Don't be sad. We'll see each other again in heaven. Now you know why I called you three times on that day you went on the picnic. Yes, we lived short lives and yes, we went to heaven ahead of you. But it's okay. Hurry home and comfort our parents. You must now be the one to show our parents the filial love we couldn't express. I wanted to love you longer, but I had no choice. Good-bye.

With these parting words in my heart, my two older brothers went down the road of no return. It was futile. "My brothers suffered so many trials!" I exclaimed as my tears fell on their faces. The more I thought about it, the more this tragedy became heartbreaking.

What a thunderbolt out of the blue! *How could this possibly be? They were blameless, model students, and so young. Why did they have to suffer such great pain and agony? Didn't the God of Love, the God of Mercy say, 'So do not fear, for I am with you; do not be dismayed, for I am your God. I will strengthen you and help you. I will uphold you with my righteous right hand' (Isaiah 41:10)? Then why did God close His eyes at the moment Matthew and John needed His helping hand most?* I didn't really understand. I just really couldn't.

19. The Voice of Young Martyrs

In hindsight, I now realize that the events of that day were by no means accidental but a work of God's perfect plan. Fortunately for me, I went on a school picnic to Sinsŏng, and since the following day was a holiday, I went straight to Aeyangwŏn, where my parents were. As always, we were financially tight and out of rice at the time. Our uncle who took care of us went ahead of me to Aeyangwŏn to get some food supplies. Tong-jang was also sent back home. Only my two older brothers and young Tong-nim were left in Sunch'ŏn. The circumstances were set in such a way that there was no one who could intervene on my brothers' behalf.

Even if someone had been there to protect them, it would not have guaranteed a different outcome. But at least I wouldn't feel this futile. At times, I often wonder what might have happened had I not gone to the picnic and instead stayed home with my brothers. In that case, though I'm not exactly sure, I too probably would've ended up alongside them in the graveyard.

Oh, how precious my two brothers were to me! I probably wouldn't have just watched them get beat. I probably would've screamed in protest. I would've fought back to stop the students from clubbing my brothers with their wooden bats. In such circumstances, who or what would I fear?

The fate of a person is such a strange wonder! Because I went on the picnic that day, my resilient life was preserved. At times, I wonder why God preserved my life. Perhaps it was because He wanted to entrust me with the responsibility of testifying to what happened on that day. So I write here about the terrible events of that day, based on the witness of Dr. Che-min Na, a classmate of John.

On the day my two older brothers died, there was no rice left in the house, so they went to the home of Pastor Tŏk-hwan Na to ask for some rice.

"Oh, Matthew, what do I do," Mrs. Na said. "I heard that the price of rice would soon drop, so I've been buying only small amounts at a time. But now, even all that is gone." She felt so sorry and didn't know what to do.

Then Matthew said in a cheerful voice, "That's quite alright. This is what a pastor's life is like." Then he turned around to leave, whistling his favorite hymn.

Mrs. Na told him that many innocent people were being hurt and killed in the midst of the riots. She warned him to forget about the rice and hide somewhere first. She told him that her son Che-min had already gone into hiding just ten minutes ago.

"God is our only refuge," Matthew replied with a bright smile. That was the last Mrs. Na spoke with him. Whenever Mrs. Na sees me, she says to me, "Tong-hŭi, I regret to this day not having been able to give your brother any rice on the day he died."

On that day, October 21, 1948, my brothers woke up early for the early morning prayer service. They woke up Tong-jang, who was still sleeping, and told him that our parents might be worried about the invasion. Both Matthew and John told Tong-jang to study hard and obey Father and Mother, and that if anything were to happen, we'd all see each other again in heaven. They sent Tong-jang home, and afterwards, they went to the well at the back of the house, washed up, and changed into some clean clothes. That day, Matthew said he had a strange dream, but he didn't say much about it when Deacon Yang asked. Matthew and John went into the prayer room and prayed together. Their prayers were far longer and more earnest than usual. When they came out, their faces were pale. Again, Matthew remained silent when Deacon Yang asked him to tell him about the dream.

On October 20, my two older brothers went to school, but Matthew returned home earlier than usual because they heard gunshots nearby. Trouble was brewing in town. Matthew had gone to Sunch'ŏn Station with a church visitor the previous day and it was there that he saw a trainload of soldiers, instead of the usual passengers, arrive. A violent clash broke out between the police and the soldiers, and soon people were running in all directions to get away from the flying bullets. He saw how the Communists had already wreaked havoc in the town of Sunch'ŏn.

Matthew became anxious when all the other boys but John had returned home from school. The sound of gunshots gradually grew louder and seemed to be getting nearer to the center of town. Matthew went out and heard from the people on the streets that the Communists had revolted. The Communist rioters were spreading their propaganda saying that the People's Army had seized the 38th parallel. Taegu and Pusan had already been occupied, and Yŏsu and Sunch'ŏn were next. Hearing this, the people began to hide in our neighbor's underground cellar.

John finally returned home at dusk. He confirmed that it was, indeed, a Communist uprising, that the rioters had surrounded their school but had eventually allowed them to go home. On his way home, John said to his classmate Che-min, "I feel this is a battle between right and wrong, between the believer and nonbeliever. Therefore, we as Christians must stand firm and meet this challenge with wisdom." These were his last words to his friend Che-min. As for Matthew, Deacon Yang urged him to seek safety in the neighbor's cellar, but Matthew refused to hide, saying, "God is our only refuge. Where else would we run to hide?"

The following day, the neighbor in whose cellar the household of Deacon Yang had hid the day before came and invited my brothers to hide again, but Matthew and John refused to go. Then Deacon Yang urged them to flee to Aeyangwŏn, but full of conviction, Matthew answered, "To be caught on the run would be much too shameful, and we might even be forced to grab a gun and join them. Therefore, we will stay here and meet whatever troubles come our way."

After a quick breakfast, Deacon Yang went back to the neighbor's cellar. At about ten o'clock, a group of students surrounded the house, each holding guns and steel weapons. What Deacon Yang most feared would happen, finally happened.

"Matthew, you jerk! Come out here!"

One of them cursed and broke into the room with his shoes still on. He dragged Matthew out and bound him tightly with rope before the group began to punch him in the face and brutally assault him. The cruel and merciless beatings continued. Though very frightened, Deacon Yang rushed back to see if Matthew was okay, only to find that the students had already beaten him up badly.

"Look here, I think I have the right to know why I'm getting beat up. What did I do?" Matthew asked while receiving severe blows from every direction.

"You fool! Don't you know? I'll tell you. Since you are the president of the Christian Students Society, you're probably a pro-American Yankee-boy. Did you not say you wanted to study in America?"

"Look," Matthew replied, "I'm no Yankee-boy. I'm a Christian and I don't want any other labels. I rely on no other than my Almighty God." In spite of the endless beatings, Matthew's voice remained bold and firm.

"Shut up! So you still identify yourself with Jesus, huh? You're better off believing in the strength of my fist." They mocked him and hailed insults at him while beating him some more. Soon his body was soaked with blood. John couldn't bear to watch Matthew suffer anymore, so he tried to fight back.

"Why are you doing this to us? So we believe in Jesus. What's so wrong about that? Though you can take away our lives, you'll never be able to take away our faith!"

"This one is also a Jesus freak. Beat him up, too!" someone shouted. And another student brought in a thick board with nails with which they beat my two brothers. Blood gushed from their heads and welts rose up on their bodies.

When someone cried out, "Let's get rid of them!" they all shouted in agreement. After digging through my brothers' belongings, they collected a couple of their books as evidence for later reference and then dragged the both of them away at gunpoint. Matthew was bound with rope and John was forced to walk with his hands above his head. In the meantime, Tong-nim cried uncontrollably as she stood there watching every single moment. But her tears meant absolutely nothing to the Communist students.

Deacon Yang was too afraid to follow them any further.

However, our neighborhood photographer's wife Mrs. Chŏng saw Matthew and John being taken to the Communist headquarters above the Sunch'ŏn Police Station. When Mrs. Chŏng was informed that the rioters had arrested some Christians and were taking them to the police station, she rushed out, fearing that her husband might be among them. Although she did not see her husband, who was in fact safe in hiding, she saw Matthew and John being dragged away. Blood streamed down their faces and they were being kicked and beaten with clubs and guns. But through it all, Matthew and John spoke with great earnestness to the students who were their captors. They urged the students to repent and believe in Jesus, to stop fighting against their fellow citizens, and to seek the spirit of Christ by which they would bring blessings on their nation. Mrs. Chŏng was moved to tears by what she saw and heard. She forgot her own troubles as she watched my older brothers being dragged out of sight.

The two were taken to the back of the Sunch'ŏn Police Station, where the corpses of others who had been captured were piled up all around the yard. Here, the students challenged Matthew.

"Do you still persist in holding onto your Christian faith? If you are willing to give up your Christian beliefs and cooperate with us, we will let you go. We did the same for Myŏng-sin Ko," one said as he pointed to a student who had come over to their side. However, Matthew did not budge.

Matthew spoke earnestly in a vain attempt to open the students' closed hearts. "You might succeed in taking away my life, but you can never strip me of my faith. I urge you to give up your violent and wicked ways and believe in Jesus."

The rioters were blind with rage. Clenching their fists,

they snapped out the order to kill him. Someone slammed the butt of his rifle against Matthew's face.

"Kill him, kill him!" Shouts rose here and there. "Don't waste time on him!"

"This fellow is a Jesus freak. Shoot him and kill him!" another yelled. John then went quickly over to where Matthew was standing.

"Listen," John cried, "my brother is the oldest son in our family and must take care of our parents when they are old. Kill me instead and let him return home!" John then stepped in front of Matthew. Matthew struggled, but he was too tightly bound.

"John, don't be a fool! They're not out to kill you. Go back home and look after our parents in place of me!" Matthew instructed.

One of the students pulled John away and another blindfolded Matthew. John struggled with all his might so that he wouldn't be separated from his brother. But they could not expect any sympathy from their captors. Mercilessly, the students forced John away.

Realizing that he was about to get shot, Matthew said, "You must repent and believe in Jesus! Though I die now, I shall go to heaven. But how will you escape the fearful punishment of hell?" His voice was rather calm but solemn.

"If you have any last words, speak now. Otherwise, shut up!"

Matthew, who was a professional singer at the time, requested that he be allowed to sing a hymn for the last time. They accepted his last request. Matthew began to sing his favorite hymn "Bright, Heavenly Way" with his clear and lovely voice. His blindfolded eyes looked toward heaven. His voice, singing for the last time, soared high above the clouds and resonated far beyond the earthly realms.

1. *There's a bright and heavenly pathway*
   That ever leads me on,
   Though I meet with many a sorrow
   And trials ne'er are gone.
   Heaven's glory shines afar,
   Earthly clouds all scattered are,
   Trusting Jesus as my Savior
   Ever bright my moments are.

2. *Although heavy are my burdens*
   And with cares my heart is pressed,
   Often heartache, often trouble
   Fill life with its distress,
   But my victory is sure,
   For in Jesus I'm secure,
   Trusting in His love and merit
   By His grace I shall endure.

3. *As I near the Heavenly Country*
   More clearly can I see
   All the glory of my Father,
   My heart longs there to be,
   Although I am weak and ill,
   He awaits my coming still,
   For the King of Heaven's glory
   Is my Jesus Savior still.

Once the hymn was over, one of the students yelled, "Shoot on the count of three! One, two, three!"

"Heavenly Father," cried Matthew, "receive my soul. Forgive their..." He did not finish. Matthew's body fell over as the bullets found their mark. Those who heard his last cry cursed and shouted.

John sprang away from the hands that held him and embraced Matthew's lifeless body. He cried out like a wounded lion, "Big brother, big brother! I want to follow you to heaven." He turned his head to the group and shouted, "You have killed my innocent brother. How will you justify yourselves for taking innocent blood? You must repent and believe in Jesus. It's not too late."

"Kill him, too!" they yelled. And the crowd's chants of approval began to escalate.

"My faith is the same as his. Shoot me, too! I will go where my brother has gone–to heaven," John said with his arms stretched out. "This is the way my Lord died when He hung on the cross, and in the same way, I will receive your bullets. Now shoot!"

"This fellow is even worse than his older brother," one of them said. "We can't let him live. Shoot him, too!" The order was given. John's last words were the prayer Matthew prayed. "Heavenly Father, receive my soul. Forgive the people of their sins. Help them to repent. And watch over my father and mother..."

And before he finished his prayer, the bullets penetrated through his body, causing him to topple on top of Matthew's lifeless body. Although John was already dead, one of the students put two more bullets in his body. These last two bullets belonged to Ch'ŏl-min Kang. (His name has been changed to protect the identity of his children and family.)

My brothers were at the top of the Communist students'

list of people to kill. The students may have succeeded in killing Matthew and John, but they weren't able to strip them of their faith in God.

This was the account of my two brothers' deaths, according to the testimonies of many who witnessed them face their greatest trial. One of the witnesses, Sun-ung Yun, was a school friend of theirs.

The Yŏsu-Sunch'ŏn Mutiny only lasted a week, but this storm wiped away my two brothers. They were kind to everyone and so loving that many praised them. But they were greatly hated by the leftist students because both Matthew and John made mention of God in every situation. And for being the president of the Christian Students Society, Matthew's name was the very first name on the Communist students' list of people to kill.

Earlier around harvest time while awaiting the celebration of Thanksgiving Day, John brought home a group of friends to study with. They were exchanging their ideas in anticipation of Thanksgiving. In the midst of their conversation, John glanced up at a photograph of a group of Christian workers and pastors that hung on the wall. He was reminded of the words that Jesus spoke, "The harvest is heavy, but the laborers are few!" How true these words were of Korea. For this reason, John always prepared himself for the Lord's service.

Even three years after the liberation of our country, order had not been restored. If anything, things were getting far more ambiguous than before. For one reason or another, there were frequent outbreaks of violence, even in schools. Students went against teachers; leftists against rightists; north against south; and civilians against their leaders. Innumerable divisions emerged—even the churches that preached about love and righteousness turned against one another. Before liberation, the faith of most of the elders and pastors had become very weak, and the situation was no better after gaining independence.

"What are you so glum about?" Che-min asked John.

John looked up at the photograph and answered, "We too must fight for Christ with the same conviction that those Christians had."

"Were all those men in prison?"

"No, a few of them weren't."

"Are there others?"

"Yes, many more," John replied before beginning to name some he knew of.

"Were many martyred?"

"Yes, we know of more than fifty who were martyred and there are many more who remain unidentified."

"Are you planning to go to college in the United States with Matthew?" Che-min asked out of the blue. "If you do, you'll be able to help build our country when you return."

"Yes, but I don't think we have to study abroad in order to do that. Though Matthew and I are making plans to study abroad, we are willing to stay if need be. For instance, if some form of persecution were to arise in our country, and especially if the need to fight for Jesus should arise, we would certainly give up the opportunity to study abroad, even if we were in the middle of boarding the plane. Throughout the years, I've come to see that we must fight more actively now than we had against Shinto worship and Japanese occupation."

John gazed back into the past when he and Matthew were expelled from school and when our whole family moved to Kwangju to be near our imprisoned father. We had to move to Pusan, where we lived in a shabby hut on top of a mountain because of the *kamidana* issues within the church. John reminisced of our Sunday services in the mountains; of the separation of our family when Matthew received military conscription; and of his life among the lepers in the dugout on Pukpangni Mountain. He closed his eyes. He had no idea how prophetic his words were. He didn't know that the impending Communist invasion would bring persecution.

Neither he nor Matthew had the chance to go to America. Little did they know, their daily disciplined lives of faith had been preparing them for martyrdom—all for the glory of God.

20. They Are Leaving, They Are Leaving!

Tong-jang and I were fortunate enough to have left Sunch'ŏn before the uprising and we safely made our way to Aeyangwŏn. However, our parents were still very worried because three more of their children were still in Sunch'ŏn.

On October 22, we heard a rumor that the rioters had killed Matthew and John. The lepers at Aeyangwŏn were more upset than my parents. Father couldn't believe what he heard, but he still managed to say, "It does not matter whether my children are dead or alive. There is no need to worry, for if they are dead, they will be in heaven; if they are alive, they will be giving themselves to the service of God even as we speak." And because Father refused to be shaken by the rumors, Mother and the lepers at Aeyangwŏn were able to calm down.

Everyone at Aeyangwŏn waited two days, but none of them received word from Matthew or John, or me since I left for Sunch'ŏn the day before to find out what had happened. When Mother spoke repeatedly about finding out for herself where her children were, the young male teacher, Sun-bok Hong, volunteered to go instead. But traveling was forbidden, and it was still dangerous to enter Sunch'ŏn, so the rest of them tried to stop him.

"Life and death are in God's hands," my father said, "there is no point in going out to search for them."

"But we'll have no peace until we know for certain! Isn't that reason enough, Pastor Son? Let me smear soot on my face and dress like a beggar. Because I am a leper, they will surely let me pass." Mr. Hong insisted on going. In the end, Father gave in and let him go, advising him to take his Bible as it might come in handy on the way.

On the following day, October 25, an urgent voice barged in on my mother's quiet afternoon of reading the Scriptures. "Mr. Hong has returned!" Mrs. Ch'a announced with tears flowing down her face. Mother rushed into the yard.

"Where is he?" Mother called out to her.

"Over there!" Mrs. Ch'a replied, pointing at the distant road that wound its way among the foothills. "Come on!" Mrs. Ch'a ran back the way she had come and Mother followed, still clutching the Bible she had been reading. With her heart pounding with hope and fear, Mother ran to greet Mr. Hong. At first, she could not make out the figure of Mr. Hong from a distance, but then she lost all sight of him when two women approached her and said, "Your children are coming!" Mother ran quickly but only saw her two daughters, Tong-nim and me. She was glad to see us safely return, but she was seized with fear at the same time.

Where are my sons, Matthew and John? she cried inside. She called out to Tong-nim and me, and asked us if our brothers were coming. We could not reply. Mother hurried forward and asked me, "Tell me, are your brothers dead?" Still, I could not answer. And Tong-nim began to cry uncontrollably.

"Tong-hŭi! Why won't you say something?" Mother cried. I burst into tears and couldn't bring myself to tell her the truth. "Both of your brothers must be dead. Matthew came by only a few days ago to sing for us, and John came just two weeks ago to get a change of clothes. And now they are gone, forever!" A suffocating sensation grabbed a hold of her just before she fainted. To Mother, the news of her two sons' martyrdoms made it feel like the sky was falling and the land was caving in.

No one told Father that Mother had fainted. Father had endured five dreadful years of torture and imprisonment with a faith as strong as steel, but he could not hide his grieving heart over the loss of his two precious sons. He lost his focus for a moment, but managed to pick up his mourning heart and lead all who gathered to the church.

All the lepers at Aeyangwŏn gathered at the church as if the bell had summoned them. My father said, "Let us...let us pray together." Although he could not repress his strong surge of sorrow, he uttered no reproach because through the many years of discipleship and much suffering, he had learned to accept the will of God. And now, God's Spirit touched his yielded heart and he was able to pray.

"...Dear Lord, we thank Thee that Matthew and John died as martyrs. Though we do not know who killed my sons, we forgive them. Father...Lord Heavenly Father...," he paused for a moment, "...Give us Thy love–love that can forgive them. Forgive us our sins. We ask this in Jesus' name. Amen."

It was a short prayer, but it was long in coming to an end, for it was broken by the cries of those who heard it. Everyone wanted to know what had happened, so one of the elders requested Mr. Hong, who went to Sunch'ŏn in place of Mother, to recount the story of my brothers' deaths. Knowing it would bring glory to God, Mr. Hong told the story in detail, ending it by saying that my brothers' deaths were like the death of Stephen. When Mr. Hong finished reporting the incident, my father arose from behind the pulpit where he had been praying, stood before the congregation and said these words:

Dear brethren,

I believe my two sons, Matthew and John, have gone to heaven. But those who killed them will go to hell. I cannot ignore this. Can I, who preaches the Gospel in order to save people from going to hell, go on my way, while those who killed my sons die without repenting?

Had they been strangers from another country, it still would have been my duty to try to save them, but since they are my own countrymen, I feel more compelled to reach out. When the people of a country fight against each other, who can tell where it will end? Each side will seek revenge, and this could go on until nearly all is destroyed.

Therefore, the tide of revenge must be checked. Let us send someone to go see Pastor Tŏk-hwan Na in Sunch'ŏn at once and tell him that if and when those who killed my sons are found, they must not be beaten or put to death. I will seek to convert them and adopt them as my own sons. And, because my sons used to say that they would become pastors and serve at Aeyangwŏn, where I served too, I do not want Matthew or John to be buried in Sunch'ŏn but be brought here to be buried in the hills of Aeyangwŏn. Today, I make these two wishes before you and before God.

The night passed and on the following morning of October 26, a van was arranged by the church to bring back the bodies of my brothers that were temporarily buried in Sunch'ŏn, because Father wished for Matthew and John to be buried at Aeyangwŏn. Mother had regained consciousness, but she was numb and isolated herself. She insisted that she see her sons' faces. She opened their caskets and rubbed her cheeks against theirs as she cried out, "Tong-in! Tong-sin! My precious sons!

Your mother and father are still alive. How could you die and leave us behind? Let me take another look at your faces." Mother embraced their cold, lifeless bodies and, cheek-to-cheek with her sons, she flooded Aeyangwŏn with her tears.

Mr. In-je Yi, lay preacher and Father's former classmate at P'yŏngyang Bible College, happened to be there as he was invited as a guest speaker at the revival meeting at Aeyangwŏn Church. He tried to comfort my mother by saying, "Mrs. Son, when a fruit is ripe, it is supposed to fall. We are not ripe yet. That's why we're still alive." But Mother didn't seem to be receptive to the preacher's comforting words.

My father too felt downcast. After his words at the church the evening before, so full of faith and power, he had fallen under a wave of depression. He said, "I'm given troubles and sorrows that others do not have to bear because of my great sins."

Listening to him, Mr. Yi grabbed my father's shoulders and scolded him. "Pastor Son, You must think clearly! In the past when both of us were in prison, we wanted so much to be martyred. God didn't allow for our martyrdom. Today, your two young and beautiful sons were offered as models of sacrifice and martyrdom. Surely, you do not oppose. This is not something to weep over but rather something to be glad about. They went to heaven, a much better place."

Mr. Yi felt that my father had to eat, especially since Father had not eaten a thing the evening before, so they went inside to have breakfast together.

"Will you give thanks?" my father asked. Mr. Yi thought for a moment of how he would pray in thanksgiving at such a time and then began:

Dear God, we thank Thee for Thy infinite love. We thank Thee that in Thy purpose, all things work for the good of those who love Thee. We thank Thee that it was Thy will to spare Pastor Son's life during his trials and imprisonment, and that Thou hast lifted these two precious lives. All three offered their lives to Thee, but Thou hast taken only two and spared the one. We do not know why, but we know that Thou hast a purpose in this, so we ask Thee to show us this purpose. Help us now to take this food that Thou hast given and live according to Thy will. All this we pray in Thy Son's name. Amen.

While listening to Mr. Yi's prayer, my father's gloomy outlook began to change. He felt a bright ray of hope in his heart.

To Mr. Yi's surprise, Father's eyes shined as he said with laughter in his voice, "Yi, I am truly grateful to you." Through Mr. Yi's prayer, God had lifted Father's spirits from under the guilt he piled upon himself. And instead, a sudden eagerness to see God's purpose unfold mended his broken heart. Father was no longer sorrowful about losing his sons. He was back to being himself and was truly glad to have offered his two sons as sacrifices. At that moment, my father picked up a pen and paper and began to write down ten things he was thankful for.

So sure was the strength he received from God that when he led the funeral procession on the following day, he followed the coffins, triumphantly singing, "Matthew, John, it's a glory, glory, it's my glory..." And as he walked between their coffins, holding them with both of his hands, he sang the hymn "Ten Thousand Times Ten Thousand:"

Ten thousand times ten thousand
In sparkling raiment bright,
The armies of the ransomed saints throng
Up the steep of light:
'Tis finished, all is finished,
Their fight with death and sin;
Fling open wide the golden gates,
And let the victors in.

Others at the funeral were moved and comforted by the sight of Father's thanksgiving. Up on the hills where my two brothers' bodies were to be buried, a few clouds hung in the clear autumn sky and a chilly breeze swept by. On that day, the ocean waves and the seagulls sounded unusually sorrowful to me. As I followed my father and the coffins, I was choked with so much grief and my heart trembled with so much indignation that I fainted many times. My heart was weeping for my brothers:

They are leaving, they are leaving!
Carried by the two flower palanquins,
They are leaving, far, far away!
The autumn leaves fall and the crows caw ominously
As a sudden wind begins to blow mercilessly,
Carrying my two brothers away.
The rain is trickling down on their tombs.
Could the raindrops be the tears of my brothers,
    sobbing sorrowfully
As they stop and go, stop and go?
Could they be the tears they are shedding
As they cross the Jordan River?

Brothers, how suffocating that grave must be!
Oh, how lonely it must be
In the bone-chilling temperatures below!
When spring comes,
The azaleas will bloom for you;
When autumn arrives,
Wild chrysanthemums will bloom also for you;
When a crow flies by,
I will look for you;
And when the clouds appear,
I will look also for you.
I won't forget how we rejoiced when liberation brought
  our family under one roof.
I won't forget how we all embraced Father and Mother
  in pure joy.
I won't ever forget how you swung me around in circles,
Calling out, "Tong-hŭi! Our beautiful Tong-hŭi!"
And gave me a gentle kiss.

Oh, how I begged for time to take away the grief! Who in the world wouldn't love their own brothers? Quite possibly no one. But the love between my brothers and sisters was especially strong. When our family scattered about and when I was at the orphanage, Matthew continued to express his love for me by visiting me, bringing me cookies and comforting me. Oh, how John used to climb up the snowy hill, blowing into his hands to keep the soybean cakes from the tofu factory warm for us! Oh, how difficult their short lives were!

In spite of always suffering from hunger, both Matthew and John kept their faith. They studied hard no matter how dire the circumstance. They were preparing to study abroad in

America–Matthew as a voice major and John to become a servant of God. Although they dreamed of a bright future, in the end they became like buds, picked in the early spring before they could even bloom.

For the longest time–whether I was awake or asleep, eating or walking–I always cried out, "God! Why did you take away my innocent brothers who loved me so much? It's so unfair! Why did you have to take away both of them at once? Others seemed to have forgotten the past and have been able to get on with life, but why can't I?" At the same time, a bitter rebellious seed occupied one area of my heart that declared, "You wait and see if I ever follow Jesus again !"

Finally, the funeral service proceedud with prayers, hymns, and a reading from the Bible. Mr. Yi read Revelation 11:1-11. His words were brief but full of conviction, and this strengthened our hearts with an eternal hope of glory.

As was customary, an account was then given of the lives of my two brothers, followed by a formal "memorial address." The choir sang a piece and soon it was time for my father's response. Wearing his white mourning robe and cap, he stepped forward and opened his heavy lips to speak. He seemed to be at peace and very calm, free from negative emotions.

"I do not care to give the usual long address of reply," he said. "Instead, I shall recount the many blessings I have received from God and give Him thanks for them."

First, I thank God for the birth of martyrs from blood as sinful as mine.
Second, I thank God for choosing me among His many disciples to be the keeper of these precious treasures.
Third, I thank God for giving me the privilege of giving up

> *my first- and second-born sons, the most precious among my three sons and three daughters, to Him.*
>
> *Fourth, if the martyrdom of one son is precious, how much more is that of two?*
>
> *Fifth, if it is a blessing to die in your sleep after living a Christian life, how much greater is the blessing to be martyred while preaching the Gospel! I thank God.*
>
> *Sixth, my sons had been preparing to go to America, but God has taken them to a better place—to heaven where He is. For this, my heart is at peace.*
>
> *Seventh, I thank God for granting me the grace and love to convert and adopt the boy who killed my dear sons...*

Stillness filled the atmosphere. It seemed so unnatural, so outrageous. How could he speak with so much composure?

> *Eighth, I thank God because I believe that the martyrdom of my two sons will be the means of bringing many more sons into His kingdom.*
>
> *Ninth, I thank God for a joyous heart and for revealing these eight truths to me. For this and for His abundant love, I thank God again and again...*

Father smiled as he lifted his head up to the heavens.

> *Lastly, I give thanks and glory to You for the great blessings You have bestowed upon me, for I know I do not deserve them. I believe they are the fruit of the prayers my own father and mother prayed every morning for thirty-five years, and the fruit of the prayers offered up for my family for twenty-three years by my loving*

brethren here at Aeyangwŏn. I thank you all.

When it was time to lower my brothers into the graves that had been dug by the young men of Aeyangwŏn, Mother grabbed onto each coffin with both hands and shook her head from side to side. "No! No! Matthew! John!" she cried repeatedly.

Because of the lepers' loud cries, neither the hymn nor the sound of Mr. Yi's earnest prayer could be heard. At last, the two coffins were lowered into the ground. It was then that I realized for the first time how grim death really is.

The deaths of my two brothers had a great impact not only on their schools and Sŭngju Church but also on all who lived in Yŏsu and Sunch'ŏn. The hymn that Matthew sang right before he was killed moved the entire town of Sunch'ŏn to ride the waves of God's grace. Not only the Christians but also the hearts of unbelievers were moved by my brothers' last moments. Because my two brothers were gunned down behind Sunch'ŏn Police Station, many of my brothers' friends witnessed the scene, a fact that was disclosed to me years later.

"We have never heard a hymn sung with such earnestness and conviction as when Matthew sang 'Bright, Heavenly Way' before his death." Each of the witnesses said this in admiration. We were all amazed. *How did he manage to sing with death staring him down right before his eyes at such a young age? And from where did he draw such powerful strength to sing?* I hope they now know that my brothers' strength to overcome death came from God. The name of their strength was Jesus! Because of Him, my brothers could see beyond the darkness and despair of death and were able to focus on the eternal home that awaited them in heaven.

21. Who Shot the Bullet?

For the first time in my life, I understood the meaning of death. The aftermath of my brothers' deaths persistently tormented me. I couldn't eat for a week and was severely sick. Whenever I tried to sit up, I felt as though a bullet would suddenly fly toward me. This constant paranoia of flying bullets took control of me. Every night, I had nightmares about flying bullets and heard the sound of my brothers' footsteps.

When night fell, the pitiful figures of my two brothers, staggering in pain and profusely bleeding from gunshots, never failed to haunt me. I couldn't fall asleep, but then again, I couldn't even sit still. I would shake my head from side to side to shake the sounds and images away, or toss and turn all night. I tried everything I could. I struggled with that phantom all night long, breaking into a cold sweat.

"Please, leave me alone!" I cried. But it wasn't easy to get rid of the phantom that clung onto me so tenaciously.

Even after I managed to overcome the phantom, another symptom developed. So many happy memories with my brothers passed through my mind like kaleidoscopic scenes. My brothers' voices were always flowing like a fountain from deep within my soul. I was now trapped in a fantasy. In reality, I was as good as dead.

When I was sick and unable to eat for a whole week, my best friend Sun-gŭm, Pastor Tŏk-hwan Na's daughter, came to visit me. She forced my mouth open, "Tong-hŭi, wake up! If you keep this up, you will go crazy. Now, come on, open your mouth and eat."

After eating only a few spoonfuls of rice, I leaned against her gentle body and closed my eyes. This seemed to clear my mind a bit. But still, I couldn't shake off my brothers' phantoms. It was only a matter of minutes before my mind became polluted with endless thoughts again. In that short time, I thought to myself, *Had my brothers sought refuge at the neighbor's house, they might not have died. Everyone else managed to hide themselves. Even Sun-gŭm's two older brothers had hidden themselves at the neighbor's house, and they're still alive and by their family. Why couldn't my brothers escape like Sun-gŭm's brothers? Was it because their life span was destined to be short?*

I resented my brothers for not hiding. If I had been there with my brothers, perhaps I could have made them hide with whatever strength I had. I regretted so much not being there. Since my brothers always listened to me, if I protested, "Brothers, if you don't hide, I'll die," they probably would have hidden next door.

I was so envious of Sun-gŭm because her two older brothers, Che-min and Ki-hyŏng, were still alive and living as her dependable brothers. I too had two older brothers, but now, I had no one I could call "big brother."

Whenever I saw someone who in the least bit resembled my brothers, my heart would sink and I'd become lightheaded. All strength and energy would drain from my body and I'd collapse to the ground. Whenever this happened, I would lean against a utility pole and stand there for a long time.

I became increasingly lethargic and rebellious. Though I always loved studying, I was careless about going to school. I lost interest in everything in life. My only wish at that time was that I would die as soon as possible and go to heaven to meet my two brothers.

No matter where I was, what I was doing—whether I was eating or walking—whenever my brothers came to mind, I mumbled to myself or protested in tears, "God, why did you take away my innocent brothers who loved me so much? Why did you have to take them both? They were still too young. Why did you snuff them out, and for what reason?"

I had inherited the spiritual heritage of my grandfather, but doubt began to grow more and more. And gradually, my favorite Scripture verses began to show cracks and soon became nothing more than words. Once I began to doubt, my doubts seemed to accumulate like a snowball. But I could not share my inner conflicts with anyone.

As for Father, nothing seemed to have changed. He always had the same calm countenance and he was faithful, as usual, to the task that was entrusted to him. He didn't show any outward emotion of bitterness. He didn't look at all like a person who suffered a tremendous loss. I couldn't understand my father. *How could he be like that?* I thought. *Doesn't he have any emotions? Is he cold-blooded? How could he be so calm when he's lost his two favorite children who were more precious to him than his own life? Yes, he's gladly accepted Matthew and John's martyrdom as something to be thankful for, but as a human being, as a father, shouldn't he at least mourn? How strong must one's faith be to overcome such humanly emotions?* I couldn't even begin to imagine.

My observations weren't necessarily correct. In fact, my father had lost more heart than anyone else. Only, he didn't express it outwardly. One day, not long after my brothers' funeral, the remainder of their belongings—their books, school

I am seated (right) with Sun-gŭm Na,
one of Rev. Tŏk-hwan Na's daughters.

bags, and school uniforms—were sent to our home at Aeyangwŏn from the Sunch'ŏn house.

That day, my father, who alone had remained strong despite the sorrows of the rest of the family, held their school uniforms close to his heart and burst into tears. For the first time in my life, I saw my father cry.

"Matthew, John, my sons. What happened to you?" Copious tears poured from his eyes. All the feelings that he had kept locked up in his heart suddenly erupted at that moment.

I finally realized then that my father's grief weighed no less than mine. He felt the same depth of sorrow I felt. No, his sorrow was much deeper. Only, I spilled all my overwhelming emotions, whereas Father kept them under control by faith alone. It was true, he was a faithful man. As for me, even if I were to die and be reborn a hundred times, I could never attain Father's lofty character or his strong faith.

After about a week had passed since the funeral, we heard that the police had captured the leader responsible for killing my brothers. We heard that his name was Ch'ŏl-min Kang and that he was a senior at Sunch'ŏn High School, the school Matthew attended. Apparently, Ch'ŏl-min had been severely beaten by his classmates and was awaiting execution. The news spread quickly to all the lepers, and Aeyangwŏn was boiling with hot emotions.

"Let's go right now and beat him to death!" the lepers lifted up their deformed fists and shouted.

"Yes, let's go! He must die the cruelest way possible." Even the unbelievers joined their lust for revenge.

I too felt no differently than they did. Rather, my heart was troubled with even more indignation. Ch'ŏl-min Kang! My mortal enemy! I wanted to go to him right away and kill him myself.

"I must kill him! I must! I'll kill him," I mumbled to myself as I walked on the road. I wished I could kill him myself, but I didn't have any real strength to do so.

22. Love Beyond Forgiveness

The ROK National Army was occupying Sunch'ŏn by now and was restoring order. But since it was left short-handed, the National Army gave the Student Assembly and the police the authority to search, question, and turn in all who took part in the uprising. Though some of the men they arrested were falsely accused, overall, the investigations were carefully carried out. The penalty for those proven guilty was death.

Che-min Na volunteered to help the work of the Student Assembly. On his second day at work, he heard the news that Ch'ŏl-min Kang—the boy who had played the key role in killing my two brothers—had been arrested. So Che-min put aside everything else and ran to the building that the Student Assembly was using for holding and questioning prisoners. There he sat in the corner of a room on the first floor, Ch'ŏl-min Kang, kneeling down and begging for his life. The verdict for Ch'ŏl-min: "HARD-LINE COMMUNIST. SENTENCE: DEATH." Ch'ŏl-min had been seen carrying a gun and taking part in the shootings with the other Communist students. He denied any association with the incident until Che-min confronted him about his activities on that day. Che-min testified that Ch'ŏl-min and the others had searched his house first but couldn't find him since he was hiding next door, and that they went straight to our house to capture and kill Matthew and John. Only then did Ch'ŏl-min finally admit to his crime. He admitted to beating and shooting my brothers, as well as to shooting John twice more to make sure he was dead, and to dumping their bodies on the street in front of their school.

On the following morning, Ch'ŏl-min was transferred to the National Army headquarters along with many others who had also received the death penalty. Che-min told the news to his father, Pastor Na, who then sent the news to our home. This was how we discovered that Ch'ŏl-min Kang had murdered my two brothers.

Hearing that the murderer who killed two innocent lives was begging for his life, I couldn't be still. I was filled with overpowering indignation. *If he considers his own life precious, how could he point a gun at someone else's face?* I was so disgusted with him that I remained speechless.

But my father's reaction was different. As I mentioned before, Father had already forgiven the enemy and was determined to love him. That afternoon, he called me quietly with his usual calm, low voice. But the light in his eyes was different. He looked as though he were firmly determined to do something.

"I must leave home right now because of the revival meeting, so I cannot go up to Sunch'ŏn myself. Tong-hŭi, you must go to Pastor Tŏk-hwan Na on my behalf and deliver my wishes to him."

"Your wishes, Father? What do you mean?"

"The student who killed your brothers has been arrested. Therefore, go quickly to Pastor Na and ask him to request that the student not be beaten or killed. I wish to adopt him as my own son, so don't forget to tell him to save the boy's life from execution."

I couldn't believe my ears! Father was actually about to act upon the words he shared at the funeral during his speech on his ten greatest blessings. *Adopt the enemy for whom I felt punishment and death would not be justice enough? Surely not! Does he expect me to call our mortal enemy my brother? Does he really think it's possible? Could such a thing be possible? No matter what, I can't!* I thought. But Father had already made up his mind.

"Father, listen to what you are saying! Do you really mean it?"

I questioned him with my eyes wide, breathing heavily. Father did not reply. Instead, he only gazed at me with a calm, gentle countenance. I raised my voice in protest and expressed my strong opposition.

"Father, please listen to my request! Leave him to die. If such a fellow is not punished, who shall be? He is not worthy to be left to live. I have never before disobeyed you Father, but this time, I can't listen to you."

At this point, my father and I began to argue. Father was determined to adopt Ch'ŏl-min Kang as his son. And I was just as determined to kill him. Both of us refused to yield to the other. My father then let out a heavy sigh and began to scrupulously explain his wishes with a calm voice.

"Tong-hŭi, please listen to me carefully. Think about why I let my children suffer for five years while I was in prison. Wasn't it to keep God's commandments? If the first and second commandments were for us to obey, His Word, 'Love your enemy,' are also ours to follow. How can I obey the first two commandments but disobey His Word? There is no greater contradiction than that. If we don't obey His command to love our enemies, your past sufferings and my imprisonment over the past five years all become pointless. We've come too far to fail Him now. Tong-hŭi, think about it quietly. What gain is there in killing that student? If he dies, will your brothers be brought back to life? No, they won't be. Sparing the boy's life will ring us much joy in knowing that we've obeyed God's command and saved the soul of a fallen human being. Matthew and John went to heaven. But it is obvious that their killer will be going to hell. Can I, who preaches the Gospel in order to save people from going to hell, go on my way, unheeding, while he who killed my sons dies and goes to hell?"

My father hastened me to go see Pastor Na on my way to Sunch'ŏn and he mentioned with a firm but gentle voice that it would be terrible if we could not get the word out in time to save the murderer.

But no matter how correct my father's words were according to God's Word, they didn't register in my ears. To me, Ch'ŏl-min Kang was nothing but an enemy. I felt that he deserved to die. He had to die cruelly and suffer far more pain than my brothers. Only then would my embittered heart be somewhat relieved.

I deeply resented my father's persuasion. Embittered tears welled up in my eyes once again. "Whatever the reason, I must stop this matter!" I screamed in tears. I retorted, "Father, think about it. If you want to forgive, forgive. But what do you mean when you say you want to make him your son? It's enough to forgive. If you adopt him, he will become my brother. Are you asking me to call our enemy my big brother?"

I went out of my mind. Surely, the sky above my head was falling. Even if I should die, I could not follow my father's instructions. Without hesitation, I cried and yelled at my father in protest. At that moment, I was oblivious to everything around me, even my father. I hated him for believing in Jesus. I hated him because his faith was so strong. The anger fed endlessly on itself and I finally burst into tears, stomping my feet in protest, shouting, "Father, can't you hear my brothers' cries? Can't you see my brothers who are looking down with sad, sad eyes from heaven, crying out for us to avenge their blood? Father, if you do not do such a ridiculous thing as this, will it mean you believe in Jesus any less? Other pastors are not like you. Why must you always follow Jesus to such extremes? What you are about to do is impossible on earth. Father, please don't insist on doing this!"

"Tong-hŭi, look carefully at the Scriptures. In the Bible, God clearly said, 'Love your enemy.' Our forgiving that student is not enough to keep him alive. Since God said to love our enemies, I want to love the boy and adopt him as my son. Didn't Abraham go to Mount Moriah to sacrifice his only son, Isaac, a son that was born to him at the age of a hundred? Yet he obeyed the first time God spoke to him. What do you think? Do you think this test is more difficult than Abraham's? If Ch'ŏl-min Kang is killed, your two brothers' deaths will have been in vain."

No matter how persuasive Father's words were, I couldn't hear a word he said. All that went through my mind was how much I wanted that ruthless murderer to die. I had nothing more to say, nor did I want to speak anymore. I shut my lips tightly and stared at my father. His eyes were still gleaming with conviction. His hand gently rubbed my back. It was such a gentle and loving touch that it helped me relax. But I still refused to give in.

As the time to leave for the revival meeting was fast approaching, Father seemed to get more anxious. He let out a heavy sigh and gently closed his eyes. This revival meeting Father had to go to had been scheduled several months in advance. While I was looking at my father's tired, yet highly dignified countenance, I felt as though all my strength was draining out of my body.

There was no use for all my passionate fury. I was angry with myself for being so rebellious against my father, especially since I was well aware that I could never go against his decision. Someone like me, even if there were a hundred, could never overrule Father's decision. I knew too well that my father feared a single word from God over anything else in the world. No matter what I do or say, I could never persuade my father away from God's will. So I finally yielded to his instructions.

"Father, I'll do as you say."

"Thank you. Indeed, you are my daughter. Since you must reach him before he is executed, you must leave now." My father gently wiped my tear-stained face with his clean handkerchief and hugged me tightly. He left hurriedly for the revival meeting as I grudgingly headed toward Sunch'ŏn.

When I arrived at Pastor Na's house, I could hear voices from inside. I called out to the pastor in a loud voice, "Is that you, Pastor Na?"

"Oh, look who's here! Isn't this Tong-hŭi?" Pastor Na and his wife led me into the house and looked at me with sorrowful eyes. All five of their children had safely survived the uprising, while my two older brothers—who had been left in their care— had been killed. There was no way they could have prevented the deaths of my brothers, but they still carried a sense of guilt. My coming troubled them. Pastor Na was at a loss for words to comfort me.

Mrs. Na spoke to me with tearful eyes. "Tong-hŭi, how terrible we feel for your father and mother! The morning of the day your brothers died, Matthew came to our house to ask for a little bit of rice. Unfortunately, we didn't have any left. I really regret not having any rice to give him. Why, of all days, had we run out of rice that day? Your father trusted us and sent his children to Sunch'ŏn. But now that this has happened, I really don't have the courage to face your family."

When I saw the pain on her face, I also thought about how Matthew and John must have been hungry even at the moment they faced death. My heart was torn. Tears clouded my eyes. But I quickly regained composure and, in a very calm voice, delivered my father's request.

"Pastor Na, I came to deliver my father's request. We have heard that one of the students who killed my brothers has been captured. If the rest of them are found, they are not to be beaten or killed, for Father wishes to adopt them as his sons and lead them to Christ. Father asks that you see to it that this be done."

Listening to me quietly, Pastor Na's eyes filled with tears. "Surely, there can be no other man like Pastor Son!"

But this was no surprise to him, for Father was already known for his strong faith, especially among the pastors of his day. Father spent twenty-three years in ministry to lepers; he spent five years in prison for refusing to bow down before Shinto shrines; and now, he not only forgave those who murdered his two sons but had also decided to adopt them as his own. *This*, Pastor Na thought, *is more amazing than anything I have ever done.*

Taking to heart the message my father had sent him, Pastor Na immediately began to work to save the life of Ch'ŏl-min Kang. But the task was far more difficult than he thought. The more he tried, the more difficult the task seemed. Pastor Na had often tried to help prisoners who had been falsely accused, but he was unsuccessful every time. Here he was now, trying to save someone who was, indeed, guilty!

At first, Pastor Na followed his son Che-min to the building that the Student Assembly was using for holding and questioning Ch'ŏl-min Kang. There, he found the boy, lying on the floor, severely beaten. His mother held him in her arms, crying and begging for his pardon. Ignoring his mother's pleas, the students surrounded Ch'ŏl-min to interrogate him, as a young soldier of the National Army stood by, listening and watching closely. The questioning seemed to have reached its climax.

"If you didn't shoot, who did? Many of the witnesses told us you went to Matthew and John's house. Many more saw you killing them. Will you now honestly confess?"

They were about to beat him again, but his mother intervened. Ch'ŏl-min, completely scared and trembling with fear, answered, "I just took two more shots at John's body after he fell." His confession infuriated the students even more.

"You are worse than a wild animal! How wicked you must be to have shot him after he was already dead!" yelled one of the students.

"You're a wretched fellow! How can you say you did not take part in shooting them when you, indeed, shot them after they were dead? Tell the truth!" demanded another.

Ch'ŏl-min could no longer defend himself. He knew he could no longer lie, and so he nodded at the charges made against him.

Pastor Na looked on for a while and then stepped in at that moment. "Please don't beat him anymore."

"Who are you?" one student asked.

"I am Tŏk-hwan Na, pastor of Sŭngju Church."

"You are Che-min's father, aren't you, sir?" another student asked. "Why are you here?"

"Is Matthew and John's murderer here?" Pastor Na asked.

"Yes! This is he. He has just confessed with his own mouth that he killed them."

"Is that so? I come with a special request from Matthew and John's father, Pastor Son. He has asked me to tell you that he does not want those who murdered his sons to be beaten or killed. In fact, he wants to adopt their murderers as his own sons."

The soldier in charge, who had been listening in silence, rose to leave. Pastor Na quickly grabbed a hold of him and repeated his request. The soldier turned away, dismissing the request as ridiculous. The students' responses were no different than that of the soldier. At once, there was a flurry of protests from some of the students. This was not the time to speak to them about pardon or else you'd be misunderstood as a Communist. Still, Pastor Na went out after the soldier and, without much success, repeated his request. In any case, the order had been clearly laid down and he could do nothing more.

On the following day, Pastor Na tried to discuss the matter with the police, but they too would not accept his request. The police told him that the country was under martial law, and that he would have to go see the officers of the National Army. Pastor Na called Mr. Sŏng-hwan O, a member of the National Assembly and a man with some influence, but he told Pastor Na to drop the matter as it might bring him into ill favor with the authorities. At that time, the authorities were busily engaged in searching out all the Communist insurrectionists who were involved in the Yŏsu-Sunch'ŏn Mutiny. This request did not make any sense and was rather considered a hindrance to their busy schedules. No one paid much attention to Pastor Na.

Discouraged, Pastor Na turned back on the road home,

when he was stopped by an old man who introduced himself as the father of Ch'ŏl-min Kang.

"What can I do for you?" Pastor Na asked him kindly. The old man replied that he had heard from his wife that Pastor Na had interceded for their son. He was very grateful to my father for taking the risk. Completely convinced that his son was not guilty, he asked Pastor Na to help save his son.

Pastor Na felt suddenly weary. If Ch'ŏl-min Kang was not guilty of the murder of Matthew and John, Pastor Son's request did not apply to this young man and he had no duty to save him. Ch'ŏl-min's father did not know this. If he did, would he admit that his son was guilty? Baffled and weary, Pastor Na's heart sought for some clear guidance from God, and so he led the old man to his church to pray. On the way, Pastor Na told the man about my father. It turned out that the man was at Kwangju Prison at the same time my father was also imprisoned. The man had heard about a remarkable pastor and knew, without a doubt, that the pastor he had heard so much about was Pastor Son. The old man had for so long been eager to meet this Pastor Son, and now their paths were about to cross.

At church, Pastor Na knelt in prayer. The old man had never been in a church before. He assumed that the verses of Scripture on both sides of the pulpit were there to keep out evil spirits, much like the writings he and his pagan ancestors had put up in their homes. He bowed after Pastor Na, but to him, Pastor Na's prayer was like an incantation before a charm. The man kept repeating, "Save my son!"

Strengthened through prayer, Pastor Na rose to leave the church. Suddenly, his son Che-min ran in, breathless and with more news.

"Father! Father! Ch'ŏl-min Kang has been taken to the P'alwang Café."

"Taken to the café? What do you mean?"

"The National Army has taken over the P'alwang Café. He's been taken there to be executed!" Pastor Na feared the worst and hurried to the café.

When he and Che-min arrived at the café, a guard shouted, "Who's there? What is your business here?"

Startled at first, Pastor Na regained his composure and said, "I am Tŏk-hwan Na, Pastor of Sŭngju Church. I have a message to deliver."

"What is it about?" the guard asked.

"It's something I must tell the soldier in charge." Glancing inside past the guard, Pastor Na saw the soldier he had met earlier at the Student Assembly. "There's the person I want to see," he exclaimed as he entered the building without waiting for a reply. "As I had pleaded with you before, again I ask that you please pardon that student. This isn't my request but that of Pastor Yang-wŏn Son, the father of the two boys this man murdered."

"The guilty must be punished. This case is now closed. You cannot say nor do anything about it. Return home. The truck will arrive soon to take the prisoner to the execution grounds."

No matter how hard Pastor Na pleaded, the soldier did not budge.

Inside the café, Pastor Na saw Ch'ŏl-min lying on the floor with his mother beside him, weeping and begging for his life. Ch'ŏl-min still denied all connections to the murder of Matthew and John and he said that he could not be convicted. The delay vexed the investigators.

Pastor Na asked the guard if he could have a word with Ch'ŏl-min. The soldier looked at him with irritation, but he permitted.

"I am Pastor Na. You must be honest with me and tell me everything. I have come at the request of Pastor Son, the father of the two boys for whom you are charged with murder. Did you or did you not take part in the uprising with the students who killed Pastor Son's sons?"

Ch'ŏl-min looked up in surprise because Pastor Na's voice was quite different from that of the students and soldiers, who seemed determined to convict him.

"I did not kill them," Ch'ŏl-min denied.

"Is that true?"

"Yes."

"Then there is nothing I can do for you." Everyone in the room stood still in silent astonishment. "I have come," Pastor Na explained, "not just to deliver Pastor Son's message but to see to it that his wishes be granted. He has requested that the murderers of his two sons, whoever they are, not be punished but rather forgiven. My duty applies only to the guilty. For the innocent, I can do nothing."

Right then, Ch'ŏl-min clutched onto Pastor Na and begged him. "Save me! I did take part in the uprising and I did kill Matthew and John. Save me... please save me!"

Then Ch'ŏl-min explained that when the mutineers entered Sunch'ŏn, the Communist students came to his house and forced him to take part. He went with them to our home where Matthew and John were, and with the other students, he beat my brothers because he could not do otherwise. Then when they were led to the execution ground, he was chosen among four others to shoot my brothers and, unwilling, he did so.

"How did you kill them?"

"We shot them—the five of us. I don't know whether my bullet hit them or not, but I shot John twice after he had fallen."

His story seemed to ring true. In the brief, hushed moment following Ch'ŏl-min's confession, many thoughts ran through Pastor Na's mind. Because of his intervention, the young man had now condemned himself. He would shortly be executed unless Pastor Na was successful in having him pardoned. His duty pressed urgently on him.

"If what you have told me is the truth, I shall do my best to save you," Pastor Na assured him.

Somewhere out there, there were four others with a claim on my father's pardon. If the soldiers decided to look for them, Pastor Na's duty would have to be extended to them as well. These thoughts passed through the fringes of his conscious mind, but they were lost as the path of immediate action opened clear before him.

Once more, he approached the soldier in charge and repeated his request for pardon, but the soldier reconfirmed that the case was now closed and that the young man's execution was now certain to occur because of the confession. Pastor Na pleaded, reasoning that Christian forgiveness could change guilty lives and have positive impact on others. But Pastor Na's words just seemed to annoy the soldier.

"I know nothing of the laws of God's working. I only recognize the laws of my country. If I were to pardon this guilty student, I would be breaking the law."

So Pastor Na asked for time to appeal to President Syngman Rhee. His request was yet again declined.

A jeep pulled up outside the café and an army officer entered the room.

"All is well, sir. We are waiting for the truck that will take the prisoners to the execution ground," said the soldier.

"The truck was following our jeep," the officer replied, "but it got a flat tire. The execution will be delayed by about half an hour. What are all these people doing here?"

"They are relatives of this prisoner, sir."

"Send them out. I will be back later." The officer got back into the jeep and drove off.

Pastor Na was desperate. He had been hoping to speak to the army officer, for it seemed that the final word in either releasing or executing Ch'ŏl-min was in the officer's hands. Now the opportunity was gone. The officer's words returned sharply at him. In half an hour, Ch'ŏl-min would be taken out and executed. Once again, Pastor Na turned to the soldier and made the same plea for more time to appeal to the president. Growing increasingly agitated, the soldier warned Pastor Na that he might be misunderstood for a Communist sympathizer if he persisted in pleading for this prisoner. Pastor Na was just as enraged.

Letting out a long, heavy sigh, Pastor Na retreated one step back, but he wasn't about to give up completely. In his mind, he was thinking up ways to melt their hard, stone-like hearts. Finally, Pastor Na thought of bringing me to present my father's request. He had no time to lose and he considered it his final card to cast.

"Since you consider my words silly, I will bring Pastor Son's oldest daughter Tong-hŭi here so you can question her directly to find out whether I am speaking the truth or not. She is at my house right now."

"Go ahead and bring her," the soldier readily agreed, hoping that the truck would arrive while Pastor Na was out of the way.

Pastor Na's house was located only five minutes away from the P'alwang Café. "Good! This is a good chance!" Pastor Na said as he ran home to bring me back with him.

I was sitting on the wooden floor when Pastor Na suddenly burst in and grabbed me by the hand. I was confused as to why he was taking me to the café. On our way there, he told me briefly what had happened and made me pledge to him that I would do only as I was told by my father. "When you get there, Tong-hŭi, you must not go back on your father's word. You must speak only what your father asked you to say."

From that moment on, my heart throbbed. *Should I let him die or live? Die or live?* My mind changed more than a thousand times during that short five-minute run to the café. I remember hesitating until the last second. With one word from my mouth, Ch'ŏl-min could be sent to the execution ground and face death. *Should I save him according to Father's will? Or should I just close my eyes and let my brothers' murderer be executed?* While I was running, I struggled with conflicting emotions. If it were up to me, I would choose to have Ch'ŏl-min put to death, but if I did, I would not be able to ever face my father. Pastor Na earnestly entreated me. My heart throbbed as if it were about to burst. I couldn't make up my mind. I did not reach a decision until I arrived at the P'alwang Café.

As we opened the door and went inside, all eyes focused on Pastor Na and me. The size of the room looked to be about the same as that of a school classroom. Chairs and tables were strewn here and there, and in the center of the room, the soldier in charge was smoking a cigarette. Pastor Na took me to the soldier and had me sit down on a chair. "This is the oldest daughter of Pastor Yang-wŏn Son and the sister of John and Matthew."

Pastor Na introduced me to the soldier. Then, all attention turned to me. I lifted my head up and looked around. There were about seven other soldiers and students, and their faces were all flushed. Then, right when I looked toward the corner of the room, I nearly went into shock as I felt my heart stop. There he was, curled up in a school uniform with both hands tied with rope. He had long, snaky eyes and the white of his eyes shown more than other people. He was beaten so severely by the soldiers and students that his face was covered with wounds. His lip was torn and blood trickled down his chin. His head was face down, but when I entered, he looked at me for a moment with a sidelong glace. And just for a moment, his eyes and my eyes met. I nearly lost my mind. I thought my heart had finally stopped. Those indescribably frightful eyes! A cold shiver ran down my spine. Those eyes were that of a murderer. Without anybody having to tell me, I instinctively knew that he was Ch'ŏl-min Kang. He was the murderer who killed my two brothers. Ah, what was I to do?

I was seized with an impulsive anger that rose from deep within. I wanted to protest: *Who do you think you are? For what were you born—to kill my two innocent brothers? For what sin, with what right did you kill my brothers?* I wanted to grab him and tear him to shreds. I wanted him to answer for my brothers' deaths. But suddenly, my father's face passed before my eyes. Struggling to suppress the anger that threatened to explode, I slowly turned away from him.

It was because of father's earnest plea that I was able to calm my anger. I couldn't, no didn't want to, disappoint Father.

In that hour of hopelessness, Ch'ŏl-min might have looked at me with a thread-like hope that he just might be saved. He didn't have much time. Within ten minutes, he would be dragged out to the execution ground. Was he looking at me, the sister of the two boys he shot to death, as his savior?

He was staring at my lips the whole time, waiting for me to speak. My words, perhaps, could save him from the death penalty.

Suddenly, the air in the room weighed down. A heavy silence fell on the room.

"What is your name?" asked the soldier in charge who was interrogating.

"My name is Tong-hŭi Son, sir." My voice was surprisingly calm and controlled.

"Are Matthew and John Son your brothers?"

"Yes, sir, they are."

"What grade are you in now?"

"I am in my first year at Maesan Girls' Middle School in Sunch'ŏn."

"So, what is it that your father said that made you come here?"

"My father would like to request that the person who killed my brothers not be killed or even beaten. My father wants the person spared and desires to adopt him as his own son. He said it is because of the Word of God that commands us to love our enemies that he must do so."

I blurted it all out in one single breath. Only after I was done communicating my father's message did I break down and let my tears run down. The cross I had to bear was far too heavy and burdensome. I dropped my head to the table and cried uncontrollably.

When I was done speaking, everyone in the room seemed to have red-rimmed eyes. Even the soldiers couldn't contain their emotions. I had said no more than Pastor Na had already told them, but my words somehow softened their hardened hearts and brought out their compassion for my family's loss and suffering. They were even able to comprehend how my father could forgive someone who caused him so much pain. The interrogating soldier, who had been very cold toward Pastor Na, didn't even realize that his cigarette had dropped from his mouth. He pulled out a handkerchief, wiped away his tears, and exclaimed, "What a great man!" Ch'ŏl-min dropped his head and sobbed as well. Images of that day remain vividly imprinted in my memory, even to this day.

The soldier finally yielded. Ch'ŏl-min Kang was saved from execution only seconds before the truck that would take the prisoners to the execution ground arrived.

23. A Repentant Prodigal Son

At last, Ch'ŏl-min Kang was released from custody, saved from execution, and became a member of our family. He took all of my father's love and attention. Father always called him affectionately, "Ch'ŏl-min, my Ch'ŏl-min!" Wherever my father was, there Ch'ŏl-min would also be. Of all the memories I have of my father, the most vivid ones are of his overwhelming love for Ch'ŏl-min. *How could Father love that gruesome murderer so much?* I always wondered. I couldn't love Ch'ŏl-min at all—just looking at his face made me sick to the stomach. Even looking at him from behind filled me with absolute disgust and hatred. I even hated the way he walked. I thought Father had completely lost his mind with the loss of his two sons. Otherwise, how could he adopt such a horrible murderer as his own son? My heart screamed, *Ch'ŏl-min Kang, you murderer! For what reason did you kill my dear brothers? Why? Bring them back to life or be gone!*

After liberation, my father led more than 2,000 revival meetings, in addition to his regular services at Aeyangwŏn Church. Usually he would leave Aeyangwŏn on Monday and return on Saturday, and even after my brothers' martyrdom, there was no change in his schedule. One time, there was a revival meeting at Namdaemun Church in Seoul and I accompanied him. On the church bulletin board, a poster read: "WORLD RENOWNED SAINT, REVEREND YANG-WŎN SON." As soon as my father saw it, he insisted that it be removed, otherwise, he would not preach. At the top of his sermon notes, he wrote these words:

Read this first before preaching at revival meetings:

1. *Depend on God's wisdom, not on your own understanding.*
2. *Be careful not to glorify yourself, but instead reveal the glory of the Lord.*
3. *Do not teach out of your own knowledge, ignorant of scriptural principles.*
4. *Do not lie when sharing your testimony.*
5. *Do not burden others with legalistic rules that you yourself cannot carry out.*
6. *Speak carefully, earnestly, and faithfully, for the words of your mouth can lead to life or death.*
7. *In this hour, with a single word from the Scriptures, the soul of a person could swing between life and death and could ascend from hell or descend to hell.*
8. *Be very careful about receiving gifts and hospitality.*
    a. *Since you're receiving the hospitality instead of the Lord, you should consider whether you are worthy of such treatment.*
    b. *Do not eat and drink for the satisfaction of taste and appetite but in order to work.*
    c. *Never pay attention to material things and gifts.*

Prayer: *Oh Lord, do not let me sin against You in this hour. Help me not to be like the rainless cloud and pass by the people without giving grace. And let only the sixty-six books of the Bible be the guidebooks of my life. Amen.*

Although Father was well known as a powerful preacher in the Christian community, he was extremely cautious to stay away from mystical miracles and prosperity theology.[9] Some time ago, I heard from Aunt Ho-sun Ch'oe that at one revival meeting at Ch'oryang Church in Pusan, the church building was packed and the people were singing praises from their hearts. Father's preaching was especially powerful and moving that day. Suddenly, someone in the corner cried out in tears, "Pastor! Pastor! I can see! I can see now!" He was a blind man who now claimed to see as he jumped up and down with overwhelming joy. The church members who were gathered there began to whisper among themselves and they looked at the blind man whose eyes were now opened. The sound of awe and praise spontaneously burst out from here and there. Both the singing and the sermon stopped. Then my father calmed down the congregation:

All you saints please be quiet. And sit down, please. The fact that this man's eyes have opened has nothing to do with me. My sermon heals the sickness of the soul, not of the body. His eyes were opened by his own faith.

This statement revealed the core foundation of my father's faith. He only preached the Gospel of heaven, never once did he promise a comfortable, wealthy life on earth. Since then, people with illnesses occasionally came to visit him, asking him to put his hand on them and pray for healing, but my father did not particularly pray for their physical healing.

I consider the soul more important than the body. What's wrong with being ill? And what's wrong with being handicapped? During our brief life as a pilgrim in this world, what greater blessing is there than to live joyfully, even as a disabled person, and go to heaven? What more could we ask for?

With these words, Father sent the visitors home. Living among lepers all his life, Father took care of them with love and never considered their disease as something to be frowned upon. The father I remember wasn't one who liked signs and miracles. His focus was always centered on the Word of God.

Rumor had spread quickly that my father took Ch'ŏl-min wherever he went in order to help his adopted son grow spiritually. At every revival meeting, many people encircled Ch'ŏl-min–some out of curiosity and some out of hatred. I remember how Father said, "As soon as the worship service is over, people gather around Ch'ŏl-min as though he were some kind of animal at the zoo. It's not good for him. Even if he hides somewhere else, people always manage to find him. I feel bad for Ch'ŏl-min. I think it would be best not to take him around from now on."

Around that time, another rumor, which had absolutely no basis in fact, had spread. I didn't know who started such a ridiculous rumor, but it just didn't make any sense. When I first heard the rumor, I actually wished to die. The rumor had spread that my father was arranging for me to marry Ch'ŏl-min. It was ridiculous! The people went so far as to say that Father had adopted Ch'ŏl-min, not as his son, but with the intentions to make him his son-in-law. Mother was also very much upset at the thoughtless rumor. She thought it was absolutely absurd. I agreed with her.

This rumor caused me to hate Ch'ŏl-min even more.

Perhaps my father was responsible for such a rumor since he decided to adopt him as his son. No, perhaps I brought this upon myself, as it was I who had been unable to refuse my father's earnest request to save Ch'ŏl-min from execution.

Several days after Ch'ŏl-min was rescued from execution, Father decided to pay him a visit for the first time. He went to Pastor Na to ask for directions, but Pastor Na wasn't home. So Mrs. Na, instead, guided my father to Ch'ŏl-min's house. As they set out together, Mrs. Na asked, "Why do you want to visit him now? You'll meet him later." She felt it seemed quite odd for a man to consider meeting the murderer of his two sons so soon.

"There's no point in putting it off," Father answered. "I must see him at once and lead him to the Savior. I'm very busy with attending evangelistic meetings and I may not have another opportunity. Besides, Ch'ŏl-min and his family probably know that we all must meet some time. I think it would make it easier on them to get the meeting over with quickly."

Mrs. Na was silenced by Father's concern for Ch'ŏl-min and his family.

"This is the place," Mrs. Na said before she went inside to announce their arrival. Father waited at the door. The place appeared to be a small fish shop. Mrs. Na returned to the front door with Ch'ŏl-min's parents, whose eyes were wide with astonishment.

"We were planning on calling you, Pastor Son! We were waiting for the transportation routes to reopen so we could go see you. But here you are. I cannot say how sorry I am for not presenting ourselves to you first," said Ch'ŏl-min's father, embarrassed.

"Ch'ŏl-min, bow to Pastor Son," said his mother. The young man barely managed to stand up, still unable to lift his head. His face, only partly healed, still bore the marks of bruises here and there. Father felt so much compassion for him.

"Are you Ch'ŏl-min? Come here," said Father, searching Ch'ŏl-min's face. Taking a firm hold of his hands, Father continued, "Be at ease. I have already forgiven you. I believe God is also longing to forgive you."

At Father's words, tears welled up in Ch'ŏl-min's eyes. Moved with gratitude, Ch'ŏl-min's father stepped forward and said, "In our home you are like a savior. We cannot begin to express all our gratitude. I had heard of you before when you were at Kwangju Prison for refusing to participate in Shinto worship. I too was in the same prison at the same time, but for a financial crime. I wanted to meet you then, but I never got the chance. I never dreamed I would meet you this way. Indeed, it is a small world." Ch'ŏl-min's father fumbled for words and then went on with great deference. "Pastor Son, I have four sons and would like to split them with you. Will you agree to this?" Father refused the man's offer, but accepted their sincere hearts.

"No, that is not at all necessary. You are very kind, but that is not what I want. My hope is that you make good men out of your boys, that your family believe in Jesus and be saved." Father then turned to Ch'ŏl-min and said, "Young man, I shall not remember what you have done, so put all your fears and doubts behind you. Please believe in Jesus Christ and say you would carry on where my two sons left off."

Ch'ŏl-min stood silent, face down. His mother brought in a small table with tea and rice cakes. It had not been long since the riots ended, so the six o'clock curfew was still in force. It was already half past five, so Father prayed a short prayer and stood up to leave.

Mr. Kang turned to Father again and said, "Pastor Son, I have something else to request of you and I want you to accept. I heard you have a daughter who is attending high school. Can't she come and live at our home while she goes to school? We have a daughter who is also of school age."

He seemed quite determined, but father refused this also. "No, thank you. I do not wish to burden you in any way. I shall see you again."

But Mr. Kang insisted. "Pastor Son, I think you may have misunderstood me. Let me explain. Our family has already decided to go to church, though we feel ashamed to go. I do not want to do this in order to repay our debt but so that the members of our family may become better Christians. If your daughter Tong-hŭi were to stay here with us, you would visit more often and our family would be able to hear more from you about God. You must agree as it would be a great blessing to our family.

"I understand now," replied Father, "but I cannot compel my daughter to do this. I shall ask her and let you know what she says." And he left the house.

When Father returned home that evening, he asked me, "Tong-hŭi, Ch'ŏl-min's father wants you to go and live with them. He says you could share his daughter's room. What do you think?"

"Oh, Father," I burst out, "I wouldn't possibly be able to bear it no matter how much they wanted me to come live with them!" Understanding how deeply my heart ached over the death of my brothers, Father gently made it clear to me that it would be in my best interest to accept Ch'ŏl-min's father's request.

"Tong-hŭi, Ch'ŏl-min won't be there at his home much since he will be with me. Besides, there is no other place for you to stay while you go to school. It's a temporary stay. Try to set a good example for their family."

I was too afraid to stay at the house where my two brothers died and I knew I had to continue my schooling, but there was no other place for me to stay. In the end, I could not refuse to go. And this is how I came to stay for a while at the hell-like house of Ch'ŏl-min.

While I was living in their home, both my body and my spirit began to dry up. I became thin. From the time I opened my eyes until the time I closed my eyes to sleep, I spent most of my time and energy hating Ch'ŏl-min. On occasions when our eyes would meet, I would quickly turn my head away in disgust. No matter how hard I tried, I couldn't suppress my hatred for him.

But to the eyes of the outsider who knew nothing of the real story, the fact that I lived at the Kang's house and that I went to school from there appeared to be an amazingly interesting story. That's why such a ridiculous rumor had spread that I would soon marry Ch'ŏl-min.

Although Ch'ŏl-min was the murderer of my brothers, Father sought a job for him everywhere. Each time, the employers would say to my father, "Don't worry. Just wait. We'll find him something." But whenever Father took Ch'ŏl-min to meet them, they would shake their heads and give poor excuses. The more they thought about it, the more uncomfortable they felt about providing a job for a murderer.

One day, Ch'ŏl-min and Pastor Yong-jun An were on their way to Aeyangwŏn. While Pastor An was purchasing the train tickets, Ch'ŏl-min suddenly disappeared from his side. Pastor An looked everywhere for him but could not find him. After a long while, Ch'ŏl-min returned with a swollen face. Apparently, Ch'ŏl-min was lured away and beaten by a person named Sŏng-bae. When Sŏng-bae saw Ch'ŏl-min, he grabbed his neck and shook him, saying, "You fool! Were there no other men for you to kill in the world that you chose to kill two good boys like Matthew and John? Now it's your turn to taste and see for yourself what it's like to die!" Sŏng-bae dragged Ch'ŏl-min to the corner, kicked him, and beat him mercilessly with his fists. Ch'ŏl-min could not help but to endure the beating without putting up a defense. No one tried to stop Sŭng-bae, who finally quit out of sheer exhaustion.

Whenever my uncle, who used to live with my two brothers in Sunch'ŏn, saw Ch'ŏl-min, he would rush at him with a kitchen knife. "You evil person! The murderer of my nephews! I'll kill you!"

Everyone in the house would have to rush to my uncle to take the knife away and help Ch'ŏl-min to a safe place.

Our immediate family really didn't have much problems with Ch'ŏl-min, but there was tremendous opposition outside the family. Many hated him and wanted him dead. But such attacks gradually decreased as Father's true intention for Ch'ŏl-min became more clear.

With my father's support, Ch'ŏl-min was able to enter the Korea Bible Institute in Pusan. By this time, he was truly a repentant prodigal son. Although he was quite ignorant of the Scriptures, his faith burned like an oil-fed fire. Clearly, he was a changed man. Each Sunday, he walked around Pusan Station and market places, handing out gospel tracts, beating on a drum, and witnessing to those who passed by.

Whenever an acquaintance would approach him and ask how he was doing, he would cheerfully smile and reply, "I'm still too lacking in knowledge to teach the children in Sunday school, so I'm out here beating my drum in hopes that the beat of the drum would lead them to church." He also used to tell everyone how grateful he was that he had found God through the great love of my father, and that he was given the opportunity to learn the wonderful truths of God at Korea Bible Institute.

Each letter that Ch'ŏl-min sent to Aeyangwŏn was filled with praise of Jesus' love and the joy of witnessing. Indeed, he was changing. My father's heart was especially glad. He was proud of Ch'ŏl-min, not only because of his ever-deepening faith but because he never forgot to sign his name, "Your son, Ch'ŏl-min Son" at the end of his letters. Father always voiced a prayer of thanksgiving whenever he received one of Ch'ŏl-min's letters from Bible school. The following is an excerpt from one of his letters:

October 28, 1949

Dear Father,

Now that I am born again by the grace and mercy of God, I can finally see the love of God and Jesus. We must glorify our God until death. I have been lifted from death and given a new life, for which I am truly grateful. Now, by faith, I look forward to going to heaven. Even if we were to refuse going to heaven, God Himself holds our hand and guides us there. I do not purposefully look for a cross to bear, but if I am called to carry one, I will by no means turn it over to others. Your son, Ch'ŏl-min Son, will carry the cross and follow Jesus.

Your Son,
Ch'ŏl-min Son

Of course, Mother treated Ch'ŏl-min more warmly than anyone else. She gave him much love and care, concerned that perhaps he might wander out of a guilty conscience. The more kindly she treated him, the deeper the wound in her heart became. She could never erase the memory of her two sons or their wretched plight on that unforgettable day. Just looking at Ch'ŏl-min seemed to remind her of my brothers over and over again.

Mother's heart first became weak at the traumatic suffering she endured when my father was arrested and imprisoned by the Japanese. Her condition worsened into a nervous disorder after the deaths of Matthew and John. She often lost consciousness and fainted. I believe this was the result of cumulated resentment against the people and circumstances that had caused such great suffering. Treatment was impossible, even with the ever-growing faith of Ch'ŏl-min. No matter how proud my father was of him, the boy still reminded Mother of the deaths of her two beloved sons.

Occasionally, if I happened to mention my brothers, my mother's countenance would completely change and she would silence me. "Be quiet! I don't want to hear about it. Never mention anything about your brothers." But soon after, she would fall to the floor and cry.

"Oh, Matthew! Oh, John!" Springtime made her nervous disorder even worse. "What can douse this fire burning in my heart?" she used to say, beating her own chest and falling weakly on her side.

As I think back, I can see how her life was truly full of suffering. Although there were others who suffered great pain and loss, I don't believe many had suffered to the extent that my own mother did. I only know of few people who have held onto the words of Jesus deep in their hearts and have lived solely by faith as my mother did.

Father used to say to us, "Your mother's faith made me the way I am today. When I was in prison, your mother's faith kept pace with mine so that I could be released in victory. Even in faith, there must be harmony between husband and wife. Alone, it is too difficult. What's the use in getting university degrees when faith, the most essential ingredient for life, is lagging?"

Ever since father was released from prison, he would often praise my mother, "Where could I ever find such a virtuous woman? The true beauty of a woman is not in her appearance nor in her adornment or perfume, but rather in her unshakable, faithful support of her husband."

True to Father's words, Mother, who had only graduated from a Bible institute, had a deep, abiding faith that was far greater than anyone I knew. Even when my father was in prison, she led us in family worship every morning and evening and she taught us the Word of God. Whenever we prayed, she encouraged us to pray for our father so that his faith would not be weakened because of his suffering and persecution. It was vital to our mother that our father keep loyal to his faith. Mother was a woman of prayer and great faith throughout her entire life.

My mother treasured the Bible as if it were physically a part of her and she lived by the Word of God. As far as

Chŏl-min Kang with my mother and siblings, Tong-nim (upper right), Tong-yŏn (lower right), and Tong-gil (in my mother's arms).

knowledge of Scripture is concerned, there was no one who could compete with her as she knew the histories of the Old and New Testaments forwards and back. Even my father relied on her when he had difficulty remembering a particular passage for his sermons. Mother could tell him immediately the chapter and verse he was looking for. She was always correct.

"I must admit, your ability to memorize the Scripture is truly amazing. Indeed, you are a walking bible. But don't forget, your memory comes from God." My father would look at my mother with deep admiration and then burst out in delightful laughter.

Father was five years older than Mother. When he was imprisoned the first time, he was thirty-eight years old and he spent his prime years behind bars. At the time of liberation and his release from prison, he was forty-four. My mother was first left to raise us at age thirty-three. At times, she wondered whether she would become a young widow. Her youthful days as a wife and mother were taken from her, as she was subjected to constant suffering and anxiety over her captive husband and fatherless children.

There was no way she could prevent her loneliness. Although she had a husband, in reality, she was always alone. Even after Father was released from prison, her situation didn't improve much because he spent more time with the leprosy patients than he did with us.

Mother lived her life yearning for the affection of my father, who always seemed busy with the work of the church and Aeyangwŏn. We children suffered from the same longing. Father always seemed too busy with other things. He hardly had any time to spend with us. We often grumbled and complained to him about it, but Mother never once expressed to him her desire for companionship. She was used to sacrificing herself.

Mother passed away while undergoing treatment at Pusan Blue Cross Medical Clinic on November 16, 1977. She had overworked herself in order to raise money for the construction of a newly established church for lepers, and consequently, she fell ill. Tied around my mother's chest was a small bundle of bills.

"Take this money to Miryang Church," Mother said with her last breath. The lepers were helping out in the construction of Miryang Church and my mother had toiled day and night to see its completion. She had been going about in the rain for three days to raise money, when suddenly she fell ill. She was seventy-one years old at the time. She had devoted her life to spreading the Gospel and was doing just that until the very day she died. Her body was laid to rest in my father's tomb, just as she had always requested.

A few months before my mother departed for heaven, my brother Ch'ŏl-min, who worked in Seoul as an apartment security guard, came down to Pusan to see her. When he arrived, Mother happened to be out at the market. Ch'ŏl-min sat down on the wooden floor, bowed his head, and prayed for a moment. When he lifted his head, he saw a picture of my two brothers on the wall. He stared at the picture for a long time, enraptured. Then suddenly, he sprang to his feet and ran out of the house without looking back, as if he were being chased. He never came back. After hearing that she had missed him by only an hour, Mother went out to look for him, but he was nowhere to be found.

What on earth? Why had Ch'ŏl-min traveled such a long distance from Seoul to Pusan to see my mother and then just suddenly disappear without a word? What was he thinking while staring at the photograph of my brothers? What was it that made him run out?

There seemed to be no explanation other than the slight chance that he was still being haunted by his guilty conscience for the terrible crime he had committed in his youth against Matthew and John. It was obvious that he was still troubled by the blood that stained his hands. Even after repenting and receiving forgiveness, and after God's mercy had cleansed his sin, he still could not erase the memory of his sin from his conscience. Even though everyone else forgave him, he could not forgive himself. I don't believe he was innately evil. To me, he seemed more timid and cowardly than anything else.

Ch'ŏl-min married and had four children—two sons and two daughters. His oldest son Ho-kyŏng often visited me while he was attending Seoul Christian University. He would call me "aunt" and was very amiable toward me. I treated him warmly as though he were my real nephew. But he suddenly stopped coming. Later, he told me he had stopped visiting because he discovered that his father was the murderer of my two brothers. What a terrible shock it must have been to find his father's name in a book! Even to this day, I wish so much that Pastor Yong-jun An had not used the real name of my brothers' murderer in his biography of my father, *The Atomic Bomb of Love*. My heart aches when I think about the trauma that Ch'ŏl-min's innocent children had to experience upon seeing their father's name in that book. Ever since that day, Ho-kyŏng has never visited my home nor has he sent me any letters.

Rumors spread that Ch'ŏl-min had killed my father. That was nonsense! My father was martyred at the hands of the Communists during the Korean War. He had been the only person of refuge for Ch'ŏl-min. After Father was killed, Ch'ŏl-min suddenly became miserable. Ch'ŏl-min began to avoid people and seemed to always look for dark places. Even at church, he would drop his head and sit in the corner, never looking people in the eyes.

Occasionally when our siblings got together, Ch'ŏl-min would respond to our facial expressions with suspicion. "Sister, why are you looking at me like that?" he would ask. He lived in fear and in the shadows. I felt pity for him. He was poor all throughout his life, working as an apartment security guard and always living under the heavy burden of his sin.

Ch'ŏl-min came to see me about two weeks before he died. He went to the house of my sister Tong-yŏn and heard that I had come, so he came to see me. He was diagnosed with cancer. Tong-yŏn took him everywhere for treatment and even sought out Deaconess Sin-ae Hyŏn to place her hand on him and to pray that God would heal him, but his health did not improve. Dragging his weakened body, he barely managed to come inside the room. As soon as he saw me, he grabbed my hands and burst into tears.

All my life, he was the one who had driven a nail in my heart, and now he was dying right before my eyes! With faltering steps, he approached me. *Forty-six years ago, wasn't he the one whose life was spared from death because of my words at P'alwang Café?* Oh, how I wanted to curse him and hate him! *Wasn't he the one against whom I grinded my teeth and stared sharply enough to kill?* But with him pitifully before me, all of that resentment, hatred, and sorrow from the past melted away as though it had only been a dream. We embraced each other and cried aloud, finally releasing all our built-up resentment. At that moment, hatred transformed into compassion.

Brother! Brother! Ch'ŏl-min, my brother!
Why must you leave so soon?
Long ago, didn't Father admonish you to continue
*   the good work in place of my two brothers?*
Didn't you give your word that you would become
*   a great servant of God for this nation and these people?*
Why must you go so far, far away,
*   shattering that promise and that pledge?*

Saying, "Forever and ever farewell," he disappeared.
I wonder how far he has gone?
One step, two steps, leaving his footsteps behind...
He left the lonely road for the other side.

I guess that's what life is like.
Do we live 100 years? 1,000 years? 10,000 years?
The sun has set and now you are gone.
I shall also leave
  to the place of our eternal home
  where my loved ones dwell.

It is said that a person tells the truth right before death. Ch'ŏl-min spilled out his heart with a teary voice. "Tong-hŭi, when I return home, I'll soon be going to heaven. When I do, I'll kneel before your brothers and beg for their forgiveness."

Ch'ŏl-min left me with these words, and exactly fifteen days later, he left this world. Fifty-one years had passed since he was saved from execution in 1948. Perhaps right now in heaven, Father, Mother, Matthew, John, and my brother Ch'ŏl-min[10] are walking hand in hand, watching me write at this hour. Perhaps they are praising the Lord God Almighty even at this moment.

24. How Could This Happen Again?

Living in Sunch'ŏn without my two brothers was like living in hell. My physical health deteriorated most while living at Ch'ŏl-min's home, as I had become dangerously thin. Just the fact that I was living in Sunch'ŏn, the place where my two brothers left the most traces, felt like punishment. Wherever I went, I was reminded of Matthew's and John's bright smiles. I would turn around and look back while walking, delusional that they were running after me, calling, "Tong-hŭi." I often thought I would end up in a mental asylum if I continued on like this.

My father and mother understood me. They knew that I was traumatized most from the death of my brothers. They became concerned about me, their oldest daughter, because I had lost my smile, as well as my interest in life. My parents decided that I ought to leave that terrible city of Sunch'ŏn, so they sent me to Ewha Girls' High School in Seoul.

I rented a small room near the school and lived with Aunt Tŏk-sun Hwang. Although she was a leper, Aunt Hwang did not suffer much from the physical symptoms of the disease. When I entered the eighth grade at Ewha, she was enrolled in Ch'ongsin Bible College and poured herself into theological study.

I remember the first day at my new school. It was a Bible class and the teacher introduced me to the other students. "This transfer student is the one who lost her two brothers during the Yŏsu-Sunch'ŏn Mutiny. Her name is Tong-hŭi Son. I want all of you to be her friend and help her out."

The students were stirred and the room suddenly became noisy. One of the students, who was sitting in the back, stood up and said, "Teacher, we would like to hear about the mutiny from Tong-hŭi Son." The other students spoke up in agreement. The teacher nodded and gestured to me with her hand to come forward. Without any preparation and somewhat bewildered, I had no choice but to stand at the front of the class.

What would I say? I would rather die than to recount the tragedy of my brothers' deaths. I left Sunch'ŏn in order to free myself from the horrid memories. And here my new classmates were, asking me to tell them about the terrible incident. Although they were happily chattering away about the "story" I had told, I suddenly got the feeling that their world and mine were far removed from each other.

I decided at this point that I wouldn't say more. I closed my mouth tightly and stood still with my head down. Silence fell over the classroom. All eyes fixed on me, full of expectation and curiosity. I heard someone say softly, "Go ahead." I bent over the teacher's desk and finally broke down. I was sad and bitter that my family's tragedy was perceived only as a "story" that would satisfy someone's curiosity. The teacher was perplexed. She asked me to sit down.

I had left Sunch'ŏn in order to free myself from the haunting memory of my brothers' deaths, yet here I was in Seoul, forced to recall the memories yet again. Wherever I went, Matthew's and John's bright smiles followed me and made me desperately miss them. Their warm, caring smiles and their unbelievably beautiful voices constantly surrounded me.

Although I tried to forget, I was enveloped with both physical and mental pain, as my soul continuously yearned for my brothers. Aunt Hwang's love and care for me provided me with great strength. Little by little, I managed to adjust back to a normal life.

The tragedies, however, didn't end there. The tragedy of my people wasn't over yet, and the suffering of my family continued. In the early morning hours of June 25, 1950, without any declaration of war, masses of heavily armed Communist troops from North Korea crossed the 38th parallel and swept down upon the unprepared South. We had no tanks or warplanes and our army was inferior to that of the North, which was backed by the Soviet Union. Koreans began killing Koreans.

God had granted us a great and precious gift called "freedom." What were we lacking that made brother turn against brother? At a time when we should have been most grateful for liberation from the Japanese, what were the people thinking? Perhaps it was the judgment of God. Maybe it was the fiery arrow of God upon the people who not only forgot His grace and gift of freedom, but who also made themselves arrogant.

Korea became an ocean of fire. Those of the North were no longer one with the South. They had become followers of Karl Marx and Vladimir Lenin. They tried to gain strength through bloodshed. In response to these circumstances, Father prayed:

I pray for the Republic of Korea. It has been five years since Your grace and mercy lifted this nation from oppression under another nation. I believe that the increasing difficulties of our people are occurring because we Christians, who were called first, weren't righteously nor faithfully fulfilling Your purpose. Lord God, You who listened to the prayers of Abraham, have mercy on us!

Please do not make this nation like Sodom and Gomorrah but like Nineveh. Let my people wear sackcloth, sit on ashes, and repent. And Lord, please withhold Your anger.

At dawn on the third day, June 28, the great bridge spanning the Han River was bombed and destroyed. The ROK troops fought bravely in order to keep our capital city, Seoul, out of the hands of the invaders from the north who spread over us like floodwaters. But, alas, we proved to be no match for the heavily armed Communists and the Soviet T-34 tanks. The sky above Seoul was blackened by ash and smoke. Everybody scrambled to hiding places, trembling with fear for their lives. The Han River was red with the blood of thousands who died trying to escape the approaching invaders. The ROK army abandoned its attempt to guard Seoul and began retreating to the south. The government had no choice but to move to Pusan, a city on the southern coast of the peninsula. The Communists pushed us farther and farther down south.

At that time, I was only in the ninth grade. I trembled with fear whenever I saw the red communist flag hanging in front of our school. I thought to myself, *Matthew and John were killed not too long ago during the Communist-inspired riots in Yŏsu and Sunch'ŏn. Is it now my turn to die?* I may have wanted to die before, but now I wanted to live!

Seoul was already in the hands of the Communist troops. Everywhere I looked, I saw their red flags waving. Bullets were flying in every direction above our heads. Every time I saw a Red soldier, my knees gave way with fright at the thought of them capturing me and killing me. Aunt Hwang and I swore to each other that we would not be separated in the midst of all the confusion, that since we lived together, we would die together.

The night before the Communists invaded Seoul, the North Korean troops abducted all the pastors in Seoul. It was a Saturday night around 11:00 p.m. when they broke into each pastor's home and said, "We would like to interrogate you briefly." The pastors never returned. I thought to myself, *Why did they abduct all the pastors? They must be trying to get rid of the church leaders first!* The families of those pastors could not flee the burning city in hopes that their abducted men would soon return.

Aunt Hwang and I were hiding in the home of Pastor Yong-jun An along with other church members. At times, we even hid in underground caves. Occasionally, we would happen to meet an insider with access to the news and would inquire about the war efforts. The news always seemed hopeless.

We joined our hearts together in desperate prayers to God. I don't think I ever had to pray so intensely for God to save my life as I had at that time. It was, indeed, true that faith deepens through unbearable trials.

Even when we had to sleep in caves, we were always prepared to leave. We had our shoes on our feet and our belts tightly fastened around our waists. We used our backpacks as pillows. Whenever we heard someone shout, "Run!" we would all jump to our feet and run as fast as we could.

God's wrath continued for nearly three months. It seemed as though He was using a shameless despot named Il-sung Kim as His stick to discipline our arrogant nation. The invading army devastated the whole country—buildings were destroyed, corpses were scattered about, children were orphaned and left to wander the streets, and the wounded moaned in agonizing pain. It was a veritable hell on earth.

When the UN Security Council passed a resolution that

ordered the Communists to withdraw to the 38th parallel and that dispatched troops under the command of General Douglas MacArthur, the situation finally began to turn around, giving us some room to breathe. The UN troops from the United States, Britain, France, Canada, Australia, Turkey, and the Philippines took the initiative and, after a surprise landing at Inch'ŏn, pushed the Communists out of Seoul. On September 28, three months after the war had begun, the UN troops pushed the Communists up north, some as far up as the Yalu River by the North Korea-China border. It seemed unification would at last be realized. Only then, could we who were in hiding finally shake off our anxiety and look up into the blue sky again. It was indeed a clear sky! But I never would've imagined that beyond that clear sky there lurked a far greater tragedy for my family and me.

Rumors quickly spread that all the pastors who had been abducted by the Communists had been taken to North Korea and slaughtered. We also heard that as the Communists were retreating, they buried non-Communist citizens alive in mass graves. All the news we received was dismal and dark.

Hearing the fate of the pastors, I became increasingly anxious about my own father's well-being. I figured he would be safe since he was living in the extreme south of Korea, but for some reason, I couldn't shake off my last strand of foreboding.

One day, Aunt Hwang and I were in the middle of a discussion, wondering about my father's safety, when all of a sudden Reverend Yong-jun An burst into the room.

"Oh, my! What brings you all the way here Pastor An?" we asked.

He didn't say a word. His eyes spoke for him as they were

filled with tears. Always oversensitive to the word "death," I could immediately feel my heart weigh down.

"Oh, no! You mean..."

"Yes, Tong-hŭi. Your father also..." Pastor An couldn't even finish his sentence. He kept having to wipe away his tears.

I thought, *So now, Father was gone too? How could this be? How could this happen again? Oh, God!* The sky was collapsing right before my eyes. When he regained consciousness and somewhat regained his composure, Pastor An began to methodically describe how my father was martyred by the bullets of the retreating Communist soldiers.

My heart was still aching over the death of my two brothers, but now, less than two years later, even Father had became a sacrifice on the altar of martyrdom. How could this be? If the events of my life happened to be made into a novel, the book would be criticized for being unrealistic. If this were a theatrical performance, critics would have deemed it too exaggerated. It was beyond anyone's understanding how such a horrid thing could happen more than once in a lifetime.

How was I to cope with the pain again? Why had God given me such a wretched experience to endure? Not once but twice! Not one or two people but three! Not friends or distant relatives, but my own brothers and father! Not by foreign hands but by the hands of our own people!

My eyes were bloodshot with bitterness and my face turned pale. My heart burned with anger and hatred, and my head was on the brink of bursting. *How could this be? It shouldn't be this way! It's hard enough to experience such a tragedy once in a lifetime. Why has my family suffered this tragedy twice? How could He do this to us? How unfair this world is! What law moves this world? Who is really in control?*

Is there really an absolute law? Is there really a Sovereign God?
My heart now only had room for malice and bitterness. Even a mouse attacks a cat when it is cornered. I began to attack God at random:

> *God! My grandfather was faithful to You. My parents were also faithful to You. My two older brothers remained faithful to You. And that's not all, God. All of my younger siblings are fervent in their faith in Christ. But why all this bloodshed? Is this the reward for faithfulness? Is this Your prize for our obedience to Your Word? If You have eyes to see, look! If You have ears to hear, listen! If You have lips to speak, answer me! Did You really have to do this?*

I looked to the heavens with angry eyes. "In Jeremiah 33:3, You said, 'Call to me and I will answer you and tell you great and unsearchable things you do not know,' but Your answer to my call was death the first time and death yet again."

That Scripture verse left my heart and had nothing more to do with me. At that moment, Satan approached me and whispered to my ear, "Tong-hŭi, look! God claims to love you, but look at what He has done to you! Look!" It was the voice of the devil and it matched what I felt inside. My heart felt like God had fallen short of His promised mercy. My heart began to fill with greater anger and doubt.

"The God you trust demands only love and sacrifice from you and hasn't rewarded you with anything, has He? What a ridiculous answer He has given you, considering all the time you spent on your knees in prayer! You have diligently served God, but is there anyone who has become more miserable than you? It's no use I tell you," Satan continued.

I thought to myself, *God is too cruel. God is powerless. God only demands us to patiently endure — to endure suffering, to endure pain, to endure indignation. He is a selfish God who forces us to be martyrs for His name's sake. Everyone says that martyrdom is a holy thing. Oh, how they are oblivious to its absurdity!*

I could not agree to the idea that one would be rewarded only by passing through thorny paths and miserable mire. It was absurd, a complete contradiction! I didn't even want to try to understand. My mind was cluttered with a thousand thoughts:

For whom and for what purpose were my loved ones martyred? How could the driving of paramount nails into the hearts of parents, children, wives, brothers, and sisters be a sign of the Truth and love of God? Who, as a parent, could possibly ask their children to walk such a painful, thorny path in order to gain rewards after death? What kind of parent would welcome pain and suffering of their beloved children? Where in the world would you find a parent that would purposely inflict wounds with a whip so that their children could receive rewards after death? If even humans do not allow for such pain to harm their beloved children, how could God allow such things to happen in the name of His love? If that is what God's love is, humans must not accept that love.

My heart hardened and my mind failed to process any further thoughts. I found myself wrapped up in endless doubt, recklessly blaming God. The root of faith, which my parents had planted in me with such care all throughout the years, was beginning to shake. If the death of my two brothers brought deep sorrow to my soul, then the death of my father brought deadly poison that spread all over my body.

Aunt Hwang and I decided to leave for Aeyangwŏn on foot because the bridge across the Han River was destroyed. My heart was focused on one thing—to hurry and see my mother. It was far too long a distance from Seoul to Aeyangwŏn and we did not know how many nights and days we would have to walk. Still, we hastily left.

When our legs became too weary to walk any farther, we rested in the shade for a while. Whenever we spotted an ox-drawn cart, we pleaded and begged for a ride toward Aeyang-wŏn. When we got hungry, we went in search for buildings with a cross and asked for food. Although our nation was in the midst of war, the church people we encountered were usually kind to us. When Aunt Hwang told them who we were and what kind of situation we were in, the church always provided us with a place to sleep and gave us breakfast.

The road before us seemed endless. I grumbled and complained to Aunt Hwang for no reason. It must have been unpleasant to hear a grown girl whining, but she graciously received all my complaints.

Our feet were severely blistered from walking and our lips turned white and peeled away. But more than the physical pain, anger and bitterness still boiled over in my heart. While I plodded along the long road, I was sometimes seized with sorrow and broke down in tears.

We stopped any form of transportation that passed our way—trucks, jeeps, ox carts; we didn't care. It was only because of these rides that we were able to make it to Aeyangwŏn at all. Finally, under the sunset, we could see smoke rising from the chimneys of the houses at Aeyangwŏn. The dogs in the neighborhood barked louder and louder as we approached.

Aeyangwŏn was in ruins! It was as though a cyclone had swept across it. Heavy silence weighed down the entire town. It had always been so bright and warm before, but now without my father's presence, Aeyangwŏn was plunged into darkness. It was like a desert without an oasis.

Suddenly, an image of my father's gentle smile came to my mind and I heard him speak.

"Oh, my! Isn't this my daughter, Tong-hŭi? Oh, how painful it must have been for you! Dear, since Tong-hŭi has come home, make her some of her favorite sweet rice pancakes."

As we passed by the church, I imagined hearing his thunderous voice delivering God's Word from his well-worn pulpit.

Although our leper friends saw us coming, all they could do was look at us with their tearful eyes. They hesitated to express any words of welcome to us. Only after a long while did someone approach me, wrap her disfigured hands around my shoulders, and say, "Tong-hŭi, you have finally come!"

How could my mother possibly bear the deathly pain of losing, first her two oldest sons, and now her husband? Mother smiled at me with a newly revived maternal love. She was saddened that I had to live in such a harsh world. Mother began to explain the details of my father's death.

25. Endure with the Spirit of a Martyr!

On September 13, 1950, two and a half months after the beginning of the Korean War, the Communist soldiers who had infiltrated the Yŏsu Department of Internal Affairs came and arrested my father. Fifteen days later on September 28—the day Seoul was retaken by the UN forces—my father, Pastor Yang-wŏn Son, was gunned down at the age of forty-eight.

Before his arrest, Father had many chances to hide, but he firmly refused each time. When the war first began and the pastors in Seoul began to flee southward, my father was worried. "Good heavens! God took up a whip in His hand because of the sins of the people. What shall become of the sheep if the shepherd leaves them? The shepherds should remain in Seoul to preach repentance and be willing to be sacrificed as offerings."

Father never once thought to flee for safety. He had actually tried to go up to Seoul, but since the roads were blocked, he didn't make it to the city.

On July 21, Pastor Tŏk-hwan Na came down from Sun-ch'ŏn and suggested that Father flee for safety. But my father's mind was made.

"I'll pray to God and follow His directions," Father told Pastor Na. The following day, my father told Pastor Na, "How glorious it will be to die for the name of the Lord! I should have died before in prison. I'm only grateful that I lived to see the independence of our country."

A few days later, Reverend Chae-bong Pak sent Deacon

Hong-bok Kim from his church to convince my father. Deacon Kim began to implore him to flee for the future of the Korean church. "Pastor Son, just as Aeyangwŏn is important to you, isn't the future of the Korean church important also? Since the salvation of this people depends on you, wouldn't it be sensible to flee for safety, even for just a while?"

This was my father's response:

Deacon Kim, let's try to discuss the point you've made. Isn't it true that Aeyangwŏn Church is part of the Korean church? Are not the families at Aeyangwŏn a part of this nation? We cannot regard the sheep of one church less important than the Korean church. Right now, the denomination is divided and the General Assembly has been turned into a battleground. The nation has divided into North and South. As church leaders, we are obliged to remain with our flocks, not only when times are good but especially in times of danger. If we continue to abandon our members to save our own lives, I'm afraid that this nation will become like Sodom and Gomorrah. In the midst of this crisis, what would be the most urgent thing to do? The shepherd must feed the sheep in order to strengthen their faith. The blood and sweat of God's people must be offered to God now. Although I am unrighteous and inadequate, by the righteousness of our Lord Jesus Christ, I want to be His offering at this time, if the Lord wills.

Deacon Kim realized that there was nothing he could do to change my father's mind. Deacon Kim asked one final question: "Pastor Son, should we not preserve our lives in order to continue our work for the church?"

Father's faith was unshakable, even in the face of death. This was his reply:

Such reasoning is truly fallacious. As I told you before, if the Lord permits, I want to be a sacrificial offering. Christianity is a religion that does not promote living well but rather dying well for His kingdom and His righteousness. We must not think that we can only spread the Gospel by living well. As a seed must die in order to sprout new growth, so our deaths enable the Gospel to bear fruit.

On July 24, Ch'ŏl-min, anxious for my father's safety, also rushed to beg him to flee. "Father, if you remain here, it is certain that you will die. Hurry and escape to safety with me." But my father stubbornly refused. It was no use. Ch'ŏl-min, now at the end of his rope, approached my mother and begged her to flee also. But Mother simply shook her head and said, "Where else could my hiding place be? Our only refuge is our Lord. His second coming is near. Where would I go?"

The residents at Aeyangwŏn, out of concern for my father, put him on board a ship by force numerous times, but all their efforts were in vain. Each time, he jumped overboard and swam back to be with his flock. "How can I run to save my life, leaving behind the leprosy patients whose bodies are not well? If we die, we will die together; if we live, we will live together."

Therefore, my parents remained at Aeyangwŏn and courageously cared for the patients who were unable to flee, while the rest, along with the people of Chŏnju and Seoul, left for Namhaedo Island.

On July 27, Yŏsu fell to the Red Army. The city and the countryside were stained red with blood. The Communists rampaged day and night, shouting, "Long live the People's Republic!" The Communist sympathizers, who had been forced into hiding after the Yŏsu-Sunch'ŏn Mutiny, came out into the open and ran wild in triumph with the soldiers from the North. They quickly attacked the citizens of the South and slaughtered them as though they were their enemies. Rumors spread that all the police officers who were in hiding were killed, all the abducted pastors were martyred while fleeing from Seoul, and all the wealthy citizens were shot after a mock "people's court."

Each morning gave light to new carnage and death, as the streets became more and more littered with corpses. It seemed that only lawlessness and injustice ruled. The lepers, seeing the situation become more serious, dug a bomb shelter and implored my father to hide there and pray. At times, they stacked up apple crates and told him to hide behind them to pray. Father protested every time. "Why do you go through all this trouble? Please, don't do this. This is not helping me. You are making me a coward. How could I ever leave the church behind?"

Soon, Aeyangwŏn faced a serious dilemma. It was truly difficult to know just how they would treat the occupying Communist army. The army had absolutely no fear of God. It was clear that no one could escape immediate death should he dare show the slightest sign of opposition. Yet it was absolutely out of the question to welcome and support them. Most of all, my father strongly opposed them and continued to preach to his flock to remain faithful.

"Do not fear martyrdom. There is no greater blessing than to die for Christ's sake." Father would become furious if he felt someone was compromising their faith in Christ in order to save their own lives.

Actually, within the General Affairs Department at Aeyangwŏn, the administrative staff, managers, school staff, and board members—about forty in all—met together several times to discuss this dilemma. Each time, my father corrected their wavering minds and encouraged them to stand firm in faith.

"But pastor," they would object, "even if we cannot hold a welcoming party for them, couldn't we at least fly the Communist flag here in order to keep Aeyangwŏn safe?"

"No, never!" Father opposed. "If we fly their flag, it shows that we welcome them. I would rather die than do such a foolish thing!"

"What if we get hurt?" others worried.

"I will take responsibility and stand in front of you to stop them from hurting you. You do not have to worry." Even after Father had quieted the patients down, they were still apprehensive and full of anxiety.

"Pastor Son. What if they arrest you and then come back to torment Aeyangwŏn? What could we do then?"

"Die the death of martyrs," Father stated without hesitation. "Endure with the spirit of a martyr." Then he added what he would always say when preaching. "I prefer to die while preaching in the pulpit, while evangelizing in the streets or while praying in a quiet place, over dieing while struggling with an illness and holding medicine." Rather than fearing death, my father gladly anticipated that such a day would come when he would be called to martyrdom. With these words, he comforted the weak in faith.

A week before the Communists broke into the compound,

everyone at Aeyangwŏn gathered three times a day at the sound of a bell for revival meetings. Although there was no longer the accompaniment of the organ or a music director, the lepers sang triumphantly, clapping their hands. They sounded like Christian soldiers, marching as to war. On Saturday, the last day of the revival meetings, Father called everyone to attend an all-night fasting and prayer service.

Our first choice is martyrdom; our second, martyrdom; our third, martyrdom also. Be ready to die as a martyr! The time has come. Therefore, do not focus on living well but rather on dying well. Since we have been redeemed in the name of Jesus Christ, it is time for us to die in the name of Jesus.

My father lived his entire life with these words locked up in his heart. He was never all that concerned with politics, nor did he make mentions of political issues in his sermons.

During a Wednesday night service just one day before his arrest by the Communists, my father preached a sermon entitled "Be Faithful Even to the Point of Death," with a reading from Revelation 2:10. His last sermon was filled with ways to glorify our Lord and how we ought to die in order to receive the crown of life. He spoke in particular about martyrdom, perhaps sensing his own destiny. This sermon was his final gift to his beloved leprosy patients.

During the lunch hour on the following day, September 13, five Communists suddenly approached Aeyangwŏn and shouted, "Open the door!" Their loud shouts aroused the anger of the big German Shepherd that came out and barked at the men. Without much thought, they shot the dog to death. The doorkeeper, startled by their actions, made a run for the door to inform the others, but he was shot down by bullets before he could even make it inside.

"We have come to take Yang-wŏn Son," they declared as soon as they got into the compound. "We know he is here. If you don't hand him over to us, we will kill all the lepers here."

Although the lepers said their pastor was far away from Aeyangwŏn, the men didn't believe them and replied, "We know he is here! We will go inside ourselves to look for him!" Since my father wasn't a man who would hide from the Communists, there was no point for the lepers to lie anymore. Elder Pak, who was dealing with the men, had someone go to inform my father.

Father was, at the time, resting from preparing his sermons for the three-day revival meetings that were to begin that very night. He noticed a sense of urgency in the voice of the young man who called out to him from outside.

"Someone must have come to see me," Father said casually as he sat up slowly.

"Yes. Armed men from the Communist Internal Affairs Department have come for you, pastor. We told them you weren't here, but they claimed they knew you were here, so..."

Right away, Father put on his suit and placed his watch, as well as the other valuables that were in his pockets, on his desk. With a pale expression but a determined attitude, he left his room and, with unhurried steps, made his way to the church building to pray. He used to instruct everyone at Aeyangwŏn, "If anyone comes looking for me, tell him to meet me in the church where I will be praying." The armed soldiers were then led into the church and they approached my father, who was praying.

"Comrade, are you Pastor Son?" one of them asked. My father did not reply immediately, for he wanted to pray for a few more minutes. Father slowly straightened his body and nodded.

"I am Pastor Son."

"You are to come with us for a short time. We would like to investigate a few matters."

Without any resistance, fully knowing what awaited him, Father followed the armed men.

Still suffering from his usual back pains, Father walked slowly and calmly, leaning on his cane for support. The lepers at Aeyangwŏn followed after him as he was being taken away.

"Comrades," the soldiers threatened, waving their guns, "do not follow us any farther, and be quiet. Note that you are only causing Pastor Son more harm by following us. We will return him to you soon."

The Aeyangwŏn brethren couldn't do much. They could only stand still and watch their beloved pastor disappear into the distance. Little did they know, this was the last time Father walked out the gate of Aeyangwŏn, leaving behind his beloved leprosy patients. Afternoons at Aeyangwŏn were like the Garden of Eden, full of all kinds of lovely flowers and beautiful birds. I still wonder if the flowers and birds had known that my father was leaving Aeyangwŏn for the last time and heading down the road toward death.

26. My Father's Martyrdom

After spending the night at the police station in Yulch'on, Father was transferred to Yŏsu Prison. The Communist Internal Affairs Department was using the prison as their "correctional" facility at the time. When Father arrived, there was already a significant number of prisoners at that small-town prison. Forty to fifty prisoners were forced into each of the seven cells that were built for no more than twenty each.

The prisoners were not real criminals, of course. The slightest sign of ill cooperation with the Communist authorities resulted in immediate arrest. Most of those arrested were wealthy landowners or bourgeoisie, Christians, educated citizens, teachers, and right-wing students. Many of them didn't understand why they had suddenly been dragged into the prison cells.

The cells were so crowded that there was no room to lie down or even sit comfortably. It was next to impossible to fall asleep because they had to crouch down and roll up to find a hardly suitable space. They were like bean sprouts growing in a single pot. Space was very limited.

Food was scarce. Every mealtime, the prisoners received a ball of barley about the size of a duck egg and a pinch of salt. Thirst was the most unbearable pain. A small bowlful of water had to be shared among several prisoners. After a mouthful of water, their thirst returned quickly because of the salt rations. The weather was hot and they were parched, but no more water was given to them. Moreover, exhaustion overtook them because of lack of sleep. Some of them nearly slid into insanity. It was a time of agonizing pain for all the prisoners.

In prison, Father met John's classmate, Ch'ang-su Kim. Ch'ang-su was a student with strong convictions and his father was an elder at Yulch'on Church. Ch'ang-su stayed by my father until the very moment of Father's execution, though he himself was miraculously saved. He now lives in Seoul and remains in close contact with our family. I asked him to recount the events of my father's arrest, imprisonment, and martyrdom as he was an eyewitness to my father's death. I truly believe that Ch'ang-su was saved to testify of these events.

My father and Ch'ang-su were locked up in Cell #3. Since Ch'ang-su was arrested about ten days before my father, the boy was glad to see him. "Pastor Son!" Ch'ang-su cried, reaching for my father's hand and with tears welling up in his eyes. He thought to himself, *For what sin should such a saint as Pastor Son be brought here? Isn't he the one who adopted an enemy—the very one who killed his two sons—to be his own son? Why should he be treated as a common sinner?* Ch'ang-su then remembered the time when he tried to comfort my father after Matthew and John died. He remembered how he was comforted rather than a comfort when Father said, "Why should we worry? My sons have gone to heaven—a far better place. Ch'ang-su, you must grow in Jesus and trust Him fully." Ch'ang-su asked himself again, *Why should such a saint be dragged into this place?* He was filled with emotions when Father walked in, as the sight of Pastor Son reminded him of his friend, John.

On the following morning, my father was escorted to the interrogation room where photos of Il-sung Kim and Joseph Stalin hung on the wall. At first, the person in charge spoke kindly to my father, even offering him a word of consolation for his suffering during the Japanese occupation. Then, handing him a piece of paper, the officer politely requested him to write something.

When my father looked at it, he discovered it was a letter of confession in which he was to confess his past wrongs. My father believed confessions were meant to be made to God, not to these Communists, and besides, he had nothing to confess to them. At first, Father didn't want to write anything. But then he realized that it was a good opportunity for him to plant God's word into the officer's violent heart. So Father took the piece of paper and, after briefly reading the instructions, he paused to pray. The officer sneered as he watched my father pray, then he

My father, Pastor Yang-wŏn Son at the front gate of Aeyangwŏn.

took out a cigarette and lit it. After finishing his prayer, Father began to write down his confession of faith.

Father finally finished and handed the paper to the officer. After a moment, the officer angrily jumped to his feet.

"Brazen fool!" he shouted. "What kind of confession is this? Pastor Son, you obviously haven't learned your lesson." The officer's anger boiled and he tossed the paper at my father's face. "I heard you suffered severely under the Japanese, so I wanted to be more lenient with you. But I can see that you are much too corrupt. For what crime were you sent to prison by the Japanese?"

"I refused to bow down before their Shinto shrine because it is against God's commandments."

"Huh! What commandments of God? I bet they're the commandments of capitalistic America, not of God! I know you've been brainwashed by America." The officer's anger escalated and he no longer bothered to even listen to my father's answers. The officer simply persisted in trying to find some sort of basis to press charges against Father. "Don't you slander Communism when you go about preaching? Aren't you really a spy for America? Why did you allow for the printing of the book *The Atomic Bomb of Love*, which criticizes the revolutionary acts of the Communists during the Yŏsu-Sunch'ŏn Mutiny? If you are a pastor, you ought to pray quietly, not preach against Communism!"

My father, however, simply listened to the officer without much opposition. He could discern that the officer was being completely irrational. The director suddenly took a wooden stick from underneath the desk and began to beat my father mercilessly. Father did not utter a single word, not even when he was beat to the floor. Ch'ang-su told me years later that he could hardly bear to watch such a gruesome scene.

"Lord," my father began to pray, "I thank you for the privilege of carrying the cross you carry, and I thank you for letting me participate in your suffering." In spite of the agony, my father bowed down before God and openly thanked Him. Only when it was dark was Father allowed to crawl back to his cell, covered with blood. According to Ch'ang-su, my father couldn't sleep that night because the excruciating pain from the beating kept him up. He suffered from a high fever and was near death.

But in the midst of all the moaning, Father never forgot to be a witness for Christ in the cell. Talking was strictly forbidden in the cell, so he whispered in the ears of the other prisoners and avoided eye contact with the guards. Even after a momentary lapse into unconsciousness, he admonished everyone in a soft voice, "All of you, believe in Jesus, and we can go to heaven together."

Each day began with an hour of introspection. Rising at 6:00 a.m., everyone was required to sit up straight and reconsider their loyalties. Father always prayed to God at this hour. His lips would move, but he was careful not to make a sound while he prayed, as severe punishment would ensue from even the smallest sound.

Although this hour was to be spent by the prisoners for reconsidering their alleged espionage activities for capitalistic America, it was, to my father, a precious time of communion with God. While some of his inmates were filled with anxieties about their family or about what would happen to them, Father's thoughts were filled with God's words. Whenever Ch'ang-su looked over his shoulder, he saw my father with his eyes closed, deeply engaged in prayer.

The hour of reconsideration ended with the sound of aluminum scratching across the cement floor. This also meant it was time for breakfast. When the tiny barley balls were distributed, each inmate struggled to grab the biggest one, though the barley balls were all nearly the same size. The prisoners were starving, so they often argued over food. They gulped down the bland barley so quickly that after eating their own portion of food, they would still be hungry and thus cast longing looks on their cellmates' food.

My father always took what was left. At times, his prayer lasted more than ten minutes, so when he finally looked up, everyone was already finished with his own portion and was eyeing the barley ball in front of Father. At each mealtime, Father offered half of his portion to the weakest person in the cell.

"I've always been a light eater. This half is enough for me," he would say.

Of course, no one really believed him. The portions were too small to satisfy anyone's appetite. How could only half be enough? Regardless, his cellmates were too hungry to refuse his offer, oblivious now to any sense of shame.

Ch'ang-su once told me that Father gave him half of his portion saying, "Ch'ang-su, this sort of place makes you feel hungry. Eat the other half of my portion also." Ch'ang-su was, indeed, very hungry, so he ate the other half my father gave him. And to this day, his throat chokes just thinking about that day. Ch'ang-su told me he would never be able to forget the barley ball of love my father gave him in prison.

When breakfast was over, everyone was told to curl up and be as silent as the dead. They were not allowed to stretch their legs or talk with the person sitting next to them. The guards beat anyone who violated these rules. Those who were caught talking had to stretch out their hands through the prison bars, where then the guards would strike them with thick wooden rods until their bones broke or till their hands dripped with blood.

On one occasion, a guard passing by the cell heard someone whisper. He came to the cell and asked, "Who spoke?" He looked around with glaring eyes to find the violator, but no one would confess. In rage, the guard threatened the prisoners, "If no one confesses within five minutes, I will punish all of you!"

When the five minutes were up and still no one spoke a word, my father finally rose to his feet, walked forward and said, "I did it, so punish me!"

The guard looked deeply into my father's eyes and then broke into a sarcastic laugh before walking away without punishing Father. The guard must have known it was not my father who had spoken because the noise had come from the front of the cell, not the back where my father was sitting.

The inmates were called in, several of them each day, to be interrogated. They left their cells with a thread of hope that they'd be released after questioning. But when darkness fell, they were sent back to their cells, usually covered with blood. Some of them even had to be carried on the backs of other prisoners. Guilty or not, nobody was ever released.

My father was also called several times before the investigator. Just like the first day of his arrest, the same questions were repeatedly thrown at him. He was always brought back to his cell all bloody and beaten. It was truly a depressing atmosphere. The questions were so irrelevant that no one even knew how to answer them. They tried to force

Father to confess, but there was nothing to confess. Their interrogation was not based on any kind of evidence. They simply commanded him to confess and repent.

Ch'ang-su was also called in before the investigators. On one occasion, he was struck across the face the moment he stepped into the interrogation room.

"You, reactionary!" the interrogators shouted. "How many people did you kill?" Ch'ang-su stood still in utter bewilderment, while the soldiers who surrounded him mercilessly kicked him everywhere. At first, Ch'ang-su thought the interrogators had mistaken him for someone else, but they had not. They stubbornly refused to listen to him. It was useless for him to defend himself.

"You wretch! Stop giving excuses! Answer our questions! How many people did you kill?" They continued to wield their clubs against his back, legs, and face. The pain was so unbearable that death would have been more merciful. Ch'ang-su considered doing anything to avoid such torture. In order to lessen their attacks, he gave in and placed his thumb on the phony confession they had written.

When Ch'ang-su returned to the cell all covered with blood, Father laid him down and prayed for him. With tears, Ch'ang-su told my father everything that had happened in the interrogation room. My father was silent for a long while and then he spoke in a low, gentle voice: "The pain of our bodies is but for a moment, but the joy of our souls is for eternity. It is only through fervent prayers that we gain the right to be a martyr."

But Ch'ang-su didn't want to die at the age of eighteen. While listening to my father, he was constantly reminded of my two brothers, Matthew and John, and his body trembled with shame. As he looked up at my father, who seemed to have no fear of death, Ch'ang-su thought, *Indeed, like father, like son!*

Such unbearable conditions lingered for two weeks. The summer had slipped by the prisoners and now they began to feel the chill of autumn against their skin.

There was a big commotion outside in the early morning on September 28, 1950. The heavily armed Communist "underground activists" were uneasily walking about alongside the prison guards who were now dressed in army fatigues. One of them approached the cell and made an announcement: "This morning at the staff meeting, we decided to set all you comrades free, so you had better cooperate with us in an orderly manner."

The word "freedom" caused a stir among the prisoners. Oh, how long they had waited to hear the word! Throughout their torturous stay, hope had nearly faded from their hearts. Now they were about to be set free. It was as if someone had been raised from the dead. They all shouted for joy and comforted one another. Strangely, the ever-watchful guards did not restrict the prisoners' outbursts. In fact, the guards were nowhere to be seen. Generous portions of water, as well as cigarettes, were given.

The lunch hour passed and afternoon turned into evening. But still, the doors of their cells did not open. Ch'ang-su was sitting next to my father, so he asked, "Pastor Son, do you think they will really let us go?"

"The important thing," my father told him, "is not whether we are released but whether we gain our final victory. We must pray. To keep our souls from perishing, we must pray earnestly and fervently." My father held Ch'ang-su's hand firmly to calm the boy's anxious heart. Then he told Ch'ang-su about a dream he had the previous night. His two martyred sons visited him in his dream. Their expressions were strange, almost as though they were smiling but angry at the same time.

The anxious time of waiting for freedom dragged on until dinnertime. Suddenly, they heard footsteps in the corridors. The prisoners looked with anticipation for their meal, but they were met only with armed guards and those who had previously tortured them. The soldiers stood in line in front of each of the seven cells. It didn't seem as though a meal would be given. Everyone wondered what the guards were up to.

At last, the guards began to open the doors one by one and they allowed the prisoners to grab their belongings and run outside. Somehow, they all knew freedom would not come as promised, even if they made their way outside. The guards began to tie them up and push them into the auditorium.

One of the soldiers, a leader of some sort, addressed the prisoners with a shrill voice: "Listen well, comrades! Right now in Yŏsu, the aerial bombing of the Americans is so severe that we must transfer you to Sunch'ŏn. Once the bombing raids end, you will return here. Do not be stirred up, comrades. Just follow our orders. If we wished to kill you, we would have already killed you by now. We will not kill you, comrades, and we will not let you become slaves to American imperialists. Be at ease and do as we say."

The soldier who was speaking had a long Japanese sword and pistol tied to his waist. All the soldiers standing around the prisoners were heavily armed with daggers, swords, and machine guns. The leader stared coldly at the 150 right-wing prisoners as he continued to speak. "Once we arrive at Sunch'ŏn, we will educate you and have you all reconsider your thoughts, after which we will release you. But if on the way to Sunch'ŏn you open your mouth and speak, look to the side or attempt to escape, we will shoot you immediately. Do not forget!"

With those last stern words, the prisoners' hope of freedom disappeared like bubbles. No one believed their promise that freedom would be granted at Sunch'ŏn.

The guards pulled on the ropes around the prisoners' hands to make sure they were tightly tied. Ch'ang-su moved right next to my father in order to be tied with him, but somehow the two of them were separated. The soldiers had tied each man's hands behind his back and then put four prisoners together, weaving the ropes between them like strings of garlic.

The march to Sunch'ŏn began after ten o'clock at night. There was fear in the air. The armed soldiers marched on both sides of the prisoners with their guns aimed at them. In the midst of all the confusion, my father lost his shoes and had to walk barefoot on the rocky road. Seeing my father walk without shoes deeply saddened Ch'ang-su. They were miles away from Sunch'ŏn and the roads were pitted with rough stones. Ch'ang-su was concerned about how long Father would manage without shoes.

The Communist soldiers escorted the men quietly out of Yŏsu proper, but once they were clear of the city, they became beasts and openly abused the prisoners, leading them onto remote mountainous roads. "Hey, you dog! How did you manage to stay alive until now?" they taunted as they put the muzzle of their guns on the faces of the prisoners. The soldiers struck some of them against their backs with the butt of their rifles for no particular reason, perhaps to vent their anger. They tried to pick fights with the prisoners, knowing very well that these men could not defend themselves. The sound of men in agony shot out from every direction. The soldiers tripped many of the captives, bringing bundles of men to tumble down together. The Communists respected no one and no one escaped such abuse, not even my father.

It was *Ch'usŏk*[11] and the moon was exceptionally bright in the late hours. An occasional gunshot rang out while they marched along, prompting the soldiers to threaten the others.

"Someone must have attempted to escape. If you try to do the same, I guarantee that you will be shot as well!" yelled one of the soldiers.

Ch'ang-su, who was walking in front of my father, witnessed firsthand the abuse Father endured. He told me that even then, my father tried to share God's Word with those who were persecuting them.

"Comrade, what is your occupation?" one of the soldiers asked my father with a sharp voice.

"I don't really consider my work an occupation. I am a pastor," my father answered with a calm voice.

"Ah ha! You are that Pastor Son whom I've heard so much about. Even in prison, you were constantly witnessing to people so that they may also believe in Jesus. Why in the world do you witness so persistently? And for what reason?" The soldier's ear-splitting voice demanded an answer.

"I want to encourage them to believe in Jesus so that they too can go to heaven. Life in this world is short, but life in heaven is eternal. Please turn from this lawlessness and believe in Jesus."

"Outrageous! So you seek to convert me also? You must be out of your mind! Where is heaven anyway?"

"If you read the Bible, you will discover God's amazing sovereignty. You must believe in eternal life and heaven."

"Yeah, yeah! You can go to heaven and live well. As for

us, we will build our paradise on earth. You can believe that your rotten, lifeless body will ascend to heaven if you want. But who would believe in such absurd lies? Have you ever met a person who has been to heaven?"

"We mustn't believe in only what can be seen with our eyes. There is greater truth in what is unseen. Doubts in our minds are from Satan. There is no greater truth than God's Word, so we must wholly trust His Word. Jesus is the only way to heaven. Believe in Jesus. Accept Him as your personal Lord and Savior."

"Shut up! How dare you try to witness to me!" Suddenly, the soldier struck my father with the butt of his rifle and my father fell to the ground. "You worthless reactionary!" Pouncing on my father's fallen body, the other soldiers began to beat him ruthlessly.

Even though the soldiers told the prisoners that they would be taken to Sunch'ŏn, they actually only went as far as Mip'yŏng on the outskirts of Yŏsu, where they abruptly halted the procession.

"Comrades, listen well!" said the commander. "Right now, the moon is bright like the light of the sun. In order to avoid American air combat, we will divide you into smaller groups of tens. Don't you dare think about running away! I assure you, you will be put to death on the spot." For some reason, an air of anxiety passed over the faces of the prisoners.

"Group One! March forward!" The first row of people began to march forward, while the rest of them stood still. About ten minutes later, a loud series of gunshots rang, shattering the silent evening. The prisoners' hearts sank as they began to realize that everyone in Group One had been gunned down.

Extreme fear seized the Communist soldiers who remained behind too, but they concealed their fears and said, "Son of a bitch! Someone must have tried to escape. Whoever it was, he deserved to die!"

No one was at ease. They heard gunshots at various intervals as the soldiers moved from person to person to make sure they were dead. It was such a chilling moment and each man fell under a thick cloud of fear for their life. According to Ch'ang-su, my father was earnestly witnessing to the other prisoners around him with his last ounce of strength. Father knew that the time had come for him to die and so he preached with all his might, realizing it would be the last chance for many of them to be saved.

"Shut up, Comrade! Didn't I tell you not to speak?" The soldier struck my father's mouth with the butt of his rifle, breaking all his teeth and filling his mouth with blood. Soon after the first series of shots ended, the soldiers approached the next group.

"Group Two! Move forward!" Ah! I can't imagine what my father had felt in that moment between life and death. I don't think I can ever describe it in writing.

September 28, 1950, my father died as a martyr. What was I doing on that day? Was I jumping for joy because the UN forces had recovered Seoul? Was I sleeping peacefully in my room? Why did I not feel any foreboding at the moment my father was standing at the gate of death? Ah, what shall I do with this sin to assuage my remorse? How can I make it up to him for my lack of filial piety?

The following is an account from Ch'ang-su Kim:

After the second group marched forward, we heard the same sound of machine guns roar. Even from a distance, I felt as though my eardrums would burst. There was no doubt that the Communists intended to kill us all. As Pastor Son stood, he turned around to look at me and said, "Ch'ang-su, pray. No matter what the circumstance, don't forget to pray. God will give you the strength you need. Let's meet in heaven."

I began to call on the name of the Lord in my heart. As I prayed, the last words of Pastor Son kept ringing in my ears. And I thought, 'It's too late now. Let's prepare to face death bravely,' but I wasn't willing to give up living just yet. With a strong desire to live, I struggled with all my might to free myself from the ropes. After a long struggle, miraculously, I was able to free one hand.

Finally, the third group of prisoners was ordered to move forward. While I was being forced closer and closer to the firing squad, I busily moved my hands around to free my other hand. When we were led about twenty to thirty meters onto the orchard roads, the smell of blood and gunpowder penetrated our noses. And in the forest, we saw many prisoners who were tied together, curled up against one another. Some were still alive, ever so slightly crying out and faintly moaning. But when I looked ahead of me, I saw countless Communist soldiers standing around, aiming their guns at them.

So there I was, facing death. My hands became even busier. At that moment, I was standing at the far left of the front row. I thought to myself, 'If these bullets fly, they will hit me first. If I stoop, will I be able to avoid them?' I tried with all my might to free my other hand, and just before the bullets flew my way, the rope suddenly broke. It was a miracle! The firing squad had their fingers on the triggers of their guns. I couldn't think about anything but escaping. I ran as fast as I could into the darkness.

From behind, I could hear someone say, "One of them got away!" Then countless bullets began to whiz past my ears. I fell into a ditch in the field. 'I'm hit! I'm hit!' I thought. My heart was racing and my body was trembling with fear. I thought to myself, 'So this is what dying is like.' I felt around for bullet wounds but found none. I only felt a little bit of blood trickling down one side of my face. I figured the bullets must've skimmed past my ears and grazed my cheek. I must've fallen because of fear and because of the sound of gunshots, rather than because I was shot.

I was wearing a white short-sleeve school uniform. Since the color white could be easily spotted in the dark, I took off my school uniform, curled up, and began to crawl as fast as I could. I don't know how far I crawled, but I was completely covered with dirt and soaked with sweat.

I climbed the mountain, crawling all the way to the top. I could no longer hear the footsteps that had been chasing me. I squatted down behind a big rock and let out a sigh of relief. Only then did I become concerned about the fate of the other prisoners. I longed to find out about Pastor Son, but I couldn't go back down the mountain. My body was still trembling and my teeth were chattering like someone who had just awakened from a nightmare. I was shaking with fear and joy and because it was extremely cold.

Still, I could hear the gunshots and the shrill machine guns from a distance. I felt that I needed to go to Pastor

Son's house and tell his family what had happened. I ran
across a stream, cut through open fields, and ran past rice
paddies in the darkness. Finally, I reached the gate of
Pastor Son's house at dawn.

Ch'ang-su explained, "The reason I was able to survive was because I was already chosen by God to bear witness to what happened during that time." Before he came to deliver the news, my family and the people at Aeyangwŏn were optimistic that my father would return safe and sound. Since Father's arrest, every visitor had said, "Even if they kill all the other prisoners, they cannot kill Pastor Son. Why would they kill the man who adopted a former Communist boy who murdered his two sons? No matter how hardened the hearts of the Communists might be, their hearts would be moved by such a merciful act of love and forgiveness. They'll have no choice but to release him untouched." Such high hopes had spread all over Sinp'ungni, which was near Aeyangwŏn.

Mother was getting close to giving birth to another son, Tong-gil. War broke out against the Communist North Korean armies. The UN Allied Forces arrived in Inch'ŏn and successfully pushed the enemy back.

Since the morning of September 24, Mother waited anxiously for my father to return. She had heard rumors that all the prisoners would be released on that day. But her waiting was in vain. On the 25th, Mother even prepared a warm breakfast for him, but still Father did not return home. The 26th was another day of hopeless waiting. *Surely he will return home today,* my mother was thinking on the 27th, but Father was nowhere to be seen. On the 28th, my younger brother was born.

My mother, holding her newborn infant, was still

Chŏl-min Kang (wearing a mourner's hat), my mother, and siblings beside my father's body.

anxiously awaiting my father's return. Her heart was burning with a premonition that she couldn't shake from her mind.

The night passed and it was already dawn, when Mother heard a loud banging against the front gate. She thought it was perhaps my father. She hurriedly got up and went outside to open the gate. There stood a young man wearing only his underwear, his one cheek red with dried bloodstains, and his body covered with dirt. It was Ch'ang-su Kim.

"Goodness! Aren't you Ch'ang-su, John's friend?"

Mother was surprised to find him there and thought for a moment that he had come to deliver good news about my father. Mother invited him inside and he changed into some clean clothes.

"Mrs. Son, go quickly to Mip'yŏng Orchard. Pastor Son, Pastor Son..." Ch'ang-su fainted before he could even finish his sentence.

Mother knew Father had been martyred, even without hearing the news. She gathered herself and asked, "Ch'ang-su, won't you tell me what happened to my husband in the orchard?"

"I don't know for sure, but I think he's been martyred."

"Oh! My dear, God has granted you your wish. You had always wanted to die for Christ like Pastor Ki-ch'ŏl Chu," Mother mumbled. "Dear God, thank You! I thank You and thank You again for letting him serve You all his life. It has always been my dear husband's wish to die a martyr, and You have allowed it to happen." Endless tears fell from my mother's eyes.

The news traveled fast at Aeyangwŏn. Several young people went to Mip'yŏng Orchard to bring my father back. When it was about time for them to return, more than a thousand members of Aeyangwŏn Church had already gathered and stood along the levee near Aeyangwŏn, waiting for the arrival of my father's body.

From far away the people saw four young men carrying something on a stretcher. As the men drew nearer to the compound, everyone realized that it was my father's body.

"He was alive only sixteen days ago. It just can't be true. Our pastor can't be dead." All the lepers collapsed and began to cry, beating their fists against the ground in grief. Their firm belief that my father would return turned into sorrow. Father's body was lowered to the middle of the yard at Aeyangwŏn, the exact spot where my brothers' bodies had been laid only two years earlier. When Mother removed the sheet that covered his body, she could see that his mouth had been crushed and that all of his teeth had fallen out. My mother gently closed her eyes.

"Do not worry about Aeyangwŏn," Mother told Father

softly. "Go in peace to heaven." Then she prayed quietly in front of his body. "Dear God, You prepared Joshua after taking away Israel's leader, Moses. Now that You have taken away the shepherd of Aeyangwŏn, I believe You will give us the next shepherd."

This is how my father left this sorrowful world at the age of forty-eight. He returned to his earthly home as a cold corpse. Members of Aeyangwŏn Church grabbed Father's body and cried bitterly, rubbing their cheeks against his. They beat their chests and tore their clothes, while tears ran down like rain.

My mother prayed first and cried quietly as she gazed lovingly at my father's sleeping face. She thought, *Was he praying at the moment of his death?* His body was covered with blood. In the palm of both hands were holes made by bullets. There was a big bullet wound on his shoulder too. My father's body was washed clean, put into new clothes, and then placed into a coffin.

Father's coffin was left in our home for three days and then it was buried in a temporary place. Later on, we dug up his coffin and, after another funeral, he was buried in a permanent grave right behind the graves of Matthew and John.

It is hard to describe in writing the scene of sorrow where nearly a thousand Aeyangwŏn lepers were bitterly weeping in front of my father's body. It was the same as when they made a sea of tears in front of the bodies of my two brothers. Among them was one who wailed most sorrowfully, more than the rest of us—Ch'ŏl-min, my brother.

"Father, you saved me. How could this be that you died before me? How could this be?" Ch'ŏl-min grabbed onto my father's body and cried his heart out. Wearing sackcloth, Ch'ŏl-min faithfully performed all the duties of the oldest son until the funeral was over.

"Oh heaven, look down! Oh, earth, listen to the wailing sound that bursts out from the ocean by Tongdo Island." I cried.

The sound of the waves and the wailing of people reached up to the heavens and echoed throughout the distant mountains. I believe the tears we shed that day will flow forever in that deep ocean.

27. Unforgettable Names

The funeral procession was held on Friday, October 13, 1950, at 9:00 a.m. Many guests came from far and wide. Nearly a thousand believers from Aeyangwŏn gathered to say their last farewells to my father in front of his coffin, which was beautifully adorned with flowers.

In Seoul, another memorial service was held at Namdaemun Church on October 29 at 2:00 p.m. Aunt Hwang sang a solo and I spoke at the end of the service. At this memorial service, there was a man in his fifties who was sobbing remorsefully more than anyone else. His name was Sŏng-gi Kim, one of the guards who used to work at Kwangju Prison. Siding with the Japanese at the time of Japanese occupation, Mr. Kim increased his power and position by subjecting my father to all kinds of torture for his refusal to bow down before the Shinto shrine. Whenever Father refused to work on the Lord's Day and insisted on holding a worship service with fasting and prayer, Mr. Kim and the others would yell at him and torture him.

One extremely cold day in January 1943, my grandfather, then well past seventy, had traveled a long distance to visit my father in prison. Mr. Kim kept their meeting under close scrutiny and gave them only a few minutes together, hardly enough to exchange a few words about the family. Forced to leave, Grandfather stumbled out, wiping away the tears from his eyes with a handkerchief. Mr. Kim regretted not having given father and son more time together. Mr. Kim said he could never remove from his mind the image of my grandfather, walking away with a hunched back and sad face.

Mr. Kim quit his job after Korea's independence from Japan and eventually converted to Christianity through the witness of his wife. Although he became a faithful Christian, he still carried a burden of guilt for having tortured my father in the past. He intended to visit my father to ask his forgiveness, but each time, he felt too ashamed to show his face. Mr. Kim kept putting it off until it was too late. That was why he attended the memorial service and why he sobbed with such regret. He mentioned that the Japanese prison guards at Kwangju were later moved by my father's faith, that they had exclaimed, "Indeed, Pastor Son is a saint!"

How can I begin to describe the kind of life my father led on this earth? From a human perspective, his life was one checkered with hardship. Born to a poor farmer—and no money for tuition—Father delivered newspapers and milk and sold dumplings by day, just so he could attend night school. After his marriage to my mother, he moved in to the leprosarium to serve the lepers and share both their good and bad times. Because of his refusal to worship at the Shinto shrines, he was imprisoned at the age of thirty-eight. He was transferred five times from prison to prison and was finally released when Korea gained liberation from Japan.

Father never once mentioned anything about his five years of suffering in prison. I suppose the only one with a complete record of my father's trials and tribulations is none other than the Living God. I've only mentioned what I've experienced or heard from firsthand witnesses.

By faith, my father overcame the deaths of his two beloved sons. Unfortunately, he died the same death as his sons—at gunpoint. Father had plenty of chances to escape and avoid death, but he chose to walk on the road to martyrdom in the way a garden tiger moth throws its body into a burning fire. His life was far from happy. Pain and misfortune followed him everywhere. His only passion was God and he placed obedience to God's Word over personal happiness. His life was short, living only to the age of forty-eight. From the age of thirty-eight, beginning with his imprisonment by the Japanese and up until the moment he died by the bullets of the Communist North Koreans, my father's nightmarish life was like death itself.

I believe my father foresaw the storms of death, tears, suffering, and poverty that approached our family like a whirlwind. This was clearly revealed in a letter he wrote on August 15, 1934, to a friend:

> *When I ascend to heaven, my flesh and blood will sing for joy, even if this body of mine should be torn. Why should I grieve? Even death and hell will surrender before us. Through death, we will taste the greater truth that lies beyond death, and through tears, we will taste God's great love.*

And when the times grew dark and his sorrows increased, Father always turned them into songs. In his diary, dated August 26, 1950, my father wrote: "Consider poverty a beloved wife and suffering a good teacher." This was true, indeed, for my father. Whenever he faced obstacles, he never allowed himself to sink below them. Rather, he tried to discover God's will, His truth, and His love that lay beneath the surface. Even in his daily life, he was only concerned with pleasing God, bringing glory to Him, and learning how he could die to receive the crown of life.

It is said that a man's character is revealed by his relationships with his associates. My father wasn't a friend to people in power or to the wealthy; he was a friend to the lepers and he loved them deeply.

People often ask me about my father. Actually, he didn't look like a typical pastor or a saint. He was rather short and down to earth. When he was with children, he was like a child; when he was with lepers, he was like one of them; when he was with us, he was like a friend. By nature, he possessed much love and was kind to everyone. He was able to mingle with any type of person. But when he stood behind the pulpit, he became a fearless lion.

People say that my father, Pastor Yang-wŏn Son, was a saint or a great martyr who lived according to God's Word and who sacrificed his own life to keep that Word. I oftentimes think to myself, *Had my father been an ordinary father, would our family have been happier? Instead of being called "children of a martyr or saint," would we still have a father by our sides? Wouldn't we all have been much happier?*

Now, many years after my father's death, I no longer hold a grudge against him. At that time, I could not understand Father's ocean-size heart with my little mind. Now, I'm very proud of my father and respect him tremendously. I'm so proud before God because my father was found to be faithful to Him. I stand proud before all Korean churches because my father loved not only with words but through practice of true love. Although our family's happiness was shattered into pieces, Father's obedience to God's Word became a valuable fertilizer for the evangelization of our nation. I stand proud before all Christians. Quintus Septimius Florens Tertullianus—anglicized as Tertullian—once said that "in the blood of the martyrs lies the seed of the Church." I wonder how the church of our nation would have grown so rapidly without the blood of martyrs. I am now convinced that the martyrdoms of my two brothers and my father worked out according to God's will. God has shown our family His great grace.

I wonder if perhaps Father is enjoying his birthday party right now in heaven. In his diary on August 6, 1949, he wrote:

On the last day of the revival meeting, one elderly lady handed me a piece of white paper and asked, "Pastor, please write down your address and birthday here for me." It seemed as though she wanted to send me a gift for my birthday. So I wrote, "My address is in the arms of our Lord and my birthday is the day I was born again. The date of my conversion is unknown. Therefore, while I live on earth, I am but a camper, so my birthday party will be held on the day I enter heaven."

Who can be against God's sovereign will? There was one incident, however, that I look back at with some regret. Several months before the Yŏsu-Sunch'ŏn Mutiny, my family had a chance to move to Pusan. Father held a series of revival meetings at Pusan Ch'oryang Church and afterwards, the board of elders decided to invite him to be their full-time pastor. The congregation was deeply moved by my father's sermons, so they aggressively sought him. Everything was set in place. All they needed now was for Father to make his decision.

As for my family, especially us children, we were wholeheartedly for the move and were full of anticipation. I was eager to go because Ch'oryang Church had a piano. My mother also seemed to want to move there, for she began to pack little by little.

There was a big problem, however. When the news of our invitation to Pusan reached the families at Aeyangwŏn, they rushed into our home and protested everyday that no one could take away their pastor. More than anybody, Dr. Robert M. Wilson strongly advised my father not to leave Aeyangwŏn. So there began a tug-of-war between Aeyangwŏn and Ch'oryang Church. My father fasted and prayed for a week about this matter. Finally, he told us he was convinced that it was not God's will for us to move, and so we unpacked our boxes.

As I reflect upon those years, I often wonder what would have happened had we moved to Pusan. *Would my father and brothers have lived?* Pusan did not suffer the same fate as Yŏsu and Sunch'ŏn during the mutiny that killed my brothers Matthew and John. Even during the Korean War, Pusan was safe from any serious threat. It would not have been necessary for my father to go anywhere to hide. Because my father was in Yŏsu, he was killed. In fact, not moving to Pusan was a determining factor in the deaths of three members of my family.

Moving is a common occurrence for people, but in our family's case, the question of moving or not moving changed the fate of our family. Who would have thought that a move would decide between life and death? Those fateful bullets that aimed at my brothers and my father were destined to hit them, so it seems those bullets nailed our family down to Aeyangwŏn.

Death! Death! Who can prevent it? Since it is said that even a sparrow does not fall to the ground unless God allows for it, their fates must have been predestined from birth. That's why God told my father to stay in Aeyangwŏn and why my father obeyed His will. Father wrote in one of his spiritual essays:

> *I must become a Jesus-addict.*
> *As the alcoholic lives on alcohol and dies because of it,*
> *   and as the drug addict lives on drugs and dies because*
> *   of it, so we should live on Jesus and die for Jesus.*
> *If we live our entire life for Jesus,*
> *   we will experience a resurrection like His.*
> *Since we are His servants,*
> *   let us work only for our Lord and not for ourselves.*

Just as he wrote, such faith was the true experience of his being. My father was a man who was addicted to Jesus, one who could not live without Him.

As for me, however, after enduring repeated tragedies and losing my father and two dear brothers, I began to doubt my faith in God. Before their deaths, faith was my absolute purpose in life, but soon after, I gradually began to rebel against God. Although I resented God a great deal for allowing such things to happen to us, I could not completely deny Him. The faithful teaching and practice of the Word of God by my parents since my birth were too solid to let me fall completely. Maintaining my faith, however, became a tremendous challenge.

During those days, I suffered severely from insomnia, hallucinations, and persistent paranoia. Unable to sleep at night, I saw phantoms and imagined that I would be killed the following day. Each night, I would hear a tearful voice say, *Will I get through the night safely? Will I be able to see the morning light?* This fear, this uncertainty about tomorrow, poisoned each day and every conscious moment. The sound of the gunshots that killed my two brothers and my father never left me. Perhaps I will never be free from that sound until the day I die.

I lived with the constant fear that if I were out in the

streets, a bullet would fly at me from somewhere. I was convinced that I was next to die. I felt death fasten itself to me. I felt as if I were slowly dying. "Death" was the only word that filled my thoughts.

I resented God and wandered away from Him. Although I forgot Him, He never forgot me. Rather, he continued to love me. When my heart was full of bitterness and resentment toward Him, He was silent. But when my heart became utterly desolate, God visited me and comforted my wounded heart.

One day, a Scripture verse that my pastor read deeply penetrated my heart. He read Luke 12:20: "You fool! This very night your life will be demanded from you. Then who will get what you have prepared for yourself?"

That's right! I thought, *If I continue on with my rebellion against God and then suddenly die and go to hell, how will I ever be able to see my two brothers and my father again? I must go to heaven to see them. I can't die now, not like this.* I heard God's voice on that day. He promised me that those who love Him and keep His commands will be blessed for a thousand generations.

I felt my heart leap for joy. Nothing extraordinary happened nor was there any epochal event, but from that day forward, I began to heal from the fear of death. The hallucinations disappeared and the tormenting paranoia faded away. Now, after many years, I look back and finally realize that all those things that happened to my family were a part of God's perfect plan. He has entrusted me with an important mission to testify about the events of those days. Through the martyrdoms of my brothers and my father, God revealed to my people a model of faith. To the hypocritical ministers who speak of God only with their lips, He has given an example of true faith.

Soon after my father's martyrdom, I left Seoul and transferred to Sunch'ŏn Maesan High School, where I later graduated from. Later, I entered Ch'ongsin Bible College in Seoul, but during my second year, I transferred to Korea Bible College in Pusan. At the end of my third year, I withdrew from studies, partly due to financial reasons.

During that time, Pastor Yong-jun An raised some funds for the families of martyred Christians. The financial assistance we received, however, was hardly enough to put food on the table, so our family remained in dire financial circumstances.

During that time, fortunately, Pastor An introduced me to a famous pianist and missionary, Reverend Dwight. R. Malsbary, and from that time on, I devoted myself solely to becoming proficient at playing the piano. Booking lessons with Reverend Malsbary was next to impossible. It was almost like picking a star from the sky. When Matthew was alive, he arranged for me to get lessons from a woman missionary named Ms. Janet Crane, whose name we pronounced as "Gujaray." In order to become a great pianist of whom my brother would have been proud, I earnestly studied the instrument.

As for my mother, she remained at Aeyangwŏn and kept busy raising funds for the construction of the Sinp'ung Church for lepers at Sinp'ungni. With a reference letter from Reverend Sang-dong Han, Mother traveled everywhere throughout the country. Through her tearful efforts, the church was finally built. My mother lived in a two-room house that the lepers had built for her with their own hands.

My younger siblings were students at the time and lived in Sunch'ŏn to be close to their schools. Pastor Hyŏn-sik Sŏ, formerly the assistant pastor at Aeyangwŏn while my father was alive, became the senior pastor of the church immediately after my father's martyrdom.

It would probably take another volume to describe the difficult circumstances of our family after my father's martyrdom, but I'll briefly explain some of them here. As the oldest daughter, I had the responsibility of taking care of my younger siblings. Fortunately, the wife of Reverend Myŏng-dong Han of Pusan Nam Church introduced me to Deaconess Ŭn-hŭi Kim, who helped me find work as a piano teacher. She had three pianos in her home, so she was helpful not only for my personal study but also for our family's welfare, since my students paid me generously.

From that time on, I began to teach piano to my younger siblings. We didn't have a piano at first, so I drew the keyboard on a piece of paper and only taught fingering. When one of the church staff members, Miss Hyang-sik Myŏng, found out about this, she got us a piano. Thanks to her, we three sisters could practice piano. We submerged ourselves in playing the piano night and day. We were all musically talented and I believe this was the best blessing that God bestowed on us. It was by His great grace that we were given this opportunity to learn how to play the piano in the midst of extreme poverty.

As a result of God's grace and our hard work, all three of us became pianists. Tong-nim graduated from Pusan College of Education as a piano major and she served as a church piano accompanist in many churches. Tong-yŏn was the best of the three of us and graduated from Kyunghee University. After earning her masters degree, she taught at Pusan Hansung Women's College, Sejong University, and Kyunghee University. I gave many recitals in Pusan and later worked as an accompanist for many musical performances and vocal soloists.

Although I am now in my sixties, I still actively serve at Pusan Taeyŏn Central Church as the choir piano accompanist. I enjoy my work and I am grateful for the fact that I can glorify God through music.

As for my younger brother Tong-jang, who lived at the orphanage with me and who walked home alone from Sunch'ŏn on the day my brothers died, he suffered from the same mental problems I did. Just like me, he resisted God and rebelled against Him for a long time. But he too finally returned to God's arms.

Our youngest brother Tong-gil, who was born on the day my father went to heaven, later graduated from Taehan Bible College and founded Sandol Church in Sŏngnam Gyŏnggi Province. *Sandol*, which means "living stone," was my father's pen name. Tong-gil is currently serving God as a missionary in the Philippines.

In reflection, I realize that God was always there with us and I'm truly grateful to Him. Even when we were faced with the most difficult, painful, and despairing circumstances, He was near. When we were lost, not knowing which road to turn on, He had already prepared the way. As a grain of seed must die to bear fruit 100 or 1,000 fold, so my brothers and my father were sacrificed as seeds to bear much spiritual fruit and to awaken countless souls in this world.

God, indeed, fulfilled His purpose for my family. Perhaps this is the answer to the prayers of my grandfather, my parents, the families at Aeyangwŏn, and my two brothers. Although they have all left this world, they have left the fragrance of Christ all over the earth.

It is far more desirable to live a short but meaningful life than a long but meaningless life. Long life does not necessarily guarantee happiness. It is not the quantity of days that is important but the quality of your days. Although Matthew, John, and Father are gone, they will continue to shine forever as unforgettable heroes, even after I finish my race in this world, beyond the decades and centuries to come, and until the end of this world.

Memorial Poetry

A Man of Whom the World was Not Worthy

By Hun Ko
(Poet/Pastor)

Speaking of you today felt awkward;
I feel more troubled than good when I speak of you.

When you sucked filthy blood and pus
Out of the deserted lepers with your own lips,
You were not a man of this world.

When your two sons Matthew and John fell as bloody
    sacrifices, and with tears you gave thanks to God:
"Offering my son to God is glorious,
I thank God for receiving my two sons!"
You were not a man of this world.

On the day you adopted the person
Who made our blood run cold,
And who was the murderer of your two sons,
The loving bomb was detonated
And you looked up at the sky with joy,
Standing firm as a cross in this land,
You were not a man of this world.

When you were buried as a martyr with your two sons
And your wife, who lived like a living martyr and coped
    with all these sufferings
On Aeyangwŏn Hill overlooking the South Sea,
The world was not worthy of a man like you.
Speaking of you today, I felt ashamed;
I feel more troubled than good when I speak of you

Important Dates in the Life of Reverend Yang-wŏn Son

3 Jun. 1902	Born in Haman, Kyŏngnam Province, Korea.
3 Mar. 1926	Entered Kyŏngnam Bible College.
5 Apr. 1935	Entered P'yŏngyang Bible College.
14 Jul. 1939	Bible teacher (assistant pastor) at Aeyangwŏn.
25 Sep. 1940	Arrested by Yosu Police for refusing Shinto shrine worship; sentenced to life imprisonment in Kwangju Detention Center; transferred to Kwangju Prison, to Kyŏngsŏng Detention Center, then to Ch'ŏngju Probation Center.
17 Aug. 1945	Released from prison with the liberation of Korea from Japanese colonization.
Mar. 1946	Ordained at Kyŏngnam Presbytery.
Sep. 1946	Served as Dean, Korea Seminary, Pusan.
21 Oct. 1948	Two sons martyred during Yŏsu-Sunch'ŏn Munity.
28 Sep. 1950	Martyred by gunshot at Mip'yŏng Orchard.
27 Apr. 1993	Reverend Yang-wŏn Son's martyrium completed.

Footnotes

1) *Ch'ŏkhwa* (anti-appeasement) monument (*Ch'ŏkhwabi*)

   In 1871, the Taewŏn'gun set up *Ch'ŏkhwabi*, which are stone tablets inscribed with anti-Western slogans, in forty major cities in Korea.

2) Reverend Sŏn-ju Kil

   Reverend Kil was originally trained as a doctor of Oriental Medicine and was highly educated in the Chinese classics. Although he became quite well-off, he faced the prospect of gradually losing his eyesight. In 1896, he heard the Gospel(Jesus as Savior of all human beings) and converted to Christianity. He was baptized in 1897 and later became a pastor. While he was leading early morning prayers at Changdaehyŏn Church in P'yŏngyang, the famous 1907 revival broke out. This revival spread to Manchuria and even as far south as Pusan. At the March 1st Movement (1919), Reverend Kil represented the Christians of northern Korea and was one of thirty-three who signed the Declaration of Independence. Naturally, such a highly regarded pastor would have been an honored guest at Ch'irwŏn Church.

3) Training for Pastors

   This book mentions the Bible Colleges that my father, Reverend Yang-wŏn Son, attended. At that time in Korea, the curriculum of Bible Colleges focused on the exegesis of each chapter of the Bible to prepare the students for ministry. For Biblical studies at a more advanced level, students had to attend a seminary at which they learned about church history, systems, and theology.

4) Uchimura Kanzō (1861-1930)

Christian theologian, essayist and editor, and born in Edo (now Tokyo), Uchimura Kanzō converted to Christianity and studied at Amherst College and Hartford Theological Seminary in the United States. He maintained a unique position that the church is unnecessary and at times a hindrance to Christian faith. The word he used to describe this position, *Mukyokai* or "Nonchurch Christianity," is still used to distinguish the tradition of his school from that of other Protestant denominations.

5) Loss of Eyebrows

One of the symptoms of leprosy is the loss of eyebrows. This is due to a cellular reaction to the leprosy bacillus by the involved nerve. The cellular reaction continues to spread into the main trunk of the involved nerve and tends to strangle it so that impulses cannot go up or down, thereby causing loss of power in the muscles of the area, loss of sense of pain, and loss of circulation in the affected area. John once said to Aunt Hwang, "Auntie, I'll shave my eyebrows and go beg with you." John said this because he wanted to help the lepers who were looking after him. To do this, he needed to appear as a leprosy patient.

6) *Yut*

Yut is an indoor game generally played during the winter

months. Four wooden sticks are tossed and the players move their pieces however many spaces the sticks indicate. The players take turns until one reaches "home."

7) *Kamidana* idol

Kamidana is the household altar of a Shinto believer.

8) Red bean gruel

The winter solstice (*tongji*) generally falls on December 21, 22, or 23, varying from year to year and also depending on the time zone one is in. Sweet adzuki-bean gruel is served on that day. Traditionally, your bowl of gruel should contain the number of rice dumplings that is equivalent to your age in the coming year.

9) "Mystical miracles" and "prosperity theology"

The term "mystical miracles" may refer to miracles experienced by someone of great faith. There is a danger, however, if the faith worker takes credit for the miracle rather than giving full credit to Jesus who is the Lord of all miracles. "Prosperity theology" implies preaching that focuses on wealth and health rather than the cross of Jesus.

10) Ch'ŏl-min Kang

In 1953, Ch'ŏl-min Kang studied at the Shingwang Evening Bible School on Cheju Island. Ch'ŏl-min was around twenty-four years old at the time, and the students at this Bible school were mainly soldiers and people who were displaced during the Korean War. The principal of Shingwang Evening Bible School was the late Reverend Dŏk-ho Chang, who was also Ch'ŏl-min's mentor. Ch'ŏl-min later served as the assistant pastor at Shingwang Bible School Church. He married Deaconess Jae-hwa Chang in 1958 and died of tonsil cancer at the age of forty-eight in his home in Seoul. Ch'ŏl-min lives on through his two sons and two daughters; the eldest son became a pastor in accordance with his father's request.

11) *Ch'usŏk*

Ch'usŏk (lit.: "autumn night"), the fifteenth day of the eighth month of the lunar calendar, was traditionally an important festival for Korean farmers. By this time of the year, fruits and grains are ripe and the autumn harvest is near.

* The late Reverend Yang-wŏn Son was awarded the first "Love Your Enemy Award" by the Love Your Enemy Foundation and Union Church (Reverend Chung Kuhn Lee) in Los Angeles, California, on September 25, 2005. The prize was $10,000.

Kwang-jo Chu

More Than Conquerors

(in English & Korean)

Hardcover/138 pages/137 x 192mm

ISBN 978-89-954904-3-3

This biography focuses on Reverend Ki-chŏl Chu's bold walk of faith and courageous martyrdom during the most devastating years in Korean church history. Written by Reverend Chu's youngest son Elder Kwang-jo Chu from firsthand personal experiences, this book illuminates an inspirational yet historically accurate account of the martyr's walk of faith. Reverend Chu, whose name is synonymous with the expression "martyr of Korea," is a representative figure in Korean church history and his life and martyrdom has helped shape the faith of modern day Korean Christians. Readers will be inspired by Reverend Chu's display of courage and strong faith, and will be deeply moved to wonder, *What can I offer to the Lord?*

"A son's depiction of his father's martyrdom, faith, and patriotism···readers who take up the example shown by Reverend Ki-chŏl Chu will develop into world peacemakers and reconcilers in Christ."

Professor Man Yeol Lee

Professor Emeritus, Sookmyung Women's University
& Former President, National Institute of Korean History

Original Author: Kwang-jo Chu
Illustrated by: Ha-lim Jang

More Than Conquerors
- Comic Edition

Paperback/208 pages/189 x 257mm
ISBN 978-89-958974-0-9

More than Conquerors was named bestseller in the category of religion by Kyobo Bookstore and Youngpoong Bookstore, and has been a steady seller since its release in October 2004. *More than Conquerors—Comic Edition* now offers young readers a chance to read about Reverend Ki-chŏl Chu's bold resistance to forced Shinto worship during Japanese colonial power—a period of greatest hardship and suffering in Korean church history. Illustrated and rewritten to meet children at eye level, this book delivers the true meaning of the Easter faith.

"Reverend Ki-chŏl Chu stood on the front lines of Korean church history and has become a prime symbol of the glorious faith. Young readers will experience a conviction of faith through this direct account by Elder Kwang-jo Chu of his own childhood witness of his father's martyrdom."

Reverend Jung Hyun Oh
Sarang Community Church